D1631934

CASSELL'S POCKET LIBRARY

❖ ❖ ❖

HERE COMES A CANDLE

HERE COMES A CANDLE

by
STORM JAMESON

"Here comes a candle to light you to bed
Here comes a chopper to chop off your head."
Old Rhyme.

CASSELL & COMPANY LTD
LONDON, TORONTO, MELBOURNE, SYDNEY

First published in 1938
Pocket Edition, 1945
Second Edition, 1947

FOR
DOROTHY,
ROBERT
and
NICHOLAS,
not forgetting
JUDITH ANN

BOOK
PRODUCTION
WAR ECONOMY
STANDARD

THE PAPER AND BINDING OF
THIS BOOK CONFORM TO THE
AUTHORIZED ECONOMY STANDARDS

Printed in Great Britain by
Wyman & Sons, Ltd., London, Fakenham and Reading

F. 1246

CHAPTER I

AFTER A short night the dawn is not waited for. Those sleeping sleep on; the sleepless merely close their eyelids against it. Those who have not yet gone to bed do not look.

The night had been airless: about two o'clock a light breeze sprang into the street; another hour and it had departed and the early morning was left breathless, clear, warm, the sky unwrinkled, the air thin and dry. Without people—no one objects to a few policemen, street-sweepers, tramps—London is as good as any other city and better than most. Still an hour, then people began to leave the Screech Owl, stepping gingerly into the court-yard with few glances at the now fiery sky. Women who had cars hurried to get into them. It is one thing to touch up your face before a mirror in electric light and quite another to feel it naked in daylight. The rest hurried out into the street, all very lively, don't you know, talking, and laughing. Cars had to be handled cleverly to turn through the archway into the narrow street. There was the usual noise. The tenants sleeping in rooms on the other sides of the courtyard—New Moon Yard—were used to it.

The Screech Owl was not an elegant night club, but it had pretensions to smartness. Its clients—some of them—could count on appearing at intervals in the pages of illustrated weeklies, and the others liked to be able to exclaim: "Look, there's Cynthia Russell; don't you remember, we saw her at the Screech Owl last week? She was at the next table." The next best thing to being photographed with your mouth wide open, a cock-tail glass in your hand, lips and nails both coming out black in the photograph, is to know by sight the people who are.

All the cars had gone except a large shabby Bentley belonging to the proprietor of the Screech Owl. He came out and started it up with a hideous clatter, and turned it round to face the gateway. He went back into the house. Ten minutes later he came out again quickly, followed by a woman in a long evening coat. He helped her into the car, ducked in after her and drove off. He called over his shoulder:

"Thomas. I say, Thomas. Lock up the desk in my room."

Thomas came out into the yard. He was still wearing his porter's uniform; he had unbuttoned the tunic and pushed the cap to the back of his head. "Right, sir."

He straddled there, looking after the Bentley. He was big and powerful, with a big face, good-tempered, solid, the eyes and the close-lipped mouth smiling slightly. A man you could like but not quarrel with.

He turned back to the house. Bert, the kitchen-boy, was dragging out an ashbin. Close behind him Simon, the chef, and one of the waiters, a Belgian called François, carried another between them. It was Bert's job but they all liked the boy and wanted to help him to get off. He was dropping with sleep. His clumsy sunburned face wore a foolish smile. His blue eyes were fixed.

Thomas strode over and dragged out the remaining ashbins himself. He dragged them as if they were toy engines, and swung them off the step with a flourish.

"Run along," he said to Bert. "Kids ought to be in bed."

The Welshman, Simon, lounged across the hall, pulling on his jacket. He was yellow with fatigue and the heat of the stuffy kitchen. It was on the second floor, under the roof. The ranges were old-fashioned; if a fire broke out the room was a death-trap. If any of His Majesty's Inspectors saw into it at night it would be condemned out of hand. One had actually called about six o'clock one evening; he was welcomed by Simon in a cool room and told that nothing was cooked in the place, only a few sausages. Simon was an accomplished liar, a cynic, who believed that every man has a right to his own death.

"The Captain doesn't sleep at home," he said with a grave face.

Thomas smiled his tight smile, without opening his lips. "And thank God when he doesn't. Twice last month I smelled burning in his room. When I went in I found he'd gone to sleep with a cigarette in his fingers and set the blanket smouldering. This place would burn like an eggshell with all that panelling and wooden stairs."

"Plenty of staircases."

"Ha, you don't sleep in it," Thomas grinned.

Simon and François went off together. The sun was now sending rays from an invisible fist; one of them reached far into the sky and turned a cirrus cloud to fiery flakes. Thomas watched it for a second before he went in and up to his attic on the second floor. The stores room and another room, used for gambling, were between it and the kitchen.

He was thinking of the Captain. Once in the War, when they were living in huts, in rest—strange how "rest" became in your mind a place, like any other—a stove blew up and burned Ashton's hut and everything in it, clothes, papers, everything. And all Ashton said was: "A damned fine collection of accounts rendered gone west, good luck to them."

A slight smile remained on Thomas's face while he undressed. How many years was it? The Captain hadn't changed. Well, yes, he had changed. Thomas's mind jerked aside. His smile faded, and he stood a minute with bent head and fingers in a buttonhole. The Captain took the place in his life of wife and child. He worried over him, exaggerating things. He knew it.

He remembered that he had not locked up the desk. Groaning, he was half asleep, he pulled his trousers up and stumbled down the narrow stairs again to the ground floor.

Silence settled into the yard; a well of shadows in the centre of London, filled with a light like water. A stranger coming into it now, when it was empty and silent, would have seen at once, in spite of decay and alteration, that the place was originally one house, one handsome three-storied house, built at the close of the seventeenth century. It had then a narrow central part, with two longer wings enclosing a courtyard. The fourth side was a wall with fine iron gates. At the beginning of the nineteenth century when the house—it had been called New Moon House by its builder—was corrupting slowly into a miniature slum this narrow side was built-in and the entrance became an archway. A door in the right-hand wall of the arch led into a completely dark room with the staircase going from it to the upper floors.

The Screech Owl occupied the whole of the long left wing. In the wing opposite a cabinet-maker had his workshop and lived, with his family, in two rooms over it. Next door to his work-room was a wine shop, the Lunar Wine Company. The narrow part, which faced you when you entered the courtyard, was a Café Bar. Every room, on every floor, had its tenant or tenants. Dark awkward staircases had been thrust in, three of them, to reach the top floor from the yard.

Since the War the place had recovered a kind of spurious prosperity, despite the decay, the want of air, the smells. Not all the tenants were disreputable.

It was within a stone's throw of Berwick Market. In the street outside Jews and Italians skinned one another for a farthing—there were dress shops, with garments made especially for undersized tightbottomed young women, shops selling oil, *pâtes alimentaires*, mysterious sausages, a Belgian pastrycook's, a herbalist. The district throbbed like an ant-heap with human, animal, and insect life. Like New Moon Yard it slept little.

Shortly before half-past five an old man shuffled downstairs from his attic above the Café Bar and wandered across to the ashbins standing outside the Screech Owl. Although the day was already warm he felt it cool on his body inside his shirt. The air coiled like a whip round his thin flanks; he felt them shrinking and withered, as though they had a life of their own, apart from his, and a poor one. When he got out of bed in the morning he was especially conscious of his body, and that it was ageing and drying up: during the rest of the day he became used to it again and forgot it.

He lifted the lid from each bin in turn and poked about in the refuse with his bare arm, holding back the sleeve of his shirt with the other hand. If he dared he would have emptied them on to the ground. He had to tell by feel whether he had touched anything that could be sold or eaten, and he had more disappointments than lucky finds. All the time, as he probed and felt, his mind kept up a grumbling unfriendly commentary. "Oh dear, oh dear, oh dear . . . oh, my God . . . you fool, you old fool, out here in your shirt delving in ashbins —why are you doing this? Why don't you go to your cousin, the headmaster, and ask him for some money, or to your other cousin the publisher and ask him to give you some reading—why, why? Because you are a lazy disreputable self-indulgent old man . . . scratching yourself . . . you'll die here—but you'll live for years more yet, oh, my God, pity me—and you'll never know why you lived at all, or what good life was to you—Ugh!"

He wrapped his salvage in a half sheet of newspaper and went slowly back to his room, cocking an eye at the bleached cloudless sky. It was going to be another dry scorching day.

A policeman strolled past the archway, turned, and came in. He tried the door of the Lunar Wine shop, and the door next to it. This one was unlocked; it opened on to a narrow passage and a staircase. "Don't they care if they're murdered in their beds?" The cabinet-maker's was a double door, and the window thick with dust. Standing close to it the policeman saw through the dust the benches, the piled up wood, and a piece of furniture. "Burn well," he muttered. He tried the doors of the Café Bar and the Screech Owl, and departed reluctantly. A countryman, from the deep valleys of Herefordshire, he disliked and despised Londoners, the inhabitants of Soho worse than the rest. The only likeable thing he had heard about London was that it had once been destroyed by fire, and whenever he had been home on leave and came back he felt that the job would have to be done again, and thoroughly this time. Why, the air was like a dirty rag.

A lean shabby cat, its spine moving in a series of nearly imperceptible shudders, slipped across the yard.

The silence lasted a little longer. A window opened and a young woman looked out. The milk boy clattered into the yard with his wire carrier full of bottles. He climbed two narrow dusty flights of stairs and set half-pint bottles down outside three doors. Barley, the cabinet-maker, took a pint and a half; they had three children. The Café Bar took six pints on this delivery.

It was less than two hours since Simon and François walked out of the yard. The day had begun.

In the larger of their two rooms over the café Gregorio Pizetti and his wife were dressing. Maddalena rose first, and her husband watched her for a moment as she moved quickly and compactly about the room. She was small and becoming very stout. She had a large face, with incongruously delicate features, the mouth small, the nose slender and arched, grey eyes. Her face—she was forty —was as smooth as the skin of her body. She had the serene air of a Flemish, not an Italian, madonna. Gregorio was very happy with her.

He reached out his arm as she passed the bed and slapped her gently. "A fine morning, eh?"

"Too fine to be living here," Maddalena said. She and the policeman from Hereford would have one impulse in common.

Pizetti got up and looked out of the window. The sunlight was on the wall opposite. He saw an old woman come to one of the windows: she wore a black shawl, like women in his village in Italy. She was a German.

"We shall go home next year," he said, turning round.

"Why not this?" his wife asked.

"Perhaps this."

Gregorio longed for Italy quite as sharply, if in fewer words, but he had set himself a certain sum which he intended to earn before he went back. He did not want to take all his money back with him. Like many patriots he believed that it is wise, if you can arrange it, to keep a little money in another country—even if you are not, by law, allowed to have it. There are always ways. He meant to buy a little land in the Abruzzi, and a house; there he and Maddalena would live joyously until they died and were buried in friendly decent Italian soil. Sacred soil. But a little money in another country is always comforting.

He began to dress, pulling his clothes on anyhow. He was thin, a scarecrow of a man, with blue eyes and a drooping moustache. His face had the same look of patience as his wife's. It was a less shrewd face. Both were the children of peasants, but Gregorio's mother, a seamstress from Rome, had what her husband and neighbours called peculiarities. She had even a few books which she read and tried to make her son read. He could not, even to please her, sit and read, but there is no doubt that something not altogether sound got into his blood from hers. He would sometimes, not often, give away food—even money. Still, Maddalena loved him. He had a merry smile. Though he was ten years older than she was, he was as spry as a boy.

"Listen," he said. He stood, smiling, his head on one side.

"What?" asked Maddalena.

"Giulia is awake. She is singing."

"Why shouldn't she sing?" Maddalena was a good mother—and she had no complaints to make of her younger child—yet she could not help a twinge of jealousy when she saw Gregorio stand there with a foolish face of love simply because his daughter felt like singing as she dressed. *I* could sing if I had nothing on my mind, she thought quickly.

She went downstairs and began to prepare their coffee. When her husband came down she had forgotten her annoyance with him, and they stood side by side, shoulders touching, to drink coffee. There was too much to do to sit down. Pizetti dipped a piece of stale bread in his bowl and sucked it in through his moustache.

"Hurry!" Maddalena said. She smiled at him.

Gregorio opened the café door. The sun had crept half-way down the opposite wall. The air smelled dry. "It is going to be hot." His wife did not answer. She was already hard at work cleaning behind the bar.

In her bedroom Giulia Pizetti sang in a low voice. She looked at herself in the glass over the mantelshelf and smiled. At seventeen she was already a beauty; dark curling hair, immense dark eyes, a white skin—she and her parents had not a feature alike, but she had her father's twinkling merry smile and Maddalena Pizetti's air of serenity. Perhaps she would be heavy when she was older and married, but now she was charming and beautiful—and light-hearted. The minute she opened her eyes in the morning she remembered that she was happy.

She would get up, idling over her washing and dressing —no one ever scolded her—and without knowing it sing in a voice which gradually became louder as the happiness of being alive and awake seized all her senses. In her voice there was something clear and cool, something springlike, like light on running water. She sang as naturally as a thrush, and for much the same reasons.

Someone knocked on the wall of her room. She started, and blushed, drawing her fine eyebrows together.

That wretched old Mrs. Caracas. I've wakened her, she thought. Her room was divided from her father's and mother's by the staircase and a landing, but only the thinnest of walls stood between her and the old woman living in the room in the corner formed by the right-hand wing. Giulia could hear when the old woman breathed more noisily than usual, and when she talked to her cats as if they were human beings. The things she said to them!

"I'm sorry," she said under her breath. She smiled guiltily.

Now that she must not sing she began half to dance as she finished dressing. Her feet moved of themselves. Snatching up the hairbrush, she moved her arms in time to them—her excitement had to find an outlet. Even now she could not help humming a little.

She opened her door quietly, and ran downstairs to the kitchen—to drink her coffee and begin the day's work.

Mrs. Caracas, shading her eyes with her hand, knocked twice on the wall. Against the tepid air of the room her eyelids lifted reluctantly. The singing stopped at once. Drat her, drat her, drat her. I shan't sleep again, these light mornings and no night to speak of it's all right when you're young but what use is it when you're old you might as well sleep and forget yourself. Much chance I have.

She sat up, groaning, pulling the rumpled bedclothes up to her shoulder. The cat which had been sleeping on the other pillow got up and sprang from the bed to a chair. She tried to catch it, letting the blanket slip down. No use.

"Come back to mother, darling, come along, puss, puss."

Of course he won't come near me, none of them will unless I have something they want just like men like every man I ever knew I've known plenty I've O my arm what time is it then? not seven what does it matter what time

it is time time we're always thinking about it when we're
old grumbling it's too early too late when every day brings
us nearer but I don't want to think about it I'll think of
the spring mornings when I used to lie in bed on board
ship a child and hear the men swilling the deck over my
head the noises off the quay trains men shouting my
father roaring out in that voice he had Put that down I
say put it down what was it I wonder then the steward
knocking coming in with bread-and-butter on a thick plate
with the Prince of Wales feathers on it on the blankets
too I remember that morning we were in some foreign
port and the women brought their baskets of fruit on
board he had something an orange very likely holding it
behind his back he said Guess which hand and like a fool
I was I said O I've had an orange he said You don't want
any more then. I never got it.

It's been like that all my life.

"My tongue's parched," she said aloud.

She put one foot awkwardly out of bed, then the other
and stood swaying holding the head of the bed, feeling her
body pressing down on her knees so that she thought they
would give way. Her nightgown was caught between her
thighs. She freed it and tottered towards the gas ring, lit
it under the kettle, then back to the bed feeling under it
for the chamber-pot, and lowered herself gingerly, afraid
of its breaking under her, yet she felt—not happy—con-
soled, safe. It's the first thing after we're born no
wonder we, all I want is a cup of tea now the real stingo
let me up O my God my back my knees.

Reaching up to the shelf she took the tea-caddy
between both hands, anxious and quivering. The best
moment of the day.

The postman came into the yard. He took the left side
first. There were no letters for the rooms over the archway; the upper room indeed was empty since the last
tenant, an Italian, disappeared owing Pizetti money. (A

lesson, as his wife pointed out, in trusting an Italian simply because he knows someone you knew when you were a boy.)

Even the postman guessed that the letters he pushed through the door of the Screech Owl were bills. He had one letter for Pizetti. Gregorio took it with a brilliant smile and hurried into the kitchen.

"Maddalena! Here is a letter from Anita at last."

His wife put down the *fait-tout* she was polishing and held her hand out. "Why do you say at last? It is less than a month since she sent the last."

She was as pleased, but less excited. Anita was their other, older, daughter, married to a chemist. Lately she with her husband and two children had moved to Palermo and to both the older Pizettis it was as though she had gone to the South Pole. Although they lived in London it always seemed to them that their village in Abruzzi was less than a hand's reach away. But to go to Palermo, meaning to live there! It was inconceivable.

Gregorio could read but he disliked the effort. So his wife read the letter aloud. To their disappointment Anita had nothing startling to say of the natives of Palermo. It seemed that even in remote places people conducted themselves much as they did at home. A neighbour's son went off to the war, to Abyssinia, and when news came that he was dead his mother made a great deal of fuss, natural in the circumstances—he was her only child and her husband had left her—and was reproached for it by the landlord. He told her that the young man had been killed defending his country. No one had attacked us here, the woman said. The enemies of our country are everywhere, Don Sacca retorted; they are after our money. But I have no money, not ten centesimi, and no one to earn it for me, his mother said, weeping.

"Poor creature," Gregorio sighed. "But what is Anita doing?"

"She is nursing her baby," his wife said, turning the page.

"Is that all?"

"She is looking after the house and the other child and her husband. Isn't that enough? Here is a postscript. She and her husband have found a house for us to buy, close to their own. It is small and clean, there is just enough garden, and it is cheap."

"In Palermo?" Pizetti said.

"Naturally, since they are living there," his wife said dryly. She glanced at him. Her grey eyes had that fixed look which meant she was thinking how foolish and gentle he was. "Do you want to be near Anita?"

"Yes, but——"

Maddalena smiled. "Don't worry," she said softly. "*I* want to go home, too. Not to Palermo."

Pizetti turned to go back into the café. He took three dancing gliding steps, out of contentment and pleasure. He shut himself in the big cupboard he called his office and switched the light on. He was going to count his money. He kept it in a padlocked wooden box under the towels, papers and odd garments with which the shelves of the cupboard were crammed to bursting. No banks for him. He remembered too well the day when his father lost his savings in a bank failure in Abruzzi: he came home, thrashed his wife and all his six children, and went out to the back of the house and hanged himself. He was in an exalted state, his son said. Yet if he had not been ruined by the bank I should never have come to England and become a rich man. His money was all in notes. He had once had a little gold, only a very little; before the War, when he and Maddalena started, they could not save for a time. When gold began to sell for high prices he sold it. He knew exactly how much he had in the tin box. Whenever he added another pound he altered the total on the piece of cardboard lying across the bundles of notes. Once a month he counted it all again. It took him almost an hour. He was a rich man. There was eight hundred and five pounds in the box. His hopes of making it a thousand turned him giddy when he thought about it during the night. . . .

No letters for the tenants above the Pizettis. The postman turned to the right. Nothing for George Barley, cabinet-maker. He began to climb the stairs to the top floor, grunting. Place stinks of dry wood.

Mrs. Kerr, Jean-Ann Kerr, roused when the bell went. She heard the faint swish of the letter falling. Shall I get up? She lay for a minute. Might be good.

She got up and looked at herself in the glass. She pulled the net off her yellow hair. That's better. Round the nostrils and on her forehead the skin was greasy, coarsening. She looked coldly and carefully at her face. Fine rosy skin, long nose, lips too thin. There were lines under her eyes. Over thirty you have to take more care, she thought. Perhaps I'll have a facial this week—perhaps change the cream. She flexed her long arms. I'll make coffee and drink it in bed. Another brassy hot day. Glittering arrowy sea, sands, a hillside. The road goes along by the sea, and turns up. Who wants to be buried alive? This is London, this was. Cheer up. A handsome man, a Canadian, will speak to you this evening—wads of money in his hip pocket. I've forgotten that letter.

Part of the passage had been walled-in to make an entrance hall the size of a cupboard. The letter was lying on the carpet.

Before she turned it over she knew. Just touching it something said, Ken. And Ken it was. She laid it on the bed and went on preparing the coffee on the gas-ring behind the curtain. What's he want——? A dull feeling, between fear and excitement, seized her.

She got into bed with the tray, poured a cup out, and opened the letter. It was what she expected. It began with a threat and ended in one of those accusing self-exculpatory sentences her one-time husband was so fond of. Come to that, he's still my husband. She saw his face clearly. Why did I ever marry him? *I must have been bloody well barmy* . . . that's a war song. Well, cheerio—you left him. Forget him, can't you?

The coffee was good and comforting. She stroked her

knees under the sheet and began to plan her day. Last night was no go—still, I got a sleep out of it, I needed it, I'll go round to Cohen's and see if she can fix me up with a new dress, I'll sleep this afternoon and get out early— I'm going to have luck. Money. All you want. If I had money I'd be as good as gold.

She flicked the letter across the room, and started humming . . . *S.O.S. I'm falling, Hold me tight, I'm falling, falling. . . .*

Down one flight of stairs and up another. The room at the far end of the wing, facing another room across the landing. Almost the last letter in his hand.

In the instant of opening her eyes when the bell rang Harriet was at home in bed in her room at the top of the house; her mother was ringing the bell for her to get up and dress; she must hurry; she would miss the train to school. Now, with one foot already over the side of the bed, she came fully awake and saw where she was, and as her foot touched the rough carpet she had a momentary qualm of distaste. Do all I can, it's not really clean, she said to herself. Nowhere in London is clean. Her cotton nightdress was creased. Her bare arms, the elbows red like a schoolgirl's, hung awkwardly. She rubbed her eyes.

The letter was from her mother . . . "My dearest Harry" . . . she ran her eyes over the page; it was only local gossip, the new bridge, Mrs. Sanderson's new coat, the stupid thing her father had just done; it ended, "God bless you and keep you. Mother. Julia Brown." She put it down. Yawning, looking without seeing it at her rosy, childishly round face in the glass, she poured the water into the basin, threw her nightgown off, and began to wash from neck to feet, standing on one towel and drying herself very inadequately with the other. She drew her stockings on before stepping off the towel; her feet, she felt, would no longer be clean if she walked on the carpet barefoot.

How different London had seemed before she came here. She had never imagined that four pounds a week would buy so little; that she would have to choose between rooms and a watchful landlady or a room of one's own—like this one—and no comfort. Four pounds. Why, it seemed a fortune when she was writing to tell her mother. And now the care she took, and going without meals, and the rest of it, to have money for presents; she must give good presents; wasn't she the rich one of the family now? She imagined her mother's face, talking to a woman in the street . . . "My daughter, Harriet, yes she's in London now. She's doing well. No, I don't think that twenty-three is too young to be in London, she's a sensible healthy girl, she wanted to go, it's natural. . . ."

But I was going to make my fortune, Harriet Brown thought, with a little laugh. For that I gave up wide clear skies, the air like water, the deep grass under the hedges in the early morning, the road going down to the stream and up the other side to the moor, the stones, the black-faced sheep, the mountain ash; girls I went with to school have married and settled down already; they have babies; they give their orders in the shops where we used to be little girls shopping with our mothers on Saturday morning; they see the hills, the stream, the lilac and flowering currant in the gardens; they think simple everyday thoughts; they are happy or unhappy but it is always the same pattern, the same threads; it is the pattern I know, one I should have made in my turn. I was born for it. In me are trees with wide branches, lifting the mist when the sun rises; walls deep in shadow and covered with a thin moss you can peel off like soft turf; warm lingering twilights, the scent from the grass, from the peonies, floating and slipping away, half caught; hot noons in the humming silence of the moor; long still solemn frost-bound nights, when a branch snapping outside sounds like a pistol shot.

In me too is something which drove me out of my place, out of the town, the house (shabby as it is) I loved, and flung me into this room.

She looked about her. The unmade bed, the chairs—

all of them too low for comfort; she liked to sit upright —the hideous carpet, the cupboard holding pieces of a tea-service, and odds and ends of her own, not one of these objects meant anything to her: she dusted them, hating them, and they knew she hated them and responded by tripping her up or getting chipped, so that she had to replace them—as if she had nothing else to do with her money at the end of the week than buy cups and plates for another woman. The room belonged to an actress who had gone on tour.

What's going to happen to me? she cried.

To look at her, as she rushed about the room, setting it to rights, pulling her dress over her head, rubbing her knee where she had banged it—she was clumsy—against a chair, you would not have guessed at the disorder, the anguish, in her mind. She simply looked stupid. No one knew, no one ever would know, the uncertainty that tormented her, the fears—am I wasting my time here? time which is so short; no one ever has enough of it; yesterday I was a child at school, dreaming of making my fortune; to-morrow I shall be old; I shall regret that I spent any of my life here; I shall think of the road, the stream, the mountain ash; I shall think of roads, cities, mountains, I have never seen. Why am I here? What am I?

She felt imprisoned and lost. Looking at herself in the glass for the first time when it was time to do her hair, she saw an unformed face, too heavy in the forehead and the line of the jaw to be pretty, a long mouth, grey unsatisfied eyes—strange that one cannot see oneself; she knew all about her own face (and did not care for it) except what it looked like to other people. A few of them found it attractive, she knew—but that was when she smiled at them, imploring them to take to her, not to notice that she was clumsy and shabby, and had no more idea how to do her hair than a cat. She laughed at herself. Now for breakfast. A good cup of tea.

The postman shot his last letters into the letter-box of the Lunar Wine Company—the last door in the yard before he turned towards the archway. The shutters were fast. A new hinge had replaced the broken one he noticed yesterday morning. Quick work.

The sunlight had slipped down one wall of the house and was creeping across the yard. He passed through it into the shadowed archway, and stepped into the street, into early sunlight and traffic.

In her room on the first floor, above the archway, Charlotte Mannheim had listened to his footsteps passing all the way round the yard, and to the silence when he was inside the house delivering on one of the stairways. Now she heard him walk under the archway. He had gone, and there was no letter for her. No reason why there should be, she thought. Who writes to an old woman on her seventieth birthday, even when—her mind faltered—even when it is also the anniversary of the day her husband was murdered. Under her very eyes. Under these eyes, she thought.

She turned from the window and sat down.

It was a morning like this, the dry heat, the sunlight, and it was about this time, seven o'clock, and he was still in bed beside her. A lock of his dark hair was across his face turned sideways to the pillow. She had been looking at him. She slept lightly—yes, even then, as a young woman.

She caught sight of her hands, folded quietly in her lap. They were discoloured, wrinkled, the hands of an old hard-working woman. And they were quiet. They did not fly to her throat when she remembered a morning forty years ago. She could think of it, oh! not without pain, but with less pain than she would feel if she knocked her head against a beam. One forgets. One forgets even such agony.

It was like looking at an old photograph, the faces, the upraised arms, dimmed by time and distance. Time did that. It thickened the slender body, turned red hair to a hideous dark grey, and it took away even the dignity of such suffering as hers. It took everything. Soon, very soon, it would take what was left, and with the death of one old tired woman no one would know what Thomas Goltmann had looked like, what he had been, how he laughed, drank, spoke; how he died. She herself had forgotten everything but the look of it. Her eyes flinched. She saw the men coming into the room. Two of them held her, her body straining against their arms in her night-shift. "What are you going to do to my husband?" she cried, twisting her body: she was in agony. She knew. Goltmann smiled at her. He had time to give her one smile. He said one thing—"Look after Anna." It was all he said. No word for her, his wife, his comrade. She *was* his wife—not married by a state both of them detested. I helped him, she thought: we kept hidden together; we spoke at secret gatherings of friends; we were hungry, cold, frightened together. And his last message—

"Look after Anna."

It was the first moment in which she knew that he and Anna were lovers. It meant nothing. He was free—it was part of their belief as sincere anarchists—and yet it had startled her. Not then. Not in the instant when she was trying to reach him, when they lifted their revolvers, and when he fell forward, his arms stretched out, his dark hair on the floor, his hands—his poor hands—gripped.

It was vile, vile. She said it aloud. "Vile! Murderers, bullies!" But—although she hated as bitterly as ever the men who shot their fellows at the command of a government—she could not feel the monstrous tearing grief of those few minutes. Of days, weeks, after it. She had to think for herself and Anna, who could not think, she had to plan. She had to warn other people. She was busy all day; then, at night, it came back, and she saw and heard. She struck her head on the wall. Tears scalded her cheeks. She felt them scalding her inside her body, bitter unseen tears.

Now nothing was left, not even her grief. The real murderer, she thought, is time. Time.

She got up and opened the window more widely. The smell of dust and heat came from the courtyard into the little room. Walking blindly, as though she saw with her hands, she touched first this and then the other articles of furniture. They seemed to reassure her. In a drawer of the table she found a letter. It was more than a year old, but she read it again, carefully, as if it had just come. Then she began slowly to dress, lifting her garments off the chair where she had thrown them when she went to bed. She drew them on without a glance. How she looked was no longer a matter of any importance, neither to her nor anyone living.

CHAPTER II

WHEN GEORGE BARLEY began courting his wife he was a tall handsome man in khaki, with ruddy cheeks, a thick black moustache, and a ready smile. He charmed the young woman by his tales of what he was going to do in London at the end of the War; she believed him and married him, though she, her family, and most of her friends considered she was lowering herself cruelly in marrying the son of a carpenter. A good carpenter, it is true—but, still, nothing more than a common workman. Sally Frost (she was then) was obstinate. She wanted to get away from home and to live in London. And, too, the man attracted her. Without understanding it, she had a sensuous side to her nature. She really wanted marriage: the idea of it drew her and repelled her at the same time. They were married during his leave. From the first she was disappointed in him, and in his love-making. When she saw him for the first time in an

ordinary suit, after the War, she could scarcely look at him.
He looked like a workman's son. He never noticed her distaste, obvious as she made it. She got used to him again,
and in a month or two they went to London. She could
never leave him after this. He was kind, decent, hard-
working. He provided a home for her and gave her the
handling of every penny he made. She had nothing to
complain of—except that he was not the sort of man she
admired, nor was their home at all the place she had
wanted. She thought she would die of shame if any of
her friends visited her and saw that they were living in
three rooms; the room behind the workshop had to be
kitchen and living-room in one; its only meagre light came
from a window into the alley between this side of New
Moon Yard and a tall building. The two rooms upstairs,
their bedrooms, wouldn't do for them much longer when
the boy was too old to sleep in the room with his sisters.
She nagged her husband about it persistently. They must,
she said angrily, try to let these rooms which wouldn't—
apart from the worry of tenants—fetch the rent of another
larger place for themselves. Whatever were they to do?
She blamed her husband bitterly for not having foreseen
the difficulties when he set himself and his workshop down
in this yard, and began having a family for which he had
not provided decent space. And yet she was sorry for
him when she had scolded him and when she saw him
looking at her in a defeated way. She tried to soften her
voice, and to think more kindly of him. But perhaps,
she thought bitterly, he doesn't feel much.

At fifty-five George Barley's thick moustache had become a drooping grey one. He had lost most of his teeth
and it covered the gap, even when he smiled. He was still
upright and very strong. When he got up in the morning,
and went down to the kitchen to set the stove going and
boil a kettle before he washed himself at the sink, he
always lingered a minute in the workshop. He snuffed
up the smell of wood, or ran his hand over a finished piece.
He loved wood. He knew in the dark the feel of a sound

piece of wood, and he could tell you the tree it came from. He never made a mistake.

This morning he had risen at seven, waking when the postman crossed the yard. His wife was still either asleep or pretending to be. He crept from the room and downstairs, carrying his shirt and trousers, and stood a minute in the dark workroom. In the early morning, when he was alone in it, he had the sense of being in a forest; a strange painful excitement seized him at the sight of some half-finished piece of furniture which in full daylight with other people in the place meant nothing but a job of work, to be done as well as possible. He went over to a bureau in the corner, finished except for the waxing and rubbing. His hand trembled slightly on it. It was a beautiful piece of work, perfect. He had worked on it for months whenever he had time to work slowly. Pity, he thought, that so few of these jobs came his way. For he was a good craftsman, he knew, and he had good men to work with him. Men who had been cabinet-makers as long as he had himself—that is, for more than a hundred years. There were Barleys in his family who had made furniture two hundred and eighty-five years back. And one of his two workmen could say as much.

But no one would pay for such work. If they were rich enough they bought at one of the fashionable shops, like So-and-so's in Wigmore Street. And so he and his fellows were using their hands, and their inherited precious knowledge of what you could do with wood, to make road signs and whatnot for the A.A. and such jobs as that. And lucky to touch it, he thought. The trouble was there wasn't enough of it. Not to keep three men going all the year. He stood with bent head, painfully considering a problem he had slept and eaten with for the last ten years. And all the time his hand was moving, half without his being aware of it, over the surface of the bureau. Something went out of him when he touched a piece of sound wood, some virtue. Something came back, too. Between him and the nature of the wood was a subtle interchange of force. In a way he could not have put into words—it would never occur to him to put words to it—he *knew* the wood when he touched it. It was as though through it he touched a still living source of strength; as though the sap, the roots going down into the earth, were immediately under his fingers in a half-finished piece of furniture standing in his workshop. When he was choosing a piece of wood he chose it with his fingers, letting them tell his brain everything about it, where the tree had come from, from dry or wet ground, how old it was, at what season in the year it had been felled. He had no need to look at timber to know whether it was foxed or not.

He took his hand from the bureau, sighed, and went into the kitchen, still carrying his shirt. He had pulled on the trousers when he first came downstairs. His nightshirt hung down over them. How his wife hated his slovenly way of dressing. If he had a new suit it looked like a dish-rag when he had worn it twice. He *is* a workman, and he looks like one, she would think. It was the worst thing she could say about him.

In the kitchen he kneeled down and cleared the ash away from the grate before laying the fire. He sifted the cinders out carefully and put them in a special bucket to use again later, when the fire was going well. All the cooking was done on the coal range, and the hot water came from the boiler at the side. There was a gas-ring for boiling kettles, attached by a long tube to a bracket in the wall, but no gas-stove. One could not be fixed in the room. It was one of Mrs. Barley's oldest grievances. George Barley liked the range. It reminded him of his home.

When the fire was going well, he went to the sink to wash his hands and face. Then he drew his shirt on and made the tea for his wife. He looked at the clock on the mantelshelf. Seven-thirty. He had overslept.

He set the things on the little tray and carried it upstairs. Standing beside their bed, waiting for her to sit up and take it, he wondered whether she had forgotten the argument that had dragged on until he fell asleep. Not she.

She remembered as soon as she saw him. The half-sullen half-supercilious glance she gave him, turning her head away immediately, warned him. She took the tea without a word of thanks.

"Have you called the children?" she said coldly.

"Not yet."

"You'd better, then."

He crossed the room and opened the door into the slightly larger room where the three young ones slept—the two girls together, the boy in a camp bed at the foot of theirs. The boy was awake. He looked at his father with a fat sheepish smile, rosy with sleep.

"Ha, you're awake," Barley said. "Get up."

Both the little girls were asleep. He went closer and saw that the elder, Sarah, was watching him furtively through her eyelashes. He rested his hand on her shoulder under the quilt. At once she opened her eyes, with a look of alarm and resentment, and wriggled away from his touch.

"Get up now," he said, "'s time."

He was uneasy with his children, and they with him. He did not care particularly for any of them, but he talked to them and made foolish schoolboy jokes when they came into the workshop and he knew his wife was out of earshot. When she could hear him he preferred not to take any notice of them. He spoke, if he had to speak, shortly and roughly. And they on their side were shy of him in their mother's presence, and not very much drawn to him at any time. Lucy, the second girl, liked him the best of the three, but for some reason he thought she was sly and overlooked her.

He went back to his workroom. Before eight his wife came down, went directly into the kitchen, without glancing at him, and began to get the breakfast ready. He heard the children quarrelling upstairs. They argued very often, and sometimes fought each other.

During breakfast at first no one spoke. Mrs. Barley looked the two girls over coldly and told Sarah that her neck was not clean.

"A great girl of twelve," she cried, "and I can't trust you to turn yourself out decently. It's sickening, sickening."

Sarah hung her head sulkily and said nothing. Barley felt sorry for her. He saw that under her stolid look she was suffering agonies of humiliation. After all, she was the oldest. She ought not to be called down in front of the other two. He said nothing.

Suddenly Lucy looked up from her bowl of bread-and-milk. "Our Sarah woke me up last night," she complained. She fixed accusing greenish eyes on her sister. At the same time she laughed. Two dimples appeared in her plump cheeks, and she had a light, merry laugh.

Mrs. Barley lifted her eyebrows. "*Did* you, Sarah?" she said.

"I couldn't help it," Sarah mumbled. "I was dreaming."

"She said the house was on fire," Lucy said in a serious voice.

A look of impatience crossed the mother's face. Sarah's dreams were a joke in the family. They were also tiresome. She had one dream that recurred every few months, and from which often she woke crying and shivering. She gave a quite sensible account of it. It always began so well, in a feeling of warmth and happiness; she and her mother were alone in the house, and her mother was in one of her easy friendly moods, joking rather like a child (her children were perhaps the only persons who now and then saw—and without being able to recognize her—the child still living on easily in the tired body of the woman); but then she grew tired and Sarah looked after her and made her lie on the bed. And with the friendliness between them Sarah began to feel a little grief. Then she smelled fire and saw smoke curling up through the floor boards in the workroom. She said, "I must take up the boards." When she pulled them up it was like a cavern under the house and the foundations and under the yard. It was filled with all kinds of things and with beams of wood; all were smouldering and charred with the fire; she saw a hat-box of her mother's among them with the fire eating it. A man rode past in the yard in the half-darkness and offered to send help, and in the kitchen when she ran to it there was an object she knew to be a telephone; it was of a singular kind, and had to be fitted together; she was clumsy with it and took it to her mother to help; and then shouting with growing fear into the mouthpiece put into her hand by her mother—"Fire, fire. Send the engine"; and the girl at the other end answering calmly, "I'll try to get one for you, but you know we're four short"; then a wall of flame rushing from the charred beams, from the foundations of the house; her mother, who had become an old woman, looking on.

She was almost out of her mind with fear, and woke up trying to control her cries. And it's not, her mother thought, as though she was a nervous child. She very seldom cried. You could threaten her with any punishment and she only stared with her large slightly prominent grey eyes, and waited. A good sound thrashing made her cry, but that was from the pain itself: she never cried, like other children, from temper or disappointment.

Mrs. Barley blamed her husband even for Sarah's tiresome dream. Some person must have told the child that all the wood and the linseed oil and other stuff in the place would make a grand blaze. Ay, and it could, she said to herself. I hate sleeping on top of it every night. We ought to move. We ought never to have been living here.

"Eat your breakfast," she said sharply to Lucy.

"It's a hot day," George Barley ventured.

"It'll be hot enough in this kitchen," his wife said. "*I* shall know how hot it is."

Barley kept his head down over his plate. "I'll leave the door open into the workroom," he mumbled. "You'll get a bit of air from the yard then."

"And a lot of dust and dirt," his wife cried. "No, thank you."

She sat with a sullen lowered look on her face. One grievance reminded her of another.

"And what may I ask, are you going to do about Hudson," she said in a cutting voice. "Are you going to give him his notice this week, or aren't you?"

It was the old argument again, the same one that had been going on last night almost to midnight. She wanted him to dismiss one of his men, the older. It was true there was rarely enough work for all three of them. Only sometimes, if a rush order came in from the A.A. they were all three working full pitch. The rest of the time they filled in, and worked slowly. Barley felt an obstinate anger against her, and shame and embarrassment. He had given way to her on so many points, and on this one he stuck. It was not only that he was sorry for Hudson, who was a good workman and too old to get another job. But they had been in the same company in the War. They fitted in well together. If one had to go, let it be the other, the younger man. But he and Hudson alone would never be able to cope with a rush of heavy work. My, it's a fair monkey puzzler, he thought ruefully. It went on twisting in his mind day after day, and he never came to a decision. He had said nothing to either man. He knew in his heart that his wife was right. But in his heart, too, he felt that if he turned Hudson adrift he would be doing himself an injury—quite as deep as the damage to the other man. And he shrank with a really bitter feeling from speaking the fatal words to him. He would almost rather go bankrupt. But there was Sally—and after all he could not let *her* go bankrupt. In spite of their quarrels he was bound to her. He admired her; he wanted to satisfy her. And he hated her for the way she held his nose down to the problem day after day. It's none of her business, he said savagely to himself. But she would have answered that by asking him whose business it was if it was not hers, to see to it that she and her children were reasonably secure.

His helpless silence aggravated his wife. Without warning she pushed her chair back and jumped up.

"There you sit like a stone, like a stuck pig," she said in

a harsh, loud voice. "I'm going. Finish your breakfast if you can swallow—with the thought of what's going to happen to us." She struck her hands together. "I wish I was dead!" she said tragically. "I wish I'd never been born—or never seen you. I don't want to see any of you again."

She slammed the door with all her strength, making a frightful noise. They heard her walking about overhead. A chair fell over; she picked it up and banged it hard down on the floor, and a piece of the plaster fell from the ceiling on to Barley's plate.

He pushed at it with his knife. Glancing up, he saw that Lucy, and Hector, who was only five, were frightened. Sarah looked as stolid as ever. Suddenly she looked her father full in the face, a jeering, ironic twinkle at the back of her eyes. It was not in the least the look of a child. It made Barley uncomfortable.

"Get on, and get off to school with you," he said roughly.

Lucy burst into tears.

"Cry, baby, cry," Sarah jeered. She watched the younger girl with a lingering, impersonal curiosity.

Lucy cried the louder. The little boy began to giggle hysterically. Beside himself with irritation, Barley walked out into the workshop, leaving Sarah to clear the table and get herself and the other two off to school. He knew she would do it—and take good care not to annoy her mother.

CHAPTER III

THERE WAS a knock at the door. Harriet whirled round from the table, on which she was setting cups, plates, egg-cups.

"Ready," she called, "come in—it's ready."

The door opened as she was speaking, and a tall young man came into the room. He closed it with his shoulder and stood smiling at her.

"Don't fuss," he said. "Plenty of time."

"Plenty for you," Harriet retorted. "I have to be in the office at nine, and it's eight now."

"Eight, is it?"

He sat down, stretching his long thin legs, and watched her pour the water on the tea, take out the eggs, waiting for each to dry before touching it with her fingers—egg water is supposed to give you warts—and fetch salt, knives, butter. It never entered his head to offer to help. He was used to being wait on. At home, at school, in the Air Force. He had never made a cup of tea in his life, or even made his own bed. He was in love with Harriet, but he let her wait on him as a matter of course. And he had arranged with Mrs. Pizetti to keep his room clean, so that all he had to do in the morning was shave and dress. He took his bath at the aerodrome where he was assistant instructor. If it were not for Harriet he could live there, in comfort. That's what he told her. But the last thing he wanted to do was to spend his evenings with members of the flying club. He liked to get as far away from them as he could. Six days in the week he left New Moon Yard at half-past seven; it was an hour's drive to the aerodrome, and he had breakfast when he got there. To-day, Monday, was his day off.

"Why don't we go across to the Pizettis' for breakfast? Then you wouldn't have to do all this."

He had said this so many times that Harriet ignored it. She felt a familiar sense of humiliation. He ought to prefer breakfast for two in her room. Why is he so careless, so—she sought for the word—lazy-minded? He had not kissed her yet.

"What are you going to do to-day?" she asked.

"I'm taking Josephine Rapp out to lunch."

"Oh."

"Now, don't look at me like that," he said softly

"You know I only want her to put up the money for me."

"Is she as rich as that?" Harried asked, with a flick of sarcasm.

"I don't know. Her father's a millionaire. She's a rotten pilot, I can tell you that."

"But you taught her to fly," Harriet said.

He ducked his head, smiling at her through eyelashes much longer and thicker than her own. She felt her heart stirring with love.

"Bill, why do you want to make this long flight?" she said in a loud voice. "Records are silly."

"You don't understand," he said.

Do I? he wondered. He could not tell her why he wanted to fly to the Cape and back. More than he had wanted anything in his life. The wish to make this flight got up, lived, ate and went to bed with him. He thought about it even when his mind was fixed on the struggles of some pupil to remember in the air what he had been told on the ground. In some way it was to make up to him for leaving the Service. But more than that. It would give him—again he hardly knew what it would give him—security? The sense of having had something that no one could take away from him. As they could take everything else—Harriet, his strength, youth, time. Time—ah, that was the devil. I'm twenty-five now, he would think; it seemed that a lifetime had gone already between the first time he put on his uniform and the day he went to the aerodrome to be interviewed for the job of flying instructor. "Flight-Lt. Randall?" "Yes, sir." "Short Service commission, eh?" "Yes." "Special Reserve, I suppose, now?" "Yes." What an ape, how'd he get on the committee of any flying club? Oh, he owned it.

"If I don't understand it's because you don't tell me," Harriet was saying.

He caught the note of anger in her voice. It made him impatient. With so little time, she mustn't be difficult —or demand attention.

B

"I can't tell you," he said. "I want to do it. That's all there is."

"Perhaps you tell your Josephine Rapp more."

Randall stood up. Without a word he went out of the room, quietly shutting the door.

Harriet looked after him, stupefied. In the four months they had known each other she was not yet used to his silent rages, nor to the way in which, rather than have a quarrel, he would leave her—flat. She was trembling.

She pushed her plate aside. Her throat was constricted now, and she could not swallow, not even the good tea. She looked at Randall's cup, and at his half-eaten egg, and tears sprang into her eyes. It's such a waste, she thought. All the time she was clearing away the things she tried not to cry. She had to carry them out to the sink on the landing to wash up. Randall's room was at the other side of the landing, and the door was shut. That shut door hardened her—it was like his not bothering to kiss her when he came in. When she was back in her room she began to cry without meaning it. Stop, stop, you haven't time, she said angrily.

Clenching her hands she became quiet. Her face felt hot and rough. She went over to the window and leaned out, to get the air on it. The smell of dust and heat floated up.

"Miss Brown. Hi, there, Miss Brown."

She opened her eyes. Looking down, she saw that that old woman, that Mrs. Caracas, was leaning out of her window on the floor below. She waved. Mrs. Caracas shouted again. "Look at my flowers," she yelled. She grew plants in pots in her room and in a box on the sill outside.

"They're lovely," Harriet said.

"What? Wha-a-t? I can't hear you. Come to my room for a minute, and I'll give you one. I'll give you a flower."

"I'm afraid I haven't time," Harriet called back.

"Come on."

Mrs. Caracas withdrew her head. Sighing—she hated to offend people, but the old woman disgusted her—Harriet prepared to go and get her flower. To reach Mrs. Caracas's room she had to go down into the yard, past the cabinet-maker's place, and up another staircase as far as the first floor. She knocked at the door.

"Come in."

The close smell of the room knocked you down. It smelled of dirty clothes, cats—the old woman kept five—stale cooked fish, and of Mrs. Caracas. There was too much furniture in it, and every piece was draped or swathed in cretonne that had faded to the same earthy hue. A little breath of dust was expelled from any object you touched.

Mrs. Caracas's wide toothless grin. Teeth in the handleless cup by her bed. She stooped over the few ragged tulips, late blooms. One plump finger touched slowly their petals. She doesn't want to part with one, Harriet thought: why did she call me?

"Soft as a baby's bottom," Mrs. Caracas said. "I love 'em. Don't you? Don't you come from the country? Yes, I thought you did, first time I saw you."

"I shouldn't mind being there now," Harriet murmured. To walk out of the room like that, without breakfast, without a word. A pot full of good tea wasted. Poured out down the sink.

"Which colour d'you like?"

"Don't give me any," Harriet smiled. "Keep them for yourself."

"Here." She broke with difficulty the lank stalk. The petals were dry and wrinkled, ready to drop off. "Last for days yet. Take it."

Her wrinkled veinous face, her eyes, became vacant, as though she had forgotten. How old is she? Where are they when they look at nothing? She had a hard mouth, mean and small, dropping at the corners.

"Thank you," Harriet said. "I'll put it in water in my room."

"You're welcome." Mrs. Caracas came alive. "Did you see my pussens on your way here?"

"Which one?"

"The big yellow tom. He slipped out when I was getting up this morning. He'll come back. Still, you never know—I don't like them to stay away. D'you know, I'm going to leave here and go and live in the country. Buy a cottage—see? I've got the money put by. Saved it. Y'know what I was, don't you? Dresser, I was. Dresser. At His Majesty's. Now and then I got a present, but I didn't spend all I got, nor I didn't let Caracas know the half of it—he'd have cleaned me out if I—well, he's dead. I've the laugh at him."

Her eyes, quick under wrinkled sore lids, followed Harriet when the girl edged towards the door. That's right, she thought, vexed; come in here, take one of my flowers, and fly off. No manners. Her thoughts scurried frantically in search of something to keep her visitor a few minutes longer. Give her something else? What? No, no.

"You off?" she said, trying to seem casual.

"I have to work," Harriet said with an apologetic smile.

"Work, hey? How old are you?"

"Twenty-three."

Virgin, too. I can always tell. At her age I——. It's natural, isn't it? why some women make a song and dance about themselves beats me 'tis done 'tis done, I am a bride, did he know he came a long way down the list well what d'you expect?

"Twenty-three, I went out to Australia when I was twenty-three, tough place and I'd a tough time. There was me and a friend of mine, Bertha, she was called, Bertha, people took us for sisters we were that alike same hair same eyes but she was a bit taller than me. Once we were in a café Bertha said, See that tall dark fellow over there, I'm going to pull his shirt out, creeping up behind him and when she put her hand on him he grabbed her and laid her across his knee and up with her petticoat showing her white drawers to all and sundry. How we laughed. I near ended myself. . . . Well, if you must go. . . ."

"Thank you for my flower."

Gone. She said that like she was saying Thank you for nothing. What Bertha said to me that evening when she when I she shouldn't have got herself in a fix, then coming to me to help her out. As if I was made of money. Lend me ten pounds, old girl. For old times' sake. I'm desperate, I swear I am, I'll pay it back I. She looked queer I must say, that look in her eyes mine like mine but who'd have thought she'd go off and do herself in when I didn't give her the money, I hadn't it, well, I hadn't it to spare then. Pay it back, she said. Yes, when the cows come home. She was a fool. If she was alive now we could've taken the cottage together, many a laugh we'd have had out of it, why couldn't she get herself out of the fix without coming to me asking for money I won't give anybody my money it's mine I worked hard for it God knows and if she says I killed her well it's a dirty lie she can't say anything again she's gone it's years and years and years a long time a long long time.

Randall walked across to the Café Bar to get breakfast. Coffee, he only wanted coffee. The half egg he had eaten in Harriet's room seemed to be stuck half-way down his gizzard, or it might be his annoyance with her. He wanted a lot of hot milky coffee to wash it down.

The old man who had one of the attics above the Pizettis' two rooms was there, crumbling bread into his mug of coffee. He turned it into a kind of gruel, eating it off a spoon. It was his own spoon. He had a theory that the spoons in restaurants poisoned you with the stuff they used to clean them. He looked up and smiled knowingly at the young man.

"Well, Pop, how's life?" said Randall amiably.

"The same," Pop said. "Not the same as when I was

a young man like you, but the same now I am an old man. It's remarkable how soon you get used to being old—as old as I am."

"You're not so old as that," Randall said, smiling at him.

"No, I'm older. That's right."

Maddalena came herself, bringing Randall his coffee. "Don't you want to eat anything, Mr. Randall? A fried egg. I'll fry you one."

"No, no eggs—nothing, thank you."

He had a quick, brilliant smile. It meant nothing, but it gave an impression of warmth and affection. He did, in fact, like Mrs. Pizetti: she reminded him curiously of his mother when she looked at him with fixed, considering grey eyes, as though she were summing him up. She was easier to get on with than his mother. She was not intelligent—not in that way. Randall did not read his mother's novels, and he pretended to be amused by her reputation for a high degree of intellect. He admired her. He loved her, and he was influenced by her. But now that she lived abroad he scarcely ever answered her letters. When she became plaintive he sat down and wrote her one of his short uninformative letters, to keep her quiet. She had always done everything for him. His father had deserted her, and her money—she had never made very much—went almost entirely on his education and his amusements. In those days she was always shabby. Yes, she had given him everything. Everything, that is, except security. He had never had even a room of his own, since she lived in hotels and took another room for him during his holidays. She hated domesticity, she said. She worked too hard. She was always writing. There was always a book to be finished; he could see it behind her eyes when she listened to him—which she did very patiently, as though she were interested, but the whole time her mind was working, turning words over, sunk: he never succeeded in occupying the whole of her attention for more than a few minutes. Yet she loved him, and probably no one else. All the same, he couldn't write to her.

"But you should eat," Mrs. Pizetti urged him. "All you young ones, nowadays you live on your nerves, you don't eat. It's bad."

"He has to keep thin, to fly," Giulia said to her mother. She looked sideways at the young man.

"Don't talk nonsense," Mrs. Pizetti said.

"She's quite right."

"Of course I am," Giulia said, laughing, rolling her magnificent eyes at both of them, and at the old man. She walked across the room as though at any moment she might begin to dance.

"Yes, of course you are right, my dear girl," Pop said. "And your mother is right—and that settles it." He polished his spoon on a sleeve stained with food and grey with dust and tobacco ash. When he saw that Randall was watching him he smiled cunningly. I've impressed him, he thought; his body felt warm and relaxed.

Dirty old chap, Randall thought idly. Why do I go on living here? He got up to go back to his room. Outside in the courtyard the sunlight struck him between the eyes. He closed them for a minute, and walked violently into George Barley, crossing the yard from the street towards his workshop.

"Ha, steady, steady," Barley grunted. The breath was knocked out of him.

"I'm sorry," Randall said in a warm voice.

"No harm done."

Randall hesitated in the doorway of the workshop when Barley went in. The smell of shavings and oil came up thick, like the smell of wood burning on a hot day. It reminded him of something in his boyhood. What? He saw his mother's face. "Nice desk you've got there," he said, to be friendly.

Barley looked at him, pleased. "Lay your hand on it," he said softly. "You get the feel of the wood, don't you? you can feel how—well, maybe you can. Yes, it's a good desk."

A film of dust hung in the air, over the men working. Looking at it from inside the workroom, it wavered in the open doorway like water running down the flank of the sunlight.

"I haven't carpentered since I left school," Randall said.

"If you want one," Barley said, "I can copy it—any time. Some Austrian oak I've had years waiting. Never get any more. Not now."

"Why not?"

"Costs too much. Before the War we used to. It's better than ours, something in the ground, I daresay. Look, there it is."

Randall peered into the corner. Cobwebs stretched one above the other, to the ceiling. He bent his long body at the knees, hands in his pockets, to look closer. He was quite willing to seem interested. Satisfy the old boy.

"Nothing's as good since the War, is it?" They all say the same things, he thought, amused, feeling at once older and younger than these war relics.

One of the workmen, an older man, lifted his head. "Nay, that it isn't," he said, in a blurred voice.

"My grandfather had eight men working for him," Barley said. "He made doors and furniture for the gentry and for well-to-do farmers. A bride always wanted something from him for her new home. My father worked for him and went on with his business when he died, but it was going to nothing even then. Tastes have changed. They don't want to pay now for good work. Spend it other ways, a wireless set, cars. Always rushing about and moving house."

He spoke slowly, without much emphasis. His eyes stared inward. Randall was quick enough to feel that a disaster was shaping itself in the man's mind. A cold breath came from Barley, as though he were isolated. Business not paying, Randall thought. He felt sorry for the men stranded in the dusty workshop like men left behind to die when the expedition moves forward. No time for them. But his sympathy was detached and impersonal. He was pretending interest. Their fate had nothing to do with him. So far as he was touched by it, their lives might have been over for a hundred years.

He went up the stairs to his room with long slack strides.

The room on the far side of his had been empty until a week since, when an elderly negro moved in. The Rev. James Daniel. His name was on an elaborate visiting-card he had nailed on the door. Randall had not seen him. Now as he was going into his room the Rev. Daniel's door opened and he came out. He had a newspaper in his hand. He held it out to the young man, pointing at a picture on the back page. "Behold and see," he said, in a rich pleasant voice, "the end of the world." It was a photograph of a fire in a country house, with firemen jetting their hoses against the fat clouds and plumes of smoke bellying from the roof.

"Oh, do you think so?" Randall said kindly. Mad. This is a nice place, he thought. Bankrupt workmen, a night club, tarts, and now a lunatic nigger. The Rev. Daniel was a big broad man, with a face so dark that his head seemed carved out of a more solid substance than flesh. Rich and glistening, the darkness poured from it. The eyes rolling above the huge cheekbones were kind and motherly, but they gave less light than a candle in a jungle.

"The Lord has spoken to me with a strong hand."

He lifted his own hand, soft-palmed, blunt, like a thick dark leaf. He smiled triumphantly at the young man.

"Afraid I must go," Randall said. Poor devil, nothing to do with me, he thought.

He could see past the Negro's shoulder into his room. It was quite empty except for a blanket folded on the floor, and a large bowl beside it filled with grey soapy water. A shabby clerical hat hung on a nail on the wall. The Rev. Daniel wore a morning coat and grey trousers, and a lay collar and tie. His clothes were creased and dusty. Most likely he slept in them, darkness congealed into darkness in the empty room.

Randall shut the door of his room. I can't live here much longer, he thought. He hated the yard because it was airless and at night hideously noisy with the cars coming to the Screech Owl. He had borrowed the room for a week from a friend of his who had gone off to South America, and during this week he met Harriet. He stayed because she stayed. She pretends to hate it, he thought. He saw her round childish face, with the look of surprise and reproach on it, and felt uneasy. He wanted to forget that he had quarrelled with her. As much as he could he kept unpleasant and unwelcome thoughts out of his mind. Life was too short.

Giulia Pizetti knocked and came into the room. He had seen her crossing the yard, carrying the duster and mop with which she cleaned his room every morning when he went to the aerodrome. He watched her make the bed, and then he half sat, half lay on it while she rubbed the furniture with the duster and ran the mop over the floor. She talked to him the whole time.

"Do you know, I think we are really going home this year. Once I was afraid we should have to stay in England for ever. I had to work in a shop. It was terrible there, I didn't like it. But then, when people began coming here, I mean people with money, because of the Screech Owl—what is that?—we had more customers, too, in the café and I could leave the shop and stay at home to help."

"Why do you want to go to Italy?" Randall asked.

He listened to her with an indulgent smile. She made him feel an older experienced man. Her beauty did not appeal to him as a young man; it was too overwhelming; he wanted something quieter and less dazzling. Perhaps without knowing it he felt that it would be too much trouble to assert himself against such a face.

"Why do you want to go away, don't you like England?"

Giulia shook her head with so much energy that the curls sprang out round it. "I'm happy anywhere. But if I had to go back to that shop——" she lifted her hands, the fingers spreading out like seaweed in water—"if I had to listen to those girls talking of boys and clothes—and they have chilblains in winter because of their thin blood. Thin blood, thin arms and bodies, thin voices. You should hear one of them say Miss—er Pi-zetty."

She began to laugh, a clear bubbling sound; she looked like her father now, the same air of gentle friendly mockery. Her eyes gleamed.

"Do you want to stay in England ?" she said.

"No."

"No."

Randall felt a sudden pleasant excitement. We all want to get away, he thought. Away where ? No matter —they were not done for, life had not got them by the leg as it had those older men downstairs, held in their old man's world. Now the sun, rushing into his room, was a challenge. Energy came to his blood from the glittering dust-stained light outside, the heat, the cloudless sky. He looked at the young girl and laughed.

"All right," he said, laughing and then smiling, "when you go to Italy I'll fly over your house on the way to Africa. Keep a sharp look out for me."

CHAPTER IV

ON HER way out of the yard Harriet ran into Mr. Alfred Linder coming in, whistling, flower in his buttonhole, got up to kill. Linder was manager of the Lunar Wine Company. It belonged to his father-in-law and he would inherit it, and so he did all the work himself, to save expense. He had a boy to deliver the goods, but he himself unlocked the front door and took the shutters down every morning and kept the books.

He was a genial ugly young Jew. He entertained ladies
in the little back room of the shop, and he was generous
to them and made them very happy by giving to each her
favourite flowers and a birthday present, and the right
sort of delicate flattery. He had a wife, of whom he was
fond. But he could no sooner help flirting with other
women, young, old, good-looking, plain, than he would
cease to breathe and long for everyone to like and admire
him. Certainly he took pains to be liked. He was like a
child who wants every other child to like him and share
his toys.

Harriet had once spoken to him in the Café Bar. Since
then he always treated her when they met as if he were
dying to be her friend. He had given her flowers, which
she accepted because she was too shy to refuse them. And
he never forgot that she had said she came from North-
umberland, and if he came across a book about that
county he bought it and gave it to her. He asked her
about her work and took a genuine interest in it, which
was more than Randall did.

She liked him and she was ashamed of him. His kindness was genuine.

"How do you do?" he said, standing in front of her.
He had a sly friendly smile. "Why are you always in
such a hurry when I speak to you? I want to talk to
you about a great many things. Are you of-fended with
me?"

"No," Harriet said. She blushed. She was embarrassed
both by his flattery and his kindness. She smiled at him,
confused, blushing. With an awkward movement of her
head and arms—she walked like a schoolboy—she dodged
past him, and hurried into the street.

She worked in Long Acre, in an advertising office. It
was not a long walk through the narrow, already bustling
streets; foreigners begin their day early, and many of these
shops and small workshops she passed were lived in by
Italians, Frenchmen, and a great many Jews. But the
street market was English all right. The men and women

standing in front of their stalls would not have been at a
loss if Elizabethan London had slipped into place behind
their backs; they were tough, careless, quick to take offence
—one man when Harriet pushed past was bawling at a
customer who had questioned the price of his lettuces:
"If you can get them cheaper, get them; they'll be good
enough for you"—strong; they stood out here in all
weathers, old women and young, with red bare hands and
necks: a woman with grey hair falling down under her ruin
of a hat thrust a rose into Harriet's face.

"Buy a flower, lady, it'll help me an' help you."

Harriet quickened her steps to be out of hearing of the
voice, whining and jeering at once. The sight of poverty
made her guilty. It was as though she were responsible,
as though simply by having four pounds a week to spend
she were accused by all the broken creatures with trays
of matches, like the man she had seen yesterday, so sunk
in himself and his poverty that he was almost invisible;
people passed him without a glance, even touched him
with not the least recognition of the truth, that here a
human being was drowning very slowly before their eyes.
It was awful; it was unbearable.

But what can I do? she thought. She was almost running; it was hot in the streets, and as airless as though all
the air were sucked back, but without disturbing the
straws, the pieces of torn newspaper, the bus tickets, lying
in the gutter.

But if she had bought a flower out of pity, she would
then only have been exasperated by her folly in wasting
money on it. What use was threepence? And she gave
away too many threepences. Very likely that woman had
had a few of them—she avoided looking at their faces
when she laid the money in their outstretched hands or on
the tray, waving aside the proffered box of matches. I
ought to put aside so much money to give away every
week, she thought. She would never do it. Money
slipped through her fingers too quickly, and usually she
was penniless before the end of the week, or she borrowed

a shilling or two from Randall, pretending that she needed change. But I'm a bad manager, she said frowning. She caught sight of herself, hurrying, in her last year's hat, in the mirror of a shop. She thought of Josephine Rapp—probably still in bed; later she would get up in a leisurely way and put on some charming summery dress and go out to lunch with Bill Randall; while I—I, Harriet Brown—who worked to get scholarships, wanted to come to London and came, thinking myself so lucky, creep into an A.B.C. to order a glass of milk and wonder whether I dare buy a pair of shoes next week—but it's Fred's birthday the week after and I promised, what was it I promised him? They'll let me know before then. Trust them.

She had forgotten the begging woman. She forgot that to possess—if you could call it possession, with so many eyes fixed on her to see what she did with it—the large sum of four pounds every week was a crime against society, to be expiated by giving away more of it. Now she knew that she would not be satisfied unless she had a chance to become rich, famous, respected. People must know about her and listen to her. She must have money, plenty of money, and time—time to read, travel abroad, buy clothes. And that was not all.

There must be excitement in her life. I want, she thought—but she did not know what it was. Something that was just round the corner. Her thoughts shot off in pursuit of it, rising suddenly like the swan she had seen hurl himself from the dark stagnant water in a strong curved sweep that carried him across the trees while she watched, hardly able to breathe, the blood knocking in her veins, in joy and terror. What is it? what is it? she said to herself. The pavement rocked a little under her feet. The house fronts, the shops, the face of a child hurrying to school with his books, were all outlined by the sudden flame. I shall be rich, she said to herself. I shall be respected and famous, people will ask my opinion, and I shall have power over them.

She saw Randall's face as he got up, pushing his chair

back. And in spite of it I shall be lonely, she thought. She saw herself, still a young woman, surrounded by friends, self-assured, elegant—but alone. Then one day she came face to face with him. A look was enough. Their love—it was like nothing that commonplace men and women could feel; it burned them up—drove them into each other's arms—My love, my love.

She could not help smiling.

There were two ways she could reach her room in the office. To-day she chose to go in by the side door and up the servants' staircase of the dingy old house. As she pushed open the door of the small room she shared with two persons—another copywriter and a typist—she felt the familiar unhappiness. What am I doing here? Why waste any more time, my precious time, writing lying descriptions of face creams to tempt other women into spending money? The room was very stuffy and dusty. The window was half open; it had jammed and refused to move any further, the other girl said, grumbling.

"It's awful," Harriet said aloud.

"I'd complain if I wasn't leaving next week."

"Oh, are you leaving?"

"Yes, I am. I'm going to get married. We meant to wait, but what's the use o' waiting when, if you believe everything, there'll be a war—or something of the sort—before you can say knife. And anyway why wait? My boy thinks a lot, and he says, What have we to wait *for*?"

Harriet murmured the proper words. She had seen the boy: two or three times during the week he came to fetch his young woman and Harriet passed him hanging about the dark staircase: he was undersized—they both were—and pale and skinny. She too would have been pale if she had not made lavish use of lipstick and rouge. What kind of children will they have? Harriet wondered. She felt sorry for them and superior. Her own future appeared so glorious, contrasted with the lives of these drab spiritless poor creatures.

"I hope you'll be very happy," she said, in a warm voice.

The other girl removed herself, suddenly and without effort, out of the reach of Harriet Brown's patronizing kindness and pity. "We'll be as happy as other people," she said, lifting her head sharply, in a gesture which Harriet now knew instinctively to be copied from one of her mother's or her grandmother's. "You can't expect a lot of happiness—not if you marry, you can't—but what's the odds? You've got to live. You've got to get on with it—that's what I say."

CHAPTER V

THE SLOW movement of the sunlight about New Moon Yard. You never caught it moving, but the shadow was driven relentlessly across the walls, and the small shadows under the windows became black and sharp. By half-past ten the sun had swallowed three sides of the yard. It filled Barley's workshop with a bronzed dust; Sally Barley jerked down the blinds in the two rooms above the workshop, to save the carpets. Pizetti's sun-blind made the café dark and tepidly cool. There were shutters, old and rotting, at the windows of their bedrooms. The sun flooded into Pop's attic above—he was out—and thrust a vibrant shaft through a triangular slit in the linen blind of the room next his.

The woman in the bed flinched, and turned over to escape it. Her head ached and she felt hot. The air in the room was fouler than she knew, because she was sleeping in it, but she felt it on her tongue and her eyelids. She kept her eyes stubbornly closed. My God, must I? she thought.

What sounded like a quarrel began in the yard below her window. It was only Pizetti talking with another Italian who wanted to sell him something. She listened to the

foreign voices. There was a smell of coffee. There were
trees bordering the river, she thought, and across the
square was the café where we had breakfast and my dada
said, Open your mouth and shut your eyes and see what
the gods have sent you. A piece of sugar he'd soaked in
the strong black coffee he drank, a canard he said it was,
what does that mean, canard? did he tell me? I can't
remember, it's like a picture or something, the leaves, the
dusty ground, white, mother's hat and blouse, I can't see
her face, though, the hot sky, burning hot, blue, like glass,
I see it as if I, oh my God it's years ago, twenty years or
something of that, I was a kid of eight.

She opened her eyes, reluctantly, and lay for some
minutes with her back to the window, watching the yellow
light on the wall. With sudden resolution she rolled sideways out of bed and stood yawning. Her feet, puffy and
not over clean, curled back from the rug.

She began to dress, taking her garments from the end
of the bed—chemise, stays, knickers. The stockings lying
there had kept the shape of her feet. Looking at her face
in the glass, she thought, I shan't wash, it only brings the
rash out. There were creases in the skin near her mouth,
where she had lain with her face pressed into the pillow.
She opened her mouth widely, trying to see the hollow
tooth at the back that ached whenever she drank anything cold.

She felt about under the pillow for a handkerchief,
moistened a corner of it between her lips and worked
round her eyes. Stepping back, she said aloud: "That's
better. Now shall I slip m'dress on and go down to the
café, or make m'self a cup of tea?" She was in the habit
of talking aloud to herself; it made her feel less neglected.

She decided to make the tea, because it was cheaper and
put off the trouble of dressing and doing her hair. While
she drank it her glance wandered rather vacantly about
the room. The big heavy bed took up a third of the
space. There was a dressing-table, a cupboard, a washstand, a slop-pail with combings of hair floating on top,

and behind the screen a shelf and a gas-ring. The door of the cupboard was open. Shoes, dirty clothes, and some cups and plates were at the bottom under the clothes hanging up. On the washstand was a badly-burned milk pan and a jug with a little milk. She poured the milk into her tea; there was scarcely enough to colour it, and she made a disappointed face.

"Hard luck I can't even have a decent cup."

She began to draw the blind up, but stopped it half-way. "Fry m'self like an egg under this roof," she said in a grumbling voice.

She looked down at her knees, at the flesh bulging before it was squeezed into the elastic of her knickers. They seemed to her pathetic, and she rubbed them gently with her free hand. "Whoops, dearie," she said to encourage them. She stood up, and tilted the mirror so that it reflected the lower half of her body, narrow waist and disproportionately heavy thighs straining against the fawn silk. "They skimp the stuff in these artificial knickers. If I had the money now I'd get another flowered ninon, the set, with open legs. Or I could rub out those I have —they'd dry in this sun."

She rummaged in a half-hearted way among the pile of dirty garments. "No, I'll do the room. Couldn't bring anyone in in this state, even if I—I've still got six quid, by the time it's spent I'll—blast this dress——"

With a weak fury she dragged her dress down over her shoulders, tearing it across the front. Pin it. Her hand felt over the dressing table for a safety-pin, and in the drawer. No luck. She worked her feet into the slippers lying half under the bed and slodged to the door. It was locked, and the key, as usual, had fallen out of the lock. She groped for it on the floor.

Her room opened straight on to the passage. One day she had amused herself by making a name-plate on one of those machines, and it was nailed under the number. Miss Enid Jones. Each time she noticed it she thought, complacently, Lots wouldn't have bothered with the Miss.

She hesitated outside Mrs. Kerr's door, uncertain of her welcome, then pressed the bell with nervous boldness. It was one of those bells which ring just the other side of the door, and made her jump. Mrs. Kerr opened the door.

"Oh, it's you, is it? Come in."

She was cool and offhand. Snooty, almost. Aggrieved Enid Jones pushed past her into the room, pretending not to notice. What's the matter with her? she thought moodily: I'm as good as she is.

"Lend me a safety-pin, will you? I tore m'dress."

"Where? Oh, I see."

Jean-Ann Kerr's cold glance took in the other woman from bed-mussed hair to down-at-heel slippers. She felt distaste. In the same instant a prick of Calvinist energy started in her. Clean her up. Rouse her. "A pin's no use there," she said in an even voice, "but whip the dress off and I'll mend it for you."

Enid Jones felt comforted because trouble was being taken over her. She sat down on the bed.

"I can't take it off, it'll tear worse. Give me a pin though and I'll draw it up—it won't show in the folds."

Moving briskly, Mrs. Kerr found and threaded a needle. She sat sideways to hold the torn edges in place and stitch them together neatly. The sour smell of the other woman's body and breath offended her. She hated to have her sitting on her bed. As soon as she had finished the job she stood up and walked to the middle of the room, hoping that if she remained standing the other woman would take the hint, and go. Yet she could not resist asking questions.

"What are you doing?"

Now it's beginning, Enid Jones thought. She was half irritated—and half eager to talk about herself. Only if I talk I say too much, she thought. She suspected everybody of laughing at her behind her back.

"Well, you know I been sick, I was going to the hospital three weeks the doctor said I ought to come back but I'm not going, what's the use they can't do anything for you

when it's money you need.   Living in that room, an oven
it is now, and trailing along a passage to the closet and
now that black man I don't like sitting on it after, well do
you ?   If I had the money——"

"Well, you had that hundred pounds left you," Mrs.
Kerr said.   Her voice pounced.   "If you'd taken that
and gone home you'd be fit now."

"I *could* have gone——"

"I simply can't bear seeing a woman let herself go.
What's going to happen when you've spent it ?   Not even
a decent dress to show.   And a stomach like a barrel You
ought to be ashamed at your age to have such a figure.
What man's going to go with you looking like you look ? "

"Mind your own business," Enid Jones said.

She was ashamed and hurt.   She got up, trying to seem
dignified, and went out of the room.   What did I come
for ?   Her arm knocked over the flimsy table that filled the
space between the two doors.   Have I broke it ?   No—
and I don't care.   But she was mortified by her clumsi-
ness.   She rushed back to her room.   Her heart was beating
"like one o'clock."   She knelt down and opened the cupboard of the washstand, and took out the small flat bottle
of brandy.   A bowl with a few lumps of sugar was still on
the chair beside her used cup.   She poured brandy on
three of them and crunched them between her front teeth
with eager enjoyment.   "Does you more good, they say,
than drinking it."   But her knees were shaking still.   The
thought jumped into her head that she would go down
and pay a visit to the doctor living on the floor below.
She felt excited at once.   It was the thought of talking
about herself to a man, a doctor—if he was really a doctor.
She would feel better, soothed.   He must be something if
he isn't a doctor, she thought; he must know something,
calling himself that.   Well, they could punish him.

She spread cream on her face and neck, and rubbed in
the Coty powder, with a flat soiled pad.   "No colour.
Rachel.   The paler I look, the better.   Make him look
hard at me."

It meant going out into the yard, in the sun, burning on her face and the back of her neck, past the workshop—she thought the men there must be staring after her and she swung her hips, taking slow short steps—then up a staircase as narrow and bare as her own, to the first floor. Plain as the nose on your face. Dr. Cleveland. A proper printed visiting-card. No bell, though. Summoning all her impudence, she knocked. *Is* he a doctor? she thought quivering. If he is, what's he doing here unless he, the same old game I suppose, I could have gone to him instead of going to Mrs. Haveyouthemoneyready? the old whore, if only I'd thought.

"Come in."

She sent an appraising glance over the room. It was uncomfortably tidy. There was a desk, a shabby sofa, a cupboard, chairs, table. Part of the room was curtained off. Must be the bed, she thought.

"Please sit down."

"Thank you," she said, trying to make her voice sound well. You can tell a lady by the way she speaks. I suppose you know I'm a lady.

Dr. Cleveland sat heavily behind his desk, heavy body buttoned into a grey coat, heavy dark face, thick hands and thighs. She had never seen him before without his hat. He had thick black hair, glossy and yet dead-looking. Perhaps he dyes it. He might be any age; his face was well-nourished and almost unlined; aquiline nose jutting between bright grey eyes; a long mouth; but it looked used. By the look of it, he might have been using it for an extremely long time. He's impudent, she thought. But, no, it was not that, not impudence. Well, what's he doing here? The answer came too pat, from some darkness in her own body. Living, I suppose—like the rest of us: what are any of us doing? She felt oppressed and queasy, and wished she had stayed in her room.

"Here," she said suddenly: "here—before I start, what's your fee?"

She forgot completely to speak in a ladylike voice. The

doctor's eyes had been inquisitive; he looked at her with a sardonic smile, but his voice was polite enough.

"What do you want me to do? What's the matter with you?"

She felt the excitement again. "That's for you to say. I been ill on and off for months, after I had a—miscarriage. I don't seem to get m'strength back. I——"

"How old are you?"

"Twenty-three."

"How old are you really?"

"Twenty-eight if you must know."

The excitement went out of her; she felt wretched again. What d' I come for, it's no use, is it? She was full of self-pity, thinking of the pain when the woman, the big smiling woman, what d' she smile for, it isn't funny. There's no fun in having that done to you, I said, but perhaps you're thinking of the money. It was all she could do to keep from crying when she thought how she had been hurt, and no one cared. Kindness I want, a little kindness. I've been hurt. She looked imploringly at the man.

"Aren't you going to examine me?"

He shook his head, slowly.

"Here—I can pay." She began to fumble in her bag, among the keys, *papier-poudré*, soiled handkerchief, lipstick.

"I don't examine patients here," he said.

She stared at him. "Well, where do you then?" I'm not going to pay twice.

"I have a consulting room." He kept his eyes on her, as sharp in his head as needles. "I may need an assistant. But perhaps your friend——?"

"What d'you mean my friend?" she said aggressively.

He lifted his hand, jerking his head at the window. "I mean the young lady I've seen you with in the Café Bar. Perhaps I'm making a mistake."

"You are if you think I go round with a nurse." She was disappointed; the interview had fallen flat, and she felt that in some way she had been insulted—it was a feeling she often had, and it always made her cry. She turned very red, and got up to go.

The doctor stood up, too. He came up to her, put his big hand on her cheek and pulled down a lower eyelid. "Ever have headaches?" he asked.

"Oh, shocking—fit to split. Feels as if m'head was opening from front to back. And m'knees—why, I——"

"All right. Undo your dress."

She lay down on the couch, and watched him open the door of the cupboard. There was a row of steel instruments and a basin or two. He was lying all the time, she thought. Now she felt a flutter of happiness, and her body was flaccid and relaxed. She expected him to pity her. She always expected people to pity her, and the numerous disappointments she suffered only made her more eager and hopeful with each new person she met. "I'm as weak as a titty," she said, giggling.

The doctor's examination was careless. He did not ask her when she had had the abortion which had completed the ruin of her health; she was so played out now that there was nothing he could have done for her, even if he had been able to treat her. He wasn't able. And would it be worth it? To survive as a professional tart you needed to be tough in mind as in body. He looked down at the young woman's yellow sagging body, and wondered with half-surprised contempt why all this fuss about human life.

"You can't stand the life you're leading," he said.

"Well, what am I to do?" She looked at him with one arm dangling outside her dress. A drop of sweat ran down her face. Isn't he going to do anything? she thought.

He took a card out of a drawer in the desk and handed it to her. "Call there any afternoon. I'll give you a tonic containing the juice evaporated *in vacuo* of camomile, elder berry, dandelion, ragwort, wormwood, gentian and St. John's wort. It will penetrate every passage in your body. You'll be a new woman. And you owe me"

—his cold unfriendly glance passed over her again—"five shillings down now."

She took the money out of her handbag and gave it to him. Her hands were shaking. She felt that she had been treated rather badly, but when she read the card after he had shown her out of the room she thought, Why not give it a try? Dr. Cleveland, Herbalist, 198 Brewer Street. Female pills. He must make a pot with all those things.

The air was like stepping into a hot bath. Her eyelids fluttered. A tiny prick of excitement moved in her again. Try it. She walked slowly, deliberately, looking in front of her.

CHAPTER VI

BARLEY LOOKED up from the bench, and saw two men standing outside the window. Their faces were distorted and obscured by the layer of dust on the glass. Then he looked at his watch. It was close on half-past eleven.

The men outside went through an elaborate business of looking for matches and lighting cigarettes, and all the time they were staring through the dusty window into the workshop. Both men were Jews. The elder, a man close on fifty, was short, with a lean face like a sheep, yellow and wrinkled. He was carefully dressed, but he had high heels on his shoes. He had quick, sneering eyes. The other man was fresh-coloured and handsome in the face; he was tall and broad-shouldered—in the middle thirties. He must have put on flesh lately, because his jacket was tight for him: he undid it when he was searching in his pockets for matches, and displayed a violently striped shirt and plaid braces.

He jerked his head towards the Café Bar, and they sauntered towards it. Pizetti glanced at them when they came in. They came in slowly, standing long enough in the doorway to look round the room. The older man's eyes took in everything. Then they sat at a table in the window. Pizetti came over at once to take their order. He never let Giulia wait on the tougher customers of the café. Neither did he try to discourage them from coming. He did not want trouble. Besides, the people who dropped in because they had noticed the place when they were going into the Screech Owl expected to see a few what they would call "underworld" faces. It was part of the fun.

He served them and went back behind the bar.

"Is this the place, Ben?"

The younger man nodded. "That's it. Noticed it last March when I dropped in here with Maurice. A week ago I was passing, I went in, the boss was out, and talked to one of his men. He said the work was slack—take on anything."

"It's a fifty pound job," the other man said. "Your sort of job." He smiled without humour. His smile showed a fine set of artificial teeth.

"It's only one place," Ben said mildly. "I was asking round about the club. Place behind you."

Both men stared, in the same meditative way, at the front of the Screech Owl.

"Well?"

"They say the fellow who runs it is short of money. Doesn't pay his bills. Ex-officer."

"What is it?"

"Usual thing. Drinks out of hours. Spieler in a back room."

Both men had the same habit of speaking without looking at each other. They looked instead into the yard; their eyes would follow a man crossing the yard until he was out of sight. To the onlooker—Pizetti—there was a curious suggestion of weight in these fixed glances, as though an identical and menacing train of thought lay behind them.

"Another fellow, bogey, was nosing round in Hackney last Friday," Ben said. "Maurice spotted him, what he was after. Same thing. Maurice let on he was a bit worried himself, but didn't know anything, only worried. From what the fellow said the insurance companies been told by Scotland Yard they *knew* someone was raising fires. All this fellow wanted was the evidence, see? Maurice doesn't have no evidence either, he's just worried. Maurice says——"

The older man cut him short, with a gesture of two fingers. "The insurance companies should worry. They raised the premiums to two guineas per cent, didn't they?"

"Yeah, but——"

"Listen, Ben. It doesn't matter what they *know*—they haven't got their evidence and they won't get it. Who's going to hand it to them? If you're windy step out here. I'm not worried." He smiled amiably. "That's all at present from yours truly Con Franklyn."

The younger man stretched an arm across the table and patted Franklyn's sleeve. "Oh, you know I'm not windy, Con," he said with a broad smile. It creased his face into a mask of good humour.

Franklyn looked at him briefly. "Still thinking of buying a garage?"

"Saw the very place I want last week," Ben smiled. "Place in Essex. Cross-roads. Blue and white painted. The identical place."

"The mug's dream," the older man said softly.

"No, but, Con. You got everything you want in that house in Stoke Newington. Marble steps to the door. Fourteen rooms, is it? I don't want nothing like that. Ruth don't want it."

He was speaking with a certain eagerness. Franklyn opened his mouth, shut it like a lid snapping, opened it. "So I've got everything I want?" he said under his breath. "Everything I want. You would know."

The younger man looked at him and looked away.

"Now if I had a house in Park Lane," Franklyn said in

the same voice, "and a yacht, a couple of cars, and a place in Surrey, then maybe I would get what I——"

He broke off as Pizetti, on his way to the door, passed close enough to the table to overhear. His glance followed Pizetti across the room to the door, and outside, resting on him until he saw that the Italian was absorbed in an argument with the man who had beckoned him into the yard. Ben finished his drink and looked round. Giulia came over to him at once. He looked up at her with the smile that made him seem frank and good-tempered.

"Thirsty weather," he smiled.

Giulia laughed back. "I like it," she said. She put her hand on her forehead and pushed back the tiny damp curls clinging there.

Ben talked to her easily and gaily for a minute, and she answered in a friendly voice. The older man watched them with sardonic indifference.

"Could I have another cup of coffee?" Ben said.

"You could," the girl laughed.

She went away. In the meantime Pizetti came back, and it was he and not his daughter who brought the cup over.

"Nice place you got here," Ben said.

"Yes, it is nice," Pizetti said, with his twinkling smile.

"Insured?" asked Franklyn.

Pizetti looked at him. "No. No, why should I pay money to insure a place which doesn't belong to me? Besides, I go back to Italy very soon."

"Made your fortune, eh?"

"No," Pizetti said quietly. "No, I made no fortune."

His thoughts flew to the box hidden under the towels in the "office." The life of a capitalist is a wearing one. If you put your money in the bank you may lose it any day, and keeping it at home there are burglars. He had suspected this pair as soon as they came in. He went back to the bar and stood with his back to the cupboard.

Franklyn drummed with his fingers on the table. He seemed sunk in thought, and the other man did not dare to interrupt him, but he was tired of sitting here.   He thought of his wife, who was expecting a baby.   Although they had been married eight years, it was her first, and she was nervous.   This morning she had complained of a pain in her back, but it was too soon yet—but he wondered Is she all right?

"Maurice was talking to the detective, eh?" Franklyn said.

"Not exactly," Ben said easily.   "He was talking to Maurice.   He thinks Maurice is worried like he is.   See? He mentions your name to Maurice.   Mr. Constantine Franklyn, he says.   Mr. Franklyn has one fire in his house in Stoke Newington and two fires in his factory in Hackney. Maurice says, Oh, has he? he says; maybe someone started those fires like they started all the fires?   Or maybe——"

Franklyn's mouth drew into a cold line.   "Maurice should take care he isn't too clever," he said in a dry voice.

Ben didn't speak.   He had few fears and no conscience— the only person he had ever considered since he was a boy was his wife; and she was an extension of himself in female form.   But he was afraid of Franklyn's colder angers.   He admired him, too.   He tried not to fidget in the prolonged silence.   Was it true that Con had nothing in his bank but an overdraft?   He spent freely on his house, on himself, good wines, cigars, plenty of posh clothes, and on a big talkative wife and two daughters.   Ben's mind flickered and took another turn.   No East End Jew would give the bogies the evidence they were looking for.   But maybe if someone, some woman, dropped a wrong word——   His face had lost its pleasant expression; it became mean and avid.   But he was physically unable to contemplate a dis-agreeable future; after a minute he began thinking with a reckless optimism about the garage he was hoping to buy and start a (more or less) honest life.   Unconsciously, as he sprawled in his chair, he began knocking one heel on the floor.   Franklyn suddenly snarled at him.   He stopped at once.

Franklyn got up and walked over to the bar.   Pizetti

watched him anxiously. His thin scarecrow body stiffened. He would defend the "office" with his life. His life, his future, was inside there, locked in a shabby wooden box.

All Franklyn did was to lean with one elbow on the bar and order coffee. Ben had followed him, like a dog; he sprawled across the counter and took an egg from the dish and began peeling it. He ate it in silence and Franklyn drank in silence. Finally he pushed his empty cup aside, and spoke to Pizetti.

"What sort of a place is it?" He jerked his head over his shoulder in the direction of the Screech Owl.

"How should I know?" Pizetti said. "I have never been inside."

"But you know something about it," Franklyn said. He gave Pizetti a cold glance.

Pizetti's faded blue eyes sparkled with a rash courage. "I tell you—what should I know about the place? It has plenty of customers. They get drunk, they dance—I suppose they pay for it. I don't know anything."

He looked quickly from one to the other, meeting from each the same cold, meditative glance. Ben spoke.

"I heard the fellow who runs it can't pay his bills," he said.

"Ah." Pizetti's face changed with relief. He smiled almost merrily. So he thought, they had been sent to spy on Ashton. Everyone for himself in this world. And the proprietor of the Screech Owl was not his friend. "I've heard that." He felt a twinge, a sudden compunction. His face became grave. "But perhaps it isn't true. You can't believe much you hear."

CHAPTER VII

AT TWELVE o'clock Randall brought his car into the yard from the garage and began to look over the plugs. He was surprised, and not very pleased, to see Josephine Rapp come in. He didn't expect her for an hour. His hands were greasy; he wiped them roughly clean, picked up his jacket from the seat, and took her over to the Café Bar for a drink.

"Well," she said, with a smile. "I thought you would be waiting for me—impatient."

"I'm never impatient," he said. "I wait for things and they come."

She was piqued by his calmness. Quite often, when she had been thinking of him as young and immature, he made a remark which seemed to open up an abyss of indifference, to her and other people.

She was twenty-five—his age. She expected men to want to make love with her. She could fall in love with any reasonably attractive man who took an interest in her; the reason she had not fallen for Randall was that beyond taking pains with her as a pupil he did not notice her. After some time she had the idea of talking to him about record flights. Then he became interested. Like any adolescent, she thought scornfully. He talked to her. He showed her maps. He was more patient with her mistakes in the air.

She hinted to him that her father might be induced to put up the money for a flight to the Cape and back.

It was not a bad idea. She played with it sometimes when she was bored. She had moments when she wanted to break through her present life into a future, indistinct, of effort and glory. She imagined herself flying on a forlorn hope. Probably in war time. She succeeded. Of course she succeeded.

She sat on one of the high stools at the bar, and wrinkled her eyes at Pizetti. She liked him. He reminded her of a character in a French film. He was agile, shabby, and childishly friendly.

"I'll have tomato juice."

Randall went through to the kitchen to wash his hands at Mrs. Pizetti's sink. Maddalena tilted her head backwards to see whom he had brought into the café with him. She looked at him with a searching, placid glance. She did not like Josephine. He knew it because she said nothing.

Giulia came in. "What lovely clothes she has," she whispered.

"Yes," Randall said. He looked at Mrs. Pizetti with a faint smile.

"Fine tails make fine birds," Maddalena said.

Drying his hands, he could see Josephine talking to Pizetti. She'll flirt with anyone, he thought. He was amused, and indifferent.

When he went in she turned her charm full on him. She was looking well, and she knew it. Her hair, thick, sleek, alive, was fresh from Mr. Charles's hands; she had a skin too good to need touching, and fine eyes. Her mouth was small, and she used a lipstick that made it geranium pink and moist. Yes, she was well turned-out.

"Where are we lunching?" she asked.

"Where you like. Ivy?"

"The last time I was there I was with a man who joined Mosley later."

"I shan't do that," Randall said. "What did he do it for?"

"I don't know. He took me down afterwards somewhere near Winchester and made me climb a hill he said was where the Anglo-Saxons defeated the Danes. He fought it all out for me. I could see he thought he was charging at the head of his men. Poor darling, he's colour-blind, he won't be able to tell a red flag from a blue one."

Randall laughed. She acted the story as she told it,

with comic vigour. She was good fun. He saw her look at herself in the mirror behind the bar.

"Why didn't you turn up for your lesson yesterday?"

"My dear Bill, I'd spent the night until six a.m. dancing with two Americans my parent was entertaining. Steel men, he said. They danced like it. My God, I thought I'd fractured every bone. I couldn't lift my head in the morning."

"You'll never fly properly unless you work at it harder," he said.

She smiled at him from the corners of her eyes. "Dear Bill. You think nothing else is worth doing. Don't you?"

"No. I wouldn't say that," he said judicially. "There's science—and doctors. But not dancing with fat old men."

"I never said they were old or fat," she protested.

"You don't dance, do you, Bill?" she said.

"No," he said, "I don't."

"Why don't you dance? We could've gone places."

"I don't like it," he said. Actually, he was a little ashamed of not being able to dance. He would never take the trouble to learn. He thought he ought to be able to dance without learning.

"Don't like it. Don't like it," Josephine mocked. "You're uncivilized, my dear." She saw that she had annoyed him, and turned deftly to the one topic which was certain to please him.

"I've asked Father to come with me to the Screech Owl to-morrow night. Can you be there?"

"Yes," Randall said. He swallowed his sudden anger. He forgot it in the excitement started up by her words. He quelled that, too. Blessed is he that expects nothing. Since his childhood he had inured himself not to give away hope or disappointment. Then no one would know too much about him.

"Of course I should like to meet your Father," he said. His cigarette had gone out, and he lit another. He hardly ever smoked one to the end. Too much trouble to go on with it.

"You can speak to him about wanting to break the Cape record."

"Have you spoken to him?" Randall asked. He did not look at her.

"I said something about it." What an infant he is, after all, she thought. She felt sorry for him.

"Look what's coming into the yard," she cried. Randall turned his head to look. Pizetti, the other customers, Giulia, all turned to look through the door when she cried out in her clear, emphatic tone. She was delighted, Randall saw, to have produced an effect. Maddalena even came out of the kitchen.

A dozen or more men and women had trooped into the yard and were standing there in a bunch, like cattle on a country road, their heads turning this way and that. There were only three men: two of them hung back diffidently, and the third, a short, plump, red-cheeked man in frock coat and top-hat, seemed to be in charge of the party. He raised his arm. He swung round, like a mechanical toy, pointing this way and that, and all the women turned as he turned. They screwed their eyes against the sun. Smiles, like torn pieces of paper, fluttered on their faces. In the dazzling sunlight all of them, except the man in the frock coat, appeared slightly distorted, like leaves floating under water.

"What are they? Who are they?" Josephine said.

She sprang from her high stool and walked quickly, her legs pressing against the white linen skirt, into the courtyard. Randall watched her walking boldly up to the group. She bent her head to speak to the leader. Among all those middle-aged and downy women she was like a dancer in a ballet. She walked with short, jerky, dancing steps. He thought suddenly of Harriet; she walked with her head down, awkwardly, as though she had to force her way through a crowd without looking at anyone. What a bore all this is, he thought.

Josephine had come back. An ironical smile drew down the edges of her mouth.

c

"They're the Society for the Preservation of Ancient Monuments," she said. She announced it to the café. Standing there, she showed herself off with a half-innocent gaiety; she wanted to be admired for her enterprise; and, yet, she was friendly; she liked people.

"They are going to preserve me!" Pizetti said, smiling. His eyes shone. That was the kind of simple joke he enjoyed.

"Come along," Randall said to Josephine.

She did not want to leave. But he had paid for their drinks, and he walked with his long, careless strides to the door. She had to follow him. Passing the preservers of ancient monuments she sent a dazzling smile towards the little man; he lifted his top-hat, and bowed. He was ridiculous. She wanted Randall to notice him, but he had stalked ahead of her to the car and was waiting with an aloof air. Is he jealous? she thought. The thought pleased her.

The little man put his hat on again hurriedly. He was afraid of sun-stroke in this heat. He looked round him at the listening faces of his flock. Almost for the first time he consciously disliked them. None shared his love—it was passion—for the houses men had built themselves so many many years ago. For reasons of their own they pretended to. One, a schoolmistress, had joined his society to be instructed. Another, elderly woman, came because she had lost her husband and all her sons in the War; she joined societies and attended lectures so that she need never be at home. Not one, he felt certain, had known the acute joy of touching the past at its quick in some old building. It was the simple natural happiness he had expected from a woman, and had not had: his wife was a pleasant woman, willing, but he had taken in her only a moderate pleasure. No doubt, he used to think, it is my own fault.

But to step into this yard, and feel, on his flesh, the breath of a man living in the seventeenth century—his mind darkened with ecstasy. He breathed deeply, almost panting. The next instant, he thought, would bring him a revelation.

"It's been altered, hasn't it, Mr. Percy?"

The gushing, timid voice close to his ear shocked him. He turned round. Smile, smile, he said savagely to himself.

"Alas, yes, Mrs. de Corson. But you can still see plainly what a beautiful house it was. New Moon House. It's the only house of its character in the centre of London. What we've to do, now, is to prevent it's being torn down to put up a cinema." He shuddered deeply. "I think a letter to his Grace—he showed himself interested and amenable when I approached him in March——"

So interested that he fell asleep during the interview. Mr. Percy had felt like a mother whose son has been laughed at. He watched stupefied. And yet he reverenced the upper classes.

"Oh, dear, it's hot."

"Shall we examine one of the staircases?" he said mechanically. "It will be cooler."

At twelve-thirty the Café Bar was empty. Maddalena brought in a steaming bowl of macaroni, cooked with cheese, eggs, and tomatoes, and she and Giulia sat down, at the table nearest the kitchen. Gregorio was about to join them when he saw Charlotte Mannheim crossing the yard towards the café. He welcomed her with his kind smile.

"I will have coffee," she said, in her precise thick voice.

She noticed that they were eating lunch and felt uncomfortable. But she did not know how to excuse herself for coming in now. She had no little polite speeches.

It was less and less easy for her to talk to an acquaintance. She had little practice. Days passed during which she spoke to no one, and then, perhaps, she would go to some room or to an obscure hall in which a meeting of anarchists was being held, and she would make her speech, and afterwards talk to a few of them, but only about their beliefs. Never anything personal.

In the last year these meetings were more frequent. There were French and once or twice Spanish comrades, and the meetings protested against the betrayal of the revolution in Spain by communists acting under orders from the arch-traitor in Moscow. Charlotte Mannheim spoke at all these meetings. She spoke with a passionate bitterness. Her hearers applauded as always. And yet she felt lost, isolated. She felt that the younger women and men respected her as an old anarchist, one of the legendary martyrs of the faith. But she was not in their inner councils. They put her forward on the platform and let her talk. And that was all.

She saw Pizetti walking away from her, and realized that he had put her coffee in front of her, and she had not thanked him.

She raised her voice, that still resonant voice. "Thank you."

He turned back. "You have everything?" he said.

What made her say it?.."This is my birthday. I am seventy."

Pizetti's thin cheeks creased into friendly smiles. "So it is your birthday? Then you will be our guest—do you like macaroni? Giulia, fetch another plate."

Without the least confusion, she found herself sitting opposite Mrs. Pizetti, who looked at her as if she were a child. She has a good face, I can trust her, she thought. She scrutinized all faces, from a lifelong habit.

Pizetti was talking, using his free hand to gesticulate, while he swept macaroni into his mouth.

"How will you celebrate your birthday?" he asked.

"You're too inquisitive," his wife said.

"Oh, I don't mind," Charlotte said. "To-night I'm going to speak at a meeting—an anarchist meeting. I am an anarchist." They may be police spies, she thought. In that case, I am telling them nothing they don't know about me. But why tell them anything? It must be true that I'm too old now. It's no wonder no one consults me. She saw Maddalena Pizetti looking at her with calm interest. No, they are not spies, she is not a spy.

"Well, I could be an anarchist myself," Pizetti said. "If this were a reasonable world I should be an anarchist. It would suit me quite well. But, as you see, it is not reasonable. To live in it, one must hold one's tongue or one must fight. There is one thing we cannot do—that is, to think. To think is forbidden."

How weary Charlotte felt! It was as though her youth had lived on—hidden, God knows where—until to-day, and to-day it had given up its ghost. Ghost of a young slender woman, with copper-coloured hair, tireless, upheld by faith and love. She had fled now to join those other ghosts, of the dead and the living, whose only refuge on earth was in the mind of one old lonely woman.

"I am not giving in," she said, defiantly. "I shall speak so long as I have a tongue in my throat. They will have to wither it to silence me."

"Don't be afraid," Maddalena Pizetti said.

"Afraid? I? I am not afraid." She let the fork drop from her thick ugly hand. "Yes, you are right," she said in a low voice. "I was lying. I am afraid. Suppose that, when I die, I realize then that my whole life has been useless? That human beings can never be reasonable, never respect each other as—as I respect you," she finished strangely.

"Well, there is Russia," Pizetti said cheerfully.

Charlotte Mannheim's head sank lower still. "Yes, there is Russia," she said inaudibly. "I, too, once believed in Russia." She glanced up and saw that Giulia was looking at her with compassion. "You are sorry for me because I am old. No, never mind—you're only quite right." She laughed. "It's an incurable illness."

Giulia laughed gently, as though she were confused. The idea of herself as an old woman was too preposterous to be entertained. Even to be as old as her mother must be difficult.

She jumped up. Seizing the coffee-pot, she said:
"You must have some more coffee for your birthday.
I'll make it," and she disappeared into the kitchen. They
heard her whistling like a thrush.

Charlotte Mannheim said fiercely: "Stalin killed my
husband."

She saw them look at her stupefied. "What did I say?
What nonsense! I'm mad." She pressed her hand on
her head. "It is forty years since my husband was killed
—and he was killed in Hungary, by the police. Don't
take any notice. I was dreaming."

"It's the heat," Pizetti said. "Only this morning I
imagined that two nasty customers had come here to rob
the place. Or do some harm." He laughed his long
chuckling laugh, which made him seem the most lovable
of scarecrows.

"No one in this country drinks enough olive oil,"
Maddalena Pizetti said tranquilly. "It cures anything—
sleeplessness, colds, stone, everything."

Other people had come into the café. Pizetti got up to
attend to them, and his wife went into the kitchen.
Charlotte was left alone with a pot of fresh coffee. She
closed her eyes. There was a night, in Spain—how many
years ago?—when she and Thomas slept wrapped in a
thin blanket between two olive fields. It rained, a light
rain like mist. She was afraid that Thomas would be ill
from the cold, and she held him in her arms all the night.
In the very early morning she saw the grey trees as it were
floating in the mist; for no reason, ecstasy poured into her
veins from them. She trembled with it. Thomas's
weight on her numbed shoulder and arm vanished, as
though he and she had both grown into the earth, with
the roots of these tranquil, friendly trees. She understood
why the Spanish peasants had spoken of them with love, as
though they possessed natures and a will like human beings.

Oh, my love, my love, she thought.

He said, smiling: "Look after Anna." I have looked
after her, she answered. I went directly from the room

where you had been lying an hour earlier, to find her. She was mending a seam in her dress, and humming. Perhaps she was thinking about you. When I came in she did not look embarrassed or startled: as she always did, she lifted her eyebrows, and said, "Well, Lotte?" The strange thing was I couldn't speak to her as "Annie"—as she liked people to call her because of the foreign sound; I had to say "Anna." She lost her head when I told her. She cried —like a child, not like a woman. Everything rushed from her. How she loved you, how happy she had been. To take her away, I had to dress her and pack her few things myself; I tied her veil—she was the only woman we knew who wore veils—so that no one should see her eyes and her swollen cheeks and become inquisitive. We had to sit up all night in the train to Berlin. She collapsed sideways, with her head on my shoulder and she was sound asleep. She could sleep; I found a happiness in despising her for it, but perhaps if we had not been so uncomfortable, crushed with other people on wooden seats, I could have slept.

Through the half-open kitchen door she saw Maddalena Pizetti scraping vegetables with her hands in a bowl of earthy water. She looked content. I have been over-whelmingly happy, she thought, and I know what agony of mind is—but I have never understood contentment.

Josephine Rapp's father was driving, with his guest, along Conduit Street. As the car turned into Regent Street he spoke to the chauffeur, ordering him to "go round by New Moon Yard." Since they were on their way to lunch at the Carlton, it meant a tiresome detour through narrow shabby streets, jammed with slow-moving traffic. Eugene Rapp did not apologize to his guest, a Swedish iron manufacturer. Years ago, when he was a young man, he had been afraid to offend anyone. In curing himself of this, an awkward habit in a man who intended to become wealthy and powerful, he became insensitive to other people. He neither heard, or if he heard did not seem to understand a remark which conflicted with his opinions and wishes. It was a restful state of mind. He flourished. He had been a delicate young man; now, when he was over fifty, he was extremely strong and energetic.

He got out of his car in the narrow street and walked into the yard. His guest followed reluctantly; he had a sensation of being plunged into the boiling centre of London. This heat was so enervating. It was his first visit to London, and he found it majestic but certainly grim—and horribly dirty.

"I wanted to see the place," Rapp said.

"Oh, yes?" So, it must be historic.

"My agent described it to me—but you can only trust your own eyes."

An old woman, carrying a cat and followed by other two, came out and crossed the courtyard. At the same moment a big elderly Negro stepped from another doorway. He passed close to Eugene Rapp. Pausing for less than a minute he raised his arm, and intoned: "Thy pomp is brought down to the grave, *and* the noise of thy viols," and went on.

"Good heavens!"

"Mad," Rapp said, with distaste. "As I was saying to you, it's an admirable site for a large cinema. Godbell was quite right." He and his half-swooning guest were standing on the exact spot where the preservers of ancient monuments had halted on their pious errand less than half an hour since. "Excavate for an underground garage —and there you are!"

"You are going to buy it?"

"I've made an offer for it."

Through the discomforts of heat, dust, and hunger, his guest had been studying the front of the building. "This must at one time," he murmured, "have been a handsome place."

"I daresay. It's a slum now." Rapp's expression

changed. His normal look was of genial indifference; it now became severe. So he would look at a board meeting where his judgment had been questioned. He never answered the question; he simply disposed, coldly, of the questioner. "Those imbeciles of slum clearance people," he exclaimed. "My agent tells me they've been getting at the ground landlord. They say that if the place is to come down they want to build flats. There's something cursed about this country. We used to keep the working-class in its place. Now—when workers are less needed than ever—we encourage them and pamper them. It's lunacy."

Eugene Rapp had been poor himself. He knew, from an incontrovertible witness, that poor men are consumed by a murderous hatred of the rich. The only way to be safe from them is to make as few concessions as possible. Not that he would ever neglect his duty to society. Had he not just given fifty thousand pounds to cancer research?

"Your workers are not very well housed."

Rapp ignored this. "The ground landlord—he's a peer, y'know—is a bit of a fool. He's influenced by the last person who talks to him." He chuckled. "A year ago he got himself in the papers by agreeing to become vice-president of some ridiculous society for suppressing blood sports the same week as he became master of a hunt."

"Oh, yes?"

"There are even, Godbell tells me, people who want to preserve the place! Can you understand it? In what is supposed to be a civilised country."

There was no answer for a moment. Then the other man said faintly: "It's very hot."

"I like it." He nodded towards the closed door of the Screech Owl. "Night club. All kinds of people go there. My daughter's been." His voice was brisk, to conceal his foolish adoration. It was the weak place in his defence; if anything disagreeable or tragic happened to his daughter he would actually suffer. Yet he disapproved of her way of life and her friends. She did as she liked, without consulting him. "Well, I think that's all. We've seen the place."

In his relief—they were moving towards the car—his guest tried to show a polite interest in it. "What an easy place it would be to burn," he said, lightly.

"Ha, an excellent idea," Rapp laughed amiably. "Is that how you get rid of your problems in Sweden, my dear fellow?" He felt a spasm of honest regret that he could not, immediately, set a match to the place and watch it burn. It would do away with all this nuisance of solicitors and argument. He detested argument.

"Oh, I only meant," his guest said, in an alarmed voice, "that with so much wood, and in this frightful heat—it might catch fire."

Pizetti had come to the door of the café and he watched them walking away. He puzzled himself to decide who they were and what they were doing standing talking and pointing in the middle of the yard. Finally he came to the conclusion that they were preservers of ancient monuments who had become detached from the main body. It was a more comfortable notion than his first—that they were officials of some sort. He had inherited from his parents in Abruzzi a well-founded dislike of officials.

CHAPTER VIII

THE REV. JAMES DANIEL had come to London because the word of the Lord came to him in New Orleans and told him to get on a boat and go to Europe. The night before he sailed he had another vision. It concerned England in particular and it was delivered to him by a young man who announced that he was Jude the servant of Jesus Christ, and brother of James. Opening Daniel's own Bible he laid his finger on a verse, and said: "England is to die." And vanished.

The verse was: "Even as Sodom and Gomorrha, and the cities about them in like manner, giving themselves over to fornication, and going after strange flesh, are set forth for an example, suffering the vengeance of eternal fire."

What could be plainer? Europe is to die—and first England—and the Lord had chosen him, James Daniel, to be witness.

And so he walked about the streets of London, from Deptford, where he lived at first, as far as Ealing, expecting to see the fire break through the pavements. Or descend in sheaves and whorled clouds from the sky. His eyes, strangely less living than his glistening black flesh, stared with the same curiosity at the children playing in the park with their nurses, at the vast buildings going up everywhere, and at streets on streets of small tight houses, in which life after life unfolded, withered, died. He was like the ambassador, or the spy, of another type of life, at once older and younger, and helplessly savage, which was waiting to take the place of these delicate northern shoots.

All the time he was thinking: Poor creatures, so soon to be destroyed. He talked to anyone he could, warning him. After a few weeks he had very little money left. An American Negro to whom he spoke in Hyde Park, a musician, who was going to France, lent him the room in New Moon Yard for a month. It was empty, but that did not trouble him. He bought a bowl to wash in. And with that, and his blanket, he settled down to wait. It could not be long now.

In a few days, prowling in the passages and staircases— for so heavy a man he was very light, almost noiseless, in his tread—he learned what sort of people lived in the other rooms. He knew most about Mrs. Jean-Ann Kerr, whose room was across the staircase from his. He had seen the men going with her into her room, sometimes as many as five or six men during the afternoon and evening until two in the morning. To-day he saw her going out at four in the afternoon. Her three-inch heels clicked on the wooden stairs. In spite of the heat she wore furs round her shoulder—it was almost a uniform.

At six that evening he was going out. As he stood on the landing he heard this click-click of heels, and another denser tread mingled with it. He waited at the top of the stairs. The woman came up briskly, followed by a middle-aged timid man, like a schoolmaster. The man looked in an alarmed way towards the tall, strong Negro, in his clerical hat.

"Hello, darkey," the woman said.

Her voice stirred in the Rev. James Daniel an impulse like a thin snake coiled in his belly, in the folds of dark flesh. It uncoiled like a whip, sending the blood flickering through his body upwards to his brain. He sent this force against her; he felt it leave him, springing from a darkness below his breast-bone. If she had been a woman of his own race, she would, he was certain, have dropped down dead. But this woman turned her long nose towards him; her eyes like greenish stones glittered with pure female insolence and malice. The evil in her turned his force back on himself. For a moment he was afraid.

He turned to the man with her.

"My son," he began. "Lust not after this woman's beauty in your heart; neither let her take you with her eyelids. For by means of a whorish woman a man is brought to a piece of bread. And her house is the way to hell, going down to the chambers of death."

The man half turned aside when Daniel began speaking to him, trying to hide his face. A look of dismay and guilt crossed it. He was clearly undecided whether to turn tail and bolt downstairs.

Jean-Ann Kerr laughed. "Out of my way, daddy," she said with a curt good-humour. She fumbled in her bag for the key of her door.

Daniel ignored her. He knew that his chance was with the man, who stood in sullen embarrassment, waiting to whip into her room as soon as the door was open. He was already put off by the unexpected adventure. After all, a nigger! He wished himself anywhere but on this staircase with its cracked dusty panelling.

"Are you determined to sin with this woman?" demanded Daniel.

"That's enough," Mrs. Kerr said. She was angry now. "Let me get at my door."

The preacher rested his huge hand on the man's shoulder. The man looked at it for a second as if a scorpion had settled there, then turned and ran down the stairs. He looked ridiculous running away, his knees splaying sideways. Clearly he was not accustomed to running. He ran like a woman. From first to last he had not said a single word.

Daniel turned to the woman. Since he had triumphed, he was prepared to forgive her. He looked at her with a strange quiet appeal and kindness in his lifeless eyes. As if he pleaded with her. But she was outraged. She screamed at him at the top of her hard voice, using every epithet of vileness in her vocabulary of abuse.

"You'd take the bread out of my mouth," she shouted, "you——"

Again Daniel felt the whip uncoil in the darkness which was in his body, a warm living darkness he carried everywhere with him, most conscious of it in the brightest sunlight. It *was* his life; he could direct it where he pleased. But now it plunged through him in wave after red-flecked wave of anger and hatred. He hated the woman's insolence and her shrill voice.

He stepped forward and put his hand over her mouth. Instantly, at the mere touch, he recalled himself. "The Lord have mercy on me," he groaned.

He dropped to his knees on the top stair, and began praying loudly.

"Lord, I know you will come with fire, and with your chariots like a whirlwind, to render your rebuke with flames of fire. And by fire will you plead with all flesh, and your slain shall be many."

He heard the woman laughing. "Pray away, daddy,"

she cried. She had been afraid when his large hand, black and sweating, pressed over her face. Now that she saw him on his knees she was amused. What a fool!

Daniel heard her laughter, like an insect singing round his ears. Then he heard another female voice. He opened his eyes, but remained kneeling.

"What's all this noise?" Mrs. Caracas said. She came half-way up the stairs from the lower floor. Her eyes darted contempt at the younger woman. Her face was red and swollen with sleep. "A nice thing if I'm to be wakened up every afternoon with your doings," she exclaimed.

"Mind your own business," Jean-Ann Kerr said.

"Every afternoon," Mrs. Caracas repeated.

"It's six o'clock in the evening, you old fool."

Deeply insulted and wounded, Mrs. Caracas turned to go back to her room. And then, as though it had only just penetrated the fog of sleep, she was struck by the astonishing spectacle of a black man kneeling at the head of the stairs.

"Well, of all the——"

Words failed her. She stood gaping. With sudden decision, Jean-Ann Kerr pushed past the kneeling man, and stepped down the stairs to go out again on her business. As she passed Mrs. Caracas she gave her furs a sharp whisk round her shoulders which set the tails flying, and one of them flew into the old woman's face.

"Oh, excuse me," she drawled, delighted.

Trembling with fury, Mrs. Caracas shouted after her. "A fire-ship, that's what you are, my girl. A fire-ship. You'll sink one of these fine days."

She gave a little scream, and pressed her hand on the soiled lace of her bodice. The black man had risen to his feet and was looking down at her. She had the feeling that he hung over her like a thick black tree. She felt weak, like a little girl. "What are you doing? What did you say?" she asked, querulous.

"I? I said nothing," the Rev. Daniel said, in a humble voice.

"Then go away. Shoo!"

She flapped her hands at him. He turned without another word, obedient, like a large dog, and disappeared round the corner of the passage. Mrs. Caracas went back to her own room.

She shut the door quickly, and padded across to the bed, disordered by her afternoon sleep. She let herself fall on to it sideways. Her heel caught the chamberpot under the valance and gave it a smart kick. Not cracked, I hope She was too breathless to stoop down to look. Turn he gave me standing there like a great idol. What next? Catch him creeping about the place at night. You can't see them at night, yes, their eyes, like a cat's in the dark. If I saw his eyes coming at me any night I should give one scream and pass away.

She felt a half real terror. Weak on my pins now, she thought. Getting on. Seventy's a good age. Not now, of course. If you watch yourself, your goings out and your comings in, you can easy live to be a hundred. Another thirty years.

An emotion half regret half weak pleasure flowed through her. If I could have the first thirty again. You don't know you're well off. The big grocer's at the corner, Please, mother wants these. Running, running, the way the street, garden behind the house, new bread, the dressmaker a big woman with a moustache. Funny it never seems to have rained then. I was a fool. I was a fool to marry. Still we, if I had a husband now that woman wouldn't dare insult me.

Must be making money hand over fist. In and out, in and out, three to midnight. Gr-r, I think nothing of her.

The cat lying out in the sun between two flower-pots stretched himself, jumped, and walked stiffly across the floor, avoiding her outstretched arm. "Come to mother."

Not he.

She stood up slowly, and began to straighten the bed-

clothes. No point in making it again now, too near
bedtime. If Caracas was here now we'd be going out
somewhere to supper; he wanted a good feed last thing.
She saw herself walking up Regent Street in a fawn dress
and velvet coat, long since gone the way of all flesh. Wot
cheer, all the neighbours say, have you bought the street?
You never looked better, old girl.

Dejected, she let her arms flop to her sides. The room,
one pool of sunlight ebbing from the window, seemed
gloomy. It rejected her and her possessions, crowded
into it, unwanted refugees.

A bit of fire, she thought.

Feeling for matches in a cup on the mantelshelf, she
set light to the gas-fire. It was ridiculous to put it on in
this heat, but say what you like, she thought, a bit of fire
makes the difference. It pulled the room together, you
might say. She felt happier at once.

"I'll make a bit of toast at it," she said aloud.

She began to sing under her breath, like a wheezy
bellows. *When you and I were seventeen.*

Moving a chair to get at a dishcloth that had fallen
behind it, she disturbed a spider scuttling out of a nest of
cobwebs. But what use to start cleaning the place when
any day now she would be moving to her country cottage?
I'll look in on an agent to-morrow. She saw indistinctly
herself in warm sunlight standing close to the railings of a
garden. The railings would be there. And a useful
shop. Flagstones. Sunlight running across the street
like bright water. Running away. Running.

CHAPTER IX

HARRIET CAME home slower than she went. At six o'clock on a hot May afternoon the streets of Soho are no bath of milk. The air is thickened with dust, and smells of oil, bodies, old clothes: it sticks in the throat.

As she turned in at the entrance of New Moon Yard, there was Linder. He locked the door of his shop, swung round, and smiled at Harriet as though this were the best moment of the day. His kind eyes took in every detail of her looks—ink-smudged fingers, shabby dressmaker-made frock, sullen mouth. She is sulking because she knows that she is dirty and hot, he said to himself. What can I tell her to make her feel confident again?

"You are tired," he said.

"No." Harriet snapped at him without meaning it. At once she felt embarrassed. She was too young and uncertain of herself to know how to deal with people. Either she spoke to them in too friendly a way, so that they believed she liked them very much; or she was rude to them. She was ashamed of being rude. Her face, as always when she was ashamed, turned brick-red. To placate Alfred Linder when she had spoken to him like some other woman, for instance like her mother, she smiled. Her smile was another matter. If he had not known so much about young women he might have supposed she was in love with him.

"Yes, you are very tired," he insisted tenderly. "I can see it."

"It's hot in my room where I work," said Harriet.

"It is hot everywhere in London." He seemed to be thinking. He was taller than she was; he had already, though he was only thirty, a big motherly stomach, on which he liked to fold his hands. He folded them there now.

"I know what you should do," he said, with a smile. "You should change your dress—I know you want to do that, though it isn't necessary—and have dinner with me in the country. I know a place in Surrey—there is a garden and a swimming-pool. It's pleasant and cool. Now, will you come?"

"It's very kind of you," Harriet mumbled. She had not the least intention of going, to-day or any day, but she did not know how to say so. "It would be splendid —but I can't come."

"Oh, dear," Alfred Linder said. "Then another day."

"Yes. Let us go another day," said Harriett.

She smiled at him again, and rushed away. She passed Jean-Ann Kerr, who was on her way out. Yesterday evening, when they were both in Pizetti's café, Mrs. Kerr had talked to her about—of all things—Woolworth's shop in Edinburgh. She had said: "I come from Edinburgh, you know"—and then she began about Woolworth's. Harriet listened with an attentive face. She saw—a child could not have helped seeing—what the woman was. And she was all the more anxious to be sympathetic and polite. In her innocence she supposed that the other woman must feel herself a social outcast. To me, Harriet's attentive eyes said, you are not an outcast at all; you are like other women. She would have been surprised —but not in the least hurt—if she had known that Jean-Ann Kerr had spoken to her because she thought the girl looked quite simple, and she had felt a moment's pity for her.

"Good evening," Harriet said, with her generous smile.

"Lovely, isn't it?" Mrs. Kerr said. Her voice was rough and metallic. Don't hinder me, was what it said. Don't expect me to chatter with you when I'm doing my job. Her glance, more distant than a memory, took in Harriet's untidy dress and hair, and sun-scorched face, with a sort of pleasant contempt. Gives herself away, she thought.

Harriet opened the door of her room with the vague

hope in her mind that it would have altered during her absence. But of course it had not altered. The over-stuffed chairs were in a half-circle as she had left them; the table, a vase of sweet-peas placed exactly in the centre, was the same; the curtains, the sagging door of the cupboard. The room looked as though no one lived in it.

No one *does* live in it, she thought, with despair. I sleep here, on the uncomfortable divan, I keep my clothes in the wardrobe, and a jar of face cream in that drawer. But I don't live here. I live nowhere. I have no home, there's no heart to my life; I live from day to day, and hand to mouth, like any improvident undisciplined creature. I am no good at all.

She remembered her conversation with the Jew. For some reason it made her ashamed. She thought that he must despise her because she was too polite to tell him that she would never—never—accept any of his invitations. It was not that she disliked or mistrusted him. Nor because he was a Jew—horror, if he should think that! in these days when decent people must go out of their way to apologize to Jews. No, no, it was simply that she could not—it was beyond her—make friends lightly. She did not want to know many people. To feel that she owed a duty to a great many people to visit them, to spend on them time, affection, energy—it would be unthinkable, unbearable. I have all I can do to manage myself, she said—half angry with these phantoms who were going to spoil her life—without trying to manage *you*.

And that was it. It was because she did not know how to manage them that she was afraid of people. She could not accept Alfred Linder's invitation and feel at ease. She would be wondering all the time, Is he bored? Do I look very shabby, so that he is ashamed of me?

Oh, but that was not all. She did not really know what she wanted. Part of her wanted excitement, a restless life, hundreds of invitations. And it was because she was torn in half—a war to the knife going on the whole time in her—that she did not know how to talk to Alfred Linder with a cool friendliness, neither encouraging him nor being unkind.

I make a fool of myself, she thought.

She put her hat away in the drawer, beside her handkerchiefs and a jar of face cream, and looked into the glass. Unconsciously, she allowed her face to fall into lines of reserve and simplicity. This was her idea of herself—a reserved, simple-minded young woman. If anyone had told her that she was odd and deceitful she would have been shocked.

All my work is no good, she thought. It was shameful, really. To write lies—they were lies—so that young women as poor as herself should spend their money on lotions and creams to make themselves look beautiful. And even I spent four-and-sixpence last week—knowing that it is wasted money. And poor women without the food to give their children. I am not only a fool. I am a criminal.

She turned away from the glass. She saw herself running along the corridor at the university, late—she was often late—for a lecture. Just to think how hard I worked—to be able to write lies. And there was her mother watching her from the audience when she went up to receive the degree. Sure of herself as Harriet had never been, and yet—what was it in her face? why was I sorry for her that day? The professor of economics was giving a garden-party in the afternoon and I took her there; and she looked at everything, at the trees, the large, rather pretentious house, and I knew that she was feeling oppressed because I had spent three years learning (she thought) to be clever. I, clever! I, this fool, this fool!

She flung herself into a chair. But now, because she had reached the pit of despair and self-scorn, she began to feel calm. "Things are not so bad," she muttered.

She jumped up. She could not rest.

Looking through the window, she saw two men going together into the Screech Owl. The taller one must be the waiter; he wore a cap and a tweed jacket over his dress trousers. One of these days, if I want to, she thought, I shall be able to dance there every evening. But what a life! And in the meantime I have only one evening dress. Well, my dear Harriet, you have ambitions. But—so far—little else. She chuckled.

When you opened the wardrobe, you saw that two garments hung quite by themselves at one end. There was a gap between them and the rest. These two were the garments—they were a dress and a coat—which she considered good enough to wear anywhere. She hardly ever wore them. They were sacred. She looked at them with satisfaction. Then, seizing a sheet of paper and her pen, she began to make a list of the clothes she would buy as soon as she had any money. Not a great many. Enough to appear well-dressed on any ordinary occasion. Plain, good, simple things.

When the list was complete she put it away in the drawer with her handkerchiefs. She felt sensible and calm. It was almost as though the clothes were already in the wardrobe. Hung, of course, at the "good" end.

CHAPTER X

SIMON, THE CHEF, and François, arrived together, soon after six. After a few minutes—he was supposed to come earlier—Bert arrived out of breath and stuttering excuses. No one bothered to listen to them. He rushed to the top floor, to the kitchen, pulled on his overalls and rushed down again to the big room. This was on the first floor; it ran the length of the house, with the bar at one end. Bert's first job in the evening was to help François prepare the tables. These were pushed close together, to get in as many as possible, and only a small space was left in the middle for dancing. It was not a good floor, but that did not matter, since there was no room to move quickly, and the couples simply embraced each other and moved their limbs a few inches to this side or that when they could, pressing genially against the bodies nearest to them.

Bert's face had been scorched by the sun. To make up for the hours he spent at night in the stifling kitchen under the roof, he passed his afternoons helping his father to sell from a stall in Berwick Street. Beside him, François appeared ghastly pale. Even his lips were pale.

"Don't run—*think*," he said, quietly, to Bert. "You know, boy, your head should save your feet. Where would I be if I ran about without thinking!"

Bert smiled with gentle, boyish good humour, and went on running with a handful of forks, then back again for the knives, and once more for something he had forgotten. He ran to the kitchen, to the store room. And all the time he smiled, and his slightly prominent blue eyes became glazed, and sweat trickled down his neck.

François did not try again to reprove the boy. His own thoughts were not fixed on his work. He was a quiet man; thirty-five; and he had been married five years. It was his wife, a Belgian like himself, who was distracting the thoughts he ought to have given to his tables.

She was of better family than he was; he had married above him, as the saying is. But in a dozen ways every day she offended his notions of propriety and his fastidious cleanliness. She was untidy, extravagant. She wasted his money, so that he had none to send to his mother in Brussels, and he knew that she owed to tradespeople. In spite of all this he was fond of her. She was his wife; he must and did look after her as well as he could. His round pale face, with its delicate features, became paler from anxiety. Worst of all, he began to suspect that she regretted marrying him. A man, a cousin of hers, had come to live in London, and she was always going out with him. She spent every evening with him. And although she was always asleep in bed when he reached home in the early hours of the morning, he would see her listless and tired during the day, as though she had too little sleep. When he thought that she might be deceiving him, his pride, and his working-man's sense of decency were both outraged. He did not want to believe it. And then, too, he was sometimes sorry for her. After all, she had loved him enough to marry him, an ordinary waiter. And if it had turned out badly that was not her fault.

He saw that Bert had stopped work and was standing gazing out of a window towards the Café Bar. He is looking to catch a glimpse of that Italian girl, the waiter thought. For no conscious reason, this vexed him.

"Why are you doing nothing?" he said rapidly. "Quick. Run up to the kitchen and fetch more glasses. You're lazy."

The boy rushed off. When he came back François had already repented that he had lost his temper. "Don't take any notice of me," he said, in his usual quiet, deliberate voice, "my wife—is not well."

"Ar. Sorry to hear that," Bert said. "Cheer up. Soon be better. What's the matter with her?"

François looked down at his hands. "I don't know. I think it's her nerves," he said softly.

"Can't do anything for that, can you?" said Bert cheerfully. "She'll get over it." He thought it strange that any man so quiet and steady as François should have a nervous wife. He looked at the waiter's pale face and pale mouth and wondered whether, at home, he was different. Still waters run deep. Like the wind his mind rushed back again to Giulia. He did not think about her in any rational and sensible way. Simply she was in his thoughts the whole time—it didn't matter what he was doing—like a cloud, like a soft cloud, coming between him and everything else in his life. He didn't hope very clearly for anything; she was much too beautiful and wonderful. He went on dreaming about her. And if sometimes it was an agony, at other times, and these were the most noticeable, he felt drunk and silly with joy. He

couldn't help himself, in any case. He had to think
about her.

A noisy powerful car roared into the yard, driven too
quickly, and stopped with the tyres screaming for mercy.
The Captain's Bentley, he thought, excited.

"Here is the boss," François said. He made "boss"
sound like a foreign word.

John Ashton slammed the door of the car and walked
quickly to his room on the ground floor. It was to the
right, off the entrance hall. The cloakrooms were on the
left, ladies' and gentlemen's side by side.

His room, labelled Private Office, was a living-room,
with a bed in one corner. It was the only room he had in
the world, and everything he possessed was in it. His
possessions went easily into a wardrobe, a desk, and a chest
of drawers. The only books in the room were the
telephone directory and an A.A. book. It was not a
cheerful room. The only window looked out on to the
cul-de-sac behind New Moon Yard and the blank wall of
a building. Ashton kept the curtains drawn over this
window and lived even in the daytime by electric light.
The furniture was what is called modernist—that is, it
was plain without simplicity; it was equally without charm
—and the curtains and paint were all very gay in colour,
which gave the room a certain brightness, almost in spite
of itself. At least it would not shock a visitor by being
different from the millions of rooms furnished in accor-
dance with some *Zeit-geist* which began to wither English
taste about ten years ago.

He sat down at the desk and began to open his letters.
Not more than two or three of them were personal. The
rest were all bills. Account rendered . . . account
rendered. . . . He threw one after another into the
waste-paper basket. I can't pay them, he thought, so
what's the use of keeping them until I can. They'll all
come in again.

There was a knock at the door. It opened, and Thomas came in. Although he was bare-headed and in shirt sleeves he saluted. It was the most natural greeting between him and the Captain. It was not a formal salute—more a gesture reminding himself of the days when he was the Captain's servant in France. For that matter, he still thought of himself as Ashton's batman. His duties as porter and chucker-out to the Screech Owl were simply other jobs he had taken on to be useful.

His large solid body filled up the doorway. He was smiling his engaging tight-lipped smile. He looked—he was—tough.

"Get me a bottle of whiskey," Ashton said.

When Thomas came back, carrying the bottle, the Captain had turned his chair away from the desk. He was straddling it, with arms crossed on the back. How many times Thomas had seen him seated in precisely that attitude, in the dug-out, in billets! If there was a straight chair anywhere about, and he could sit as he pleased, he sat on it in this way.

"Anything to eat, sir?" he asked, relishing the question.

"No—no," Ashton said. "I don't want anything. Unless you can think of a way of choking off these damned brutes who keep asking me for money."

Thomas's large face became blank with concern. "Is it worse than usual?" he asked quietly.

"Oh, we can pay what must be paid, the electric light, rates, and so on. And that's about all." Ashton smiled with a rather singular charm, his teeth very white in a heavy, dark face. "What I want, Thomas, is a nice little fire."

Thomas laughed—less at the joke than because he had remembered that other fire which had destroyed a lot of bills.

"The place is over-insured," Ashton said.

"Do you remember when your hut caught on fire, sir?"

Ashton's expression changed. "Do I not! Those were the days. God, you knew what you were fighting then."

Thomas lowered his head, and his face took on a queerly stubborn look. "Ye-es," he said, slowly, "it might have been a lot worse war. But once is enough. You can't trust anyone these days. Not the politicians, nor anyone. That's what I think."

"You shouldn't think," Ashton said lightly, standing up. "It's perfectly useless. Put me back into uniform, with something to strafe, and field allowances, and I can promise you never to think again."

Thomas grinned. He went away, and Ashton poured himself out a drink. He limited himself in drinks, but it needed one or two to enable him to concentrate, even for a short time, on his problem. Put briefly, where the devil could he raise the money to tide him over until the club began paying? He believed that it would soon pay. He had not only friends but relatives among the people whose frequent presence at a night club or a restaurant will make it the fashion, so that other persons, stockbrokers, gossip-writers, business men and what not, become willing to pay an exorbitant price to pass hideously uncomfortable and unprofitable nights there. All these friends and second and third cousins of his owed it to him, and to themselves, as members of an invisible body, to help the Screech Owl. That very few of them had, so far, done their duty, was a social blasphemy Ashton could not forgive.

And yet, in a secret corner of his mind, he was not surprised. His recklessness, his courage, and the brutality which lay close under the surface of his good manners, were not the whole story. There was a soft place in his mental skin. It would be truer to say that he had memories which he kept continuously out of sight because they would humiliate him. But one does not kill an unflattering memory by ignoring it.

John Ashton's parents were small landowners in Dorset. They both came from families which were offshoots of the offshoots of a great family. He was their sixth child, and fourth son, and if either parent had wished for him to be born they gave him no sign of it when he was old enough to consider his place in the household. It was clearly, even sharply, a place at the back. When he was very young indeed he had a Nanny of whom he was fond. But she had grown old and feeble in looking after his elder sisters and brothers, and when he was five she vanished from the house and he became the unwanted sixth in the schoolroom, an embarrassment to tutors who did not know how to teach an infant, and a nuisance to his sisters. None of his brothers was unkind; they failed to notice him, that was all. He learned to avoid his father. He disliked having his ears pulled, and this was his father's way of showing that he knew he had a fourth son. His mother he saw so seldom that when he was still very young, not more than four years old, he failed to recognize her in a white ball-dress and rushed away when she spoke to him. After this incident, she seemed to have decided that he was a black sheep.

His eldest brother was sent to Eton; the others, and himself of course, to a much cheaper public school. He went there a year younger than the rest, to get him away from home. Of his first months there he took care never to think at all. Very occasionally, in sleep, he found himself back in a small room weeping bitterly, in an agony of despair and shame. In his dream John Ashton was both the child and an onlooker, and the onlooker was always ashamed of the child. . . .

When he left London on the first stage of his journey to Santiago his father came to the station to see him off. He had said good-bye to his mother at home; she had talked to him, for the first time, not as though he were an unattractive boy, but as though he were a visitor, someone with whom she must converse for a certain time and with an air of interest. She spoke of someone she had once known who had visited Chile, a man whose name he had never heard and in whom therefore he could only feel a

moderate interest. She discussed sea voyages, and reminded him that the time would change as they travelled
further west. "Does it get later or earlier? I can never
remember," she said, with a smile.

After twenty minutes or so she glanced at the clock.
"I'm afraid you should be going," she said, gently and
easily, as though he might be dropping in again next week.
He kissed her, and went out of the room and downstairs,
said good-bye to two of the servants, and got into the car
with his father, and that was over.

His father was silent at the station. Possibly he had
realised, with a touch of discomfort, that this package they
were shipping to Santiago was a young man of scarcely
nineteen, burly for his age, but without experience, without knowledge of the world. The elder Ashton tried to
recall what he himself had thought about at nineteen.
But he could no more feel the sharpness of that bewilder-
ing year than he could recall the taste of yesterday's
dinner. He gave up trying, and trotted out a few sentences which passed the time until the train went and he
could hurry away, stifling easily in himself the sense of
dissatisfaction and guilt. . . .

As a shipping clerk in London he would have had
nothing. In Santiago he was still only a shipping clerk, but
to the English people there he was another Englishman,
and a son of the Honourable James and Mrs. Ashton. He
was gathered into a fold as narrow as that of his public
school, but a fold of adults, with its scandals, pre-
occupations, comedy turns, even a tragedy. As a young
man he was allowed to run outside the fold. Very soon
he made friends with a Chilean of his own age, the son
of a General, who was some sort of government servant.
With his friend, whose name was Diaz, he rode, visited a
house full of young women, visited cafés, the theatre. It
was the first time in his life he had had a natural uncom-
plicated relationship with anyone.

One day he repeated to the head of his firm something
Diaz had told him. In the instant of saying it he realised

that it was important. What it signified was that Diaz's
father, and certain other people, were acting in some un-
defined way against the government. Ashton's chief became excited. He explained that there might be a chance
to sell a consignment of rifles—either to them or to the
government—Ashton had already learned that more than
one sort of trading had its headquarters in the shipping
office of this English company in Santiago. Yes, very well.
He would find out more; Diaz would talk to him about
it again when he had drunk a little. He pocketed a fiver
for his expenses, and took Diaz out to dinner.

It was amusing and exciting to play the diplomat. Easy,
too. From Diaz he learned that far more was going on
behind the scenes than he had suspected. Next morning
again it was without any sense of betraying a confidence
that he told everything he had heard.

Less than a month later, when Diaz's father, his friends,
and Diaz himself, were arrested as conspirators and shot,
he saw that he had played his part in a very curious and
strictly commercial transaction. The conspirators had
not bought the rifles, but the government had. It had
bought information at the same time. And it was he,
John Ashton, who had been the first go-between in an
affair which ended, for his friend Diaz, fatally.

He was shaken, appalled. But he was ashamed to let
anyone see what he felt. After a short time he began to
feel proud of his cynicism. In these South American
states it was every liar and schemer for himself. You
schemed, lied, and took any risks, moral and physical, to
pull off a deal. Anything, if you succeeded, could be
justified.

After less than a year of Santiago he knew that he had
always known this. . . .

He enjoyed the War. The life of an officer on active
service suited him perfectly. He had bed, board and
lodging provided for him, with honour and gratitude
thrown in. He was a competent officer. He did not
enjoy danger and discomfort, but they never affected his

nerves; he didn't resent them.   But when he went on
leave, to London, or on Paris leave, he had all the excitement of going into a conquered city.   During the War he
saw inside the dining-rooms of the Berkeley, the Savoy,
the Ritz, for the first time.   The wartime London he
knew was wide open; he rarely had to pay for a meal.   It
was as easy to sleep with a young woman as to dance
with her.   Easier—he didn't care for dancing.

At the end of the War he could have gone back to South
America—as a clerk.   He didn't go.   He had made
friends among men like himself, with expensive tastes and
no money.   Two of them started an easy-money scheme
in which he joined.   It was a worse than dubious scheme.
It came off, and he took his share of the profits, fifteen
hundred pounds, and cut out.   He preferred to gloss
over this incident in his mind.

He had definite ambitions.   He wanted money, and he
wanted it to establish himself in society.   Two of his
brothers had been killed in the War, but not the eldest,
who disapproved of him.   Then his parents died, and he
found that he had not been left anything.   All went to
his sisters and to the heir.   He felt savage.   He churned
over ways of making enough money to buy what he
wanted.   He wanted the life of an idle rich man, and the
respect of head-waiters and tailors.   At bottom, what he
wanted was a definite, well-established place in society.
A perfectly respectable ambition.

Selling motor-cars bored him.   He went on with it—
and made debts—until his godmother died and left him
precisely eighteen hundred pounds.   He put it into
renting, decorating, and advertising the Screech Owl.

Three days ago his sister-in-law had introduced him at
a luncheon party to Eugene Rapp.   I didn't get on badly
with him, he thought.   He had been able to answer a
question Rapp asked about Chile.   He pretended to know
more about the country than he did, and told Rapp an

amusing story about selling munitions to a Chilean secretary for war. The only lie in the story was that it had not happened to him but to his chief.

Rapp had laughed heartily.

He jumped up and began to walk about the room. His mind was working with the quickness born of whiskey and excitement. He saw what he had to do. He must get Rapp here, to the Screech Owl, impress him with its possibilities—as a night club different from all the others. And when Rapp became interested, slip in a word about wanting a sleeping partner. If you know anyone who has a couple of thou' idle, he would say.

A couple! He could put down five thousand easier than I can pay five bob, he thought. God damn him!

It was a rotten world in which energy, recklessness, strength, had to crawl about begging for money. If there's trouble in the world, they shout for us to put it right for them, he thought. Pity there isn't more trouble. The country's rotten at both ends. Too many self-satisfied rich men, too many bolshevik workers. If I had my way, he thought, with a sour anger, I'd make 'em both toe the line. Do 'em good.

Thomas went up to the kitchen. He found that Simon had made coffee for himself and the others. He took his mug and went to the window looking into the cul-de-sac with its blank wall. In a minute François and the boy came in. François asked what sort of a mood the boss was in.

"The Captain's all right," Thomas said.

An ironic smile crossed Simon's face. "How much longer shall we be here?" he said. "Things aren't right. You don't get the right people."

Thomas was silent. He looked from Simon's sallow lop-sided face to the waiter's sober one. He wanted to hear what they had to say.

"Some of the customers are decent people," François said. "I can tell by how they eat. But there are too

many what I call smart toughs." He had a way of
speaking as though he were finding words for some pro-
found discovery. "They have no money of their own,
and when they bring people with money it's for themselves, not for us. They're no good," he said in a flat
voice.

Simon laughed. He looked slovenly and unhealthy.
Actually, he was full of energy. He was less worried than
any of them. He was a good cook, and he could always
get some sort of job. And he had a contempt for
failures.

"Go bankrupt or be raided," he said sardonically.
"It's one or the other with these places."

Damned Welshman, thought Thomas. And brave
bloody little Belgium. He kept his head down, and
watched them as though they were enemies. Suddenly
François asked his opinion.

"If you want it, I think you jaw too much," he said
quietly. "I've seen the Captain in tight places before
now, and he's always managed to get out." He hesitated,
then went on. "There was the time he got bored and
went over to the Boche lines at night. There didn't
seem anyone about, so he drops in the trench to look
round. Then one of them comes round the corner,
alone, and before he can squeak the Captain has knocked
him cold—with his fist. Then he looks to see what
regiment he is. And comes back in."

He told the story with a smile at once cold and
triumphant. He looked round to see what effect it had
had on them. The Belgian was listening with his usual
quiet attention, much as he would listen on the Day of
Judgment. Simon's expression was a puzzle. He was
not sneering, but he remained unimpressed. Thomas
wanted to kick him.

"If the place fails we'll be out of a job," François said
quietly.

"You don't say!" Simon mocked him.

"It's not going to fail," Thomas shouted.

He looked round him for Bert. The boy always listened to him with speechless respect. He was in time to see Bert's back vanishing through the door. "Hi! Where are you off?" he called roughly.

Bert did not turn round. In a nervous voice he said: "Back in a minute," and hurried on.

Half-past six is a slack time in the Café Bar. Pizetti has gone upstairs to lie down for an hour, and his wife is preparing their supper, and chopping bacon fat for the soup. Giulia is left in charge of the café, where most likely there are not more than two customers, half asleep.

She saw Bert a minute before he came in, racing across from the door of the Screech Owl, and turned her back. He hurried in, and she looked round with a smile of surprise and pleasure. "Oh, is it you?"

"Yes," he said breathlessly, "I got ten minutes. They'll be gassing that time. They've been at it about ten now and I couldn't listen no longer. See?"

"Not any longer," Giulia said, with a smile. She gave a little touch to her black curls. She liked this smiling, clumsy, decent boy, and she liked his admiration of her. She encouraged it without meaning to be cruel at all, with an almost innocent coquetry. Not completely innocent—what young woman is? But she had never imagined what his feelings could be, and she forgot him when he was not with her.

"All right. Not any longer," he repeated.

"If you are going to be a famous chef you will have to go back to school," she said, mocking him gently.

"Come September, I'm going to a place in Westminster in the day-time. Place where you learn to cook—see?"

"Yes, I see," she laughed. "I can see you. Well, I shall teach you Italian, and you can call yourself—what?—Bertorelli, or Bertasso. Bertorelli, the great chef!"

"I'll be an English chef," he said, slowly.

She saw that his eyes had clouded like a child's. He is so good, so decent, she thought. He is as big as a man, but he has exactly the expression of a little boy. When

D

his mother looks at him, she must think he is only eight or nine.

"But how old are you?" she asked delicately.

"Sixteen," he said, with reluctance. He had meant to say "nineteen," but the truth had rushed out.

"Ah, then I'm a hundred years older than you. I'm seventeen, nearly eighteen."

He was leaning against the counter, his hands fidgeting with a glass—large, red hands, coarsened with work, but boyish, like his expression. All his movements were awkward and sudden, graceless, yet very touching. Giulia sighed. I feel so old, I might be his mother, she thought. It was an absurd thought. She smiled, feeling all at once inexplicably happy and excited—for no reason. She had almost forgotten Bert.

"What do you think about all day?" he asked her, in his usual quick mumbling voice. He ran the words together, dropping his voice before the ends of sentences so that it was difficult to hear him.

"Oh." She threw her head back, looking at him through her eyelashes. "I think about going home."

He said nothing. He looked bewildered. "Well, I got to go," he said at last. "See you later."

He blundered out of the café, knowing exactly where he was going but walking as if he did not, marching forward, head down, eyes fixed on the ground in front of him as if he thought it might begin to play him tricks if he were weak with it. Giulia watched him go with amusement. How funny he is, like a calf, she thought, smiling. She had forgotten him before he passed out of sight.

CHAPTER XI

MRS. BARLEY tried to keep her children in the yard when they came from school. She would not have them run in the streets with the foreign and Jewish children of the district. Once when she saw Sarah racing along Brewer Street with some other children, she waited for her at home and thrashed her until her own arm ached. Then she was sorry. But she could not tell Sarah what she had felt, seeing her tearing along the street—"like a pure savage." It had made her feel that they were really sunk, that her children were slum children. She thrashed her child to save her from the pit, and because she was wretched. "That we should come to this," she said again and again. She had no better words for the agony it was to her to think of her children becoming familiar with the street and the street words. She hated her husband for having brought them here.

The children were allowed to play in the cul-de-sac behind Pizetti's. It was paved, and there was a high blank wall against which they could throw balls. They played here alone, since other children preferred the wild excitements of the street.

They suffered for their mother's insistence. The children they knew in school resented the aloofness of the young Barleys, and punished them for it with the cruelty of children. They jeered at them in the school playground and tripped them up. Hector, who had just moved into the lowest class on the boys' side, was always fighting with older bigger boys; he was always beaten, and he came back to the charge again and again, angry tears running over his round red face. Plump little Lucy, with her merry eyes and infectious laugh, could have made friends, but she stuck faithfully to Sarah. Sarah would have been too much for ordinary children to swallow at any time. She was intelligent and awkward. In class she asked questions and drew the teacher's attention to herself, breaking every unwritten rule of conduct. She had no idea she was doing anything out of the way, or shameful.

Her unpopularity hurt her. Sometimes, with the freakishness of children the others would relent and let her join them. She was madly grateful. But it always ended badly. She fell, or she innocently said something at which they took offence. In a flash they swung round and began mocking and pointing at her. She answered back, shouting in a shrill voice like her mother's, cheeks crimson. The disgrace, the pain of feeling herself an outcast, was terrible.

She would pretend not to understand what they were saying. A foolish supercilious smile remained fixed on her face, but her throat was hard. Yet they never once made her cry. She managed somehow to shut away part of the humiliation, so that it was bearable. She could pretend it was not so bad, they didn't really despise her. That much was true. They didn't. But they felt something unusual in her, and it was enough for them. Heave a brick at it!

In their evenings in New Moon Yard and in the cul-de-sac they played an endless game. It was invented by Sarah. The game was to think of some difficult, or dangerous exploit, and then to do it without flinching. Once it was that each had to stand alone in the narrow alley they had to run along to reach the cul-de-sac, waiting for the other two to spring out with fearful yells and raised sticks. The victim must not even blink under the shock.

They spent weeks practising acrobatic tricks, with painful tumbles. A tear, or a cry of pain, was a mark against the weakling. The tally was kept in chalk on the blank wall. Lucy's was the longest line of white strokes. When she fell she could not help the tears rushing out of her eyes. She would say:

"I'm not, I'm not."

The other two watched her solemnly.

"Yes, you are," Sarah said cuttingly.

"Yes, you are," Hector chimed in.

Out came the piece of chalk, and another stroke was added to the tale of Lucy's failures.

They played other games, rushing with wild whoops and yells from end to end of the place, but this was the favourite. They called themselves by a special name when they played it. They were The Spunkers. At home, when one child was going to be thrashed the two others would whisper hurriedly beforehand. "Be a Spunker. Spunkers can't feel anything."

Oh, can't they? The luckless one would do her, or his, best to support the honour of the Spunkers. The strangest part was that Sarah, who could stand any amount of self-inflicted pain, cried loudest when they were being whipped. Little soft Lucy cried resentfully, and Hector roared more with rage than anything. But you would have thought that Sarah was frightened out of her wits. She—"a great girl of twelve," as Mrs. Barley said—bawled the place down.

Both she and Hector were unmoved by appeals to their better nature. If they suffered inwardly they never showed it. Lucy wept freely at these times. It was not that her nature was any better than theirs, but her feelings were much nearer the surface.

In spite of Mrs. Barley's uncertain temper, and the sporadic enmity of the other children, they were happy. They liked New Moon Yard. They liked too the feeling that the cul-de-sac belonged to them. Mrs. Caracas, hearing peals and shrieks of laughter coming from the alley below her room, would mutter:

"Mad or bad, I don't know which."

And when they trooped in home, with scarlet cheeks and hair all over the place, their mother felt that something unmanageable and dangerous had come into the house. She was relieved and glad when they were in bed. There at least they were quiet and safe.

This evening they went on playing outside until half-past nine. Their mother came to the end of the cul-de-sac. They were too deeply absorbed in their game to notice her. Lucy was kneeling on the ground with her eyes tightly shut, her round little face lifted, with a blank expression. The other two, Sarah and the boy, were standing one at each side of her, swinging their linked arms to and fro above her head, and singing in quick intense voices. Mrs. Barley listened. It went on for a long time, while Lucy kneeled without moving, not even opening her eyes.

> Gay go up and gay go down
> To ring the bells of London town
> Ha'pence and farthings
> Say the bells of St. Martin's
> Old Father Baldplate
> Say the slow bells at Aldgate
> You owe me ten shillings
> Say the bells of St. Helen's
> When will you pay me?
> Say the bells of Old Bailey
> When I grow rich
> Say the bells of Shoreditch.
> Pray when will that be?
> Say the bells of Stepney.
> I'm sure I don't know,
> Says the great bell of Bow.

Their voices cracked with hurry and excitement, and both their arms came down, sweeping down with cruel swiftness, on Lucy's shoulders. She gave a little cry of terror.

> Here comes a candle to light you to bed.
> Here comes a chopper to chop off your head.

"You're dead, we've killed you," Hector shouted.

"I'm not," Lucy said quickly. She scrambled to her feet.

"You are, you are."

They were so absorbed, so intense, that the mother felt uneasy. Ha, I don't like it, she thought vaguely; it's not a proper game. She lifted up her strong, usually harsh voice and called them to come at once. They came nervously, in silence.

"Don't you know the time?" she said sharply.

They were supposed to guess the time from the light, and by some inner sense. On these light evenings this sense deserted them.

"I s'd think it was about nine," Sarah ventured.

"Well, it's half-past," Mrs. Barley snapped.

She said nothing more, only driving them to get off to bed. I can't blame them, she thought. The two young ones should have been in bed at seven, but how could they ever sleep in a room that even drawn blinds wouldn't darken? And the evening was airless, stifling! Better let them tire themselves out.

She stood over them as they washed, urging them in a harsh voice.

"Quick, quick with you!"

When they were lying in bed she stooped quickly to kiss hot damp cheeks. She stood a second longer by the boy's bed. He lay with eyes closed and hands clenched outside the sheet. His eyebrows were drawn together in a fierce frown. To his mother he seemed far more defenceless than the two girls. Whatever happened, she was determined to get him away from these streets. He was not going simply to be a workman like his father. She had clenched her mind on this, like a fist.

She went downstairs. Her husband came in from the workshop and crossed heavily to the sink to wipe his hands. How grey he looks, she thought. She was half sorry, and half only vexed with him—as if it were his fault that he was getting old.

"Did you speak to Hudson?" she asked suddenly.

He answered without turning round. "No, I didn't."

She was ready to fly at him, but something in the set of his shoulders as he bent down silenced her. He's really older, she thought. Her heart ached a little. She remembered so well what he had been.

"Well, come and have your supper," she said in a softer voice.

He sat down to the table without looking at her. "I was thinking," he said. He hesitated. "I was thinking we s'd need Hudson until th' boy's old enough to come in. Maybe then——"

She interrupted him. "What do you mean? Hector's not going into the workshop."

He put his knife down and stared at her. "What's he to do then?" he said. He looked bewildered.

"I don't know yet what he's to do. But I do know he's not going to waste his time on something that's quite useless. No one wants men like you nowadays." She was brutal in her fear for her son's future.

Barley's expression changed to one of awkward dignity. He did not know what to say. He knew he couldn't deal with her—but he was deeply and unspeakably shocked. She had never, in her worst tempers, said anything that humiliated him as did these quietly spoken words.

He cleared his throat. "Then he'll be the first one o' the family for two hundred years who——"

He stopped. He did not know how to go on. It was no good to try explaining to Sally that she was going to destroy something actual and irreplaceable. He couldn't take it in his hand, his certainty about it, and show it to her. And in a half-formed way he knew, too, that she had other and inhuman forces on her side. It was true. Men like him were *not* wanted to-day. Time had gone past them.

He said nothing. But he felt—oh, useless. Done for.

His wife got up and began clearing the things. Frowning, she asked: "Did you send off the fire insurance to-day?"

He gave a start of guilt. "I forgot all about it," he said.

Mrs. Barley clicked her tongue in an exasperated sound. "You forgot!"

"I'll send it to-morrow without fail."

"Yes, and if the place were to get on fire to-night we

shouldn't draw a penny, because you'd *forgotten* to pay the premium," his wife said sarcastically.

Barley got up slowly. "You're right, Sally," he said humbly, "I'm a fool."

"Well, you needn't make a song about it," she answered, softening towards him. "Get the letter ready to-night, and Sarah can drop it in the post on her way to school."

Towards ten o'clock the light in the yard had a curious bronze tinge, like the water in a moor stream. It was the dust in it, and the change of light. The sun had set, but there was still warmth in the light for a few moments. This faded; the watery light became grey, unmoving. There were shadows in the yard now, but not a breath of air. It was absence of warmth, not coolness.

The first guests began to arrive at the Screech Owl. The first dozen cars were allowed to park in the centre of the yard; the rest had to go round to the garage at the back.

Mrs. Barley was undressing in her bedroom. She lifted a corner of the blind and watched an elderly man in evening dress help two women out of a car in front of the door. One of the women slipped her cloak off in the doorway, displaying bare shoulders and back.

She's as old as I am, Sally Barley thought. Older, probably; they look after themselves. "You'd wonder some of them bothered to dress at all," she said to her husband, "they're as near naked as makes no matter."

She could not imagine the life of the woman she had seen going in. It must be strange to have naught to do, she said to herself. She sneered—but she envied her. Yet by no stretch of imagination could she put herself in that woman's place. She might have been a South Sea islander for all Sally Barley knew about her. She dropped the blind and came over to the bed. Her husband was half asleep already. Slipping off the rest of her clothes, she lay down beside him.

The noise of cars coming and going, changing gear, went

on outside. It was another world. Her world was this
room, this bed, the man lying drowned in sleep beside her.
It scarcely extended now to the room in which the three
children were lying, nor to the darkened workshop downstairs. She lay with eyes open, listening, without attention. The time is so short, she thought. She did not
know what she meant—it was something to do with the
fact of her lying night after night in this room, and life
slipping away, escaping from her, so that nothing remained except the furniture in this room, the sheet on
which she pressed her hand, and her body. Even that
no longer belonged to her.

Mrs. Caracas had turned the gas off in her room, so that
she could watch without being seen the cars coming and
going to the door of the Screech Owl. Because it was a
hot night she had taken off all her day clothes except her
vest and stockings before putting on her nightgown.
Looking round her for her shawl she found it pushed down
at the foot of the bed. The devil's in things, she thought;
the mean tricks they play on you. She watched with
meditative eyes a young girl laughing half running into
the club. It was dark now, but the electric light over the
doorway made a yellow pool into which they stepped for
a minute. An anxious haggard face went in. A short
pot-bellied man in a grey overcoat, with a simpering tart.
"Bad luck to her," Mrs. Caracas said aloud. They don't
enjoy it; nobody enjoys themselves like we used to, hard
work, play hard. And cut and come again. Lobster à la
Newburg. Jokes we used to have. Nothing between the
King and Mrs. Langtry. A column of news about something or other. Then right by itself so you couldn't
miss it—Not even a night-shirt. Bertha—you can't forget her to-day can you, when I was at the theatre, and
Bertha laughing herself sick that evening at that man,
gay old boy, they haven't the spunk now, or the police
would stop it, or the newspapers lies on lies I never read
them. Nothing's like it was, nothing. If you ask me it's
not going to last. How can it last if people aren't properly

enjoying themselves, and you've only to look at their faces
to see they aren't, well I thank God I had my time when
I did. If I was young now—if I was young now——

She stood up, clutching the window-sill, and groped
towards the bed. If I was young now me ankles wouldn't
ache. She stretched herself out in bed with a voluptuous
sigh. Bed, glorious bed.

"You don't want to look at them," Randall said.

He watched Harriet with a slight smile. She dropped
the curtain across the window and turned to him.

"A lighted doorway at night, and people going in—I
like it."

"Why?"

"I don't know." She looked at him with a self-con-
scious smile. She was not always at ease with him.
Although he had said he loved her, and she ought now to
have felt surer of him, she still felt that he might tire of
her. He might notice that she was badly dressed, and not
used to meeting people, or to restaurants. She felt
happier when they were alone in her room, yet even there
she was a little anxious to find something to talk about
to him.

She wanted him now to feel that her love of lighted
doorways at night was interesting. She tried to think of a
witty or a poetic explanation, but nothing occurred to her.

"Did you enjoy your lunch?" she asked. The words
were out of her mouth before she could stop them. She
was disgusted with herself.

"It was all right. Nothing much. She's bringing her
father to supper at the Screech Owl to-morrow night—
so that I can talk to him."

She felt an acute dismay. "Oh." She made an effort
to speak in a light, gay voice. "That's what you wanted,
isn't it? It's kind of her."

Randall was half lying in one of the arm-chairs. He
stretched his arm up suddenly, caught hold of her, and
pulled her down beside him. They lay facing each other
in the chair, and he held her body along his. They lay

still. She drew light, shallow breaths, again afraid of seeming awkward. She hoped her dress was not caught up.

Randall held her closely. He kissed her on the lips and held her body fast on his. Then suddenly he let her go and lay looking down at her with the same faint smile.

She set her hand to his chest and felt his heart striking against it. This gave her an exquisite feeling of safety.

"Are you happy?" he asked, as if it were difficult to speak.

"Yes, of course."

But then he got up, leaving her. She was hurt. She turned round quickly in the chair, sitting upright, elbows on her knees. She pretended to smile.

"Harriet," Randall said. "When are you going to give up your ridiculous job? If we got married at once we could have a house near the aerodrome; it belongs to a man on the committee, but he's going to America for two years. He'd rent it to us."

"But why shouldn't I keep on with my job?"

She was glad of the chance to argue with him. It would prove to him that she had a mind of her own still. She looked at him eagerly.

"We've had that all out once," Randall said.

"Yes, I know. But we didn't agree," she said at once triumphantly. "After all, why should I give up my work and live in a small house, waiting for you to come home?"

"No reason at all—if you don't want to."

She was unreasonably disappointed. She had stiffened herself for the argument, and—it happened almost always —he had slid aside. He would be angry, or in this mood, evasive, but he would not argue. She was unhappy and felt like a child.

She supposed that if she held out long enough he would give way and agree to let her keep on with the office after she married. But she did not want that. She wanted him to approve.

"It's not fair," she cried.

"What isn't fair?" he said with good humour.

"You will have your work and I—I should only have to look after the house."

"We might have a child," Randall said.

She was silenced, her heart beating loudly; she couldn't answer it by saying that their child need not take up all her time. Or that she didn't want a child. Her mind fell into a confusion. She saw Randall yawn. At once she was ashamed. He's only bored sitting in here with me, she thought.

"Got to go," he said, smiling, yawning openly. "Up at six to-morrow, you know."

"And you'll be over there to-morrow night until all hours." She jerked her head in the direction of the Screech Owl.

"We'll have dinner together first."

"Perhaps."

"No perhaps about it. We'll go over to Pizetti's and have dinner. I'll come for you." He ducked his head to kiss her firmly on the lips. "Good night."

"Oh. Good night."

He had gone. She clenched her hands and ran to the window, to distract herself by looking. There was the lighted doorway; two people, a man and a girl, were arriving on foot. She stared. I don't know what's the matter, she thought; I don't know. She wanted to run out, to laugh. The room was too small to hold her life. She pressed both hands to her chest, and stood there, watching, watching.

At eleven the Café Bar was crammed with customers; Pizetti ran about, making jokes, his lean body jerking between the tables like a puppet. His patient blue eyes shone with a friendly laughter. His wife stayed behind the counter, as calm in the confusion as always. Her face was colourless under the sharp light; her eyes watched everything with an unwavering scepticism, like an old child; her tiny mouth, made more delicate by the width of

her face, folded in an ironical line. She had her own
opinion of the customers, and where Gregorio wanted
them to be happy she would have preferred to make them
good. She was never shocked; she expected people to be
silly, to hurt themselves, to steal and tell lies. She did
not hate them for it.

Dr. Cleveland had been sitting at the counter, almost
facing her, for more than an hour. Before he came, he
had drunk himself into a visionary state, and he saw the
café as a bed the size of London, crammed with bodies,
like infusoria pushing against each other in a drop of water.
In Maddalena Pizetti's face he saw cruelty and serenity.
He began to talk to her, and she listened rather as if he
were a child.

"You see all these people'" he said, rolling his lips,
laughing. "What could one expect from them but grief
giving birth to grief? They are short-lived—a tree will
outlive generations of them—and to give themselves dignity for this short time they imagine that the teacupful of
life in their veins renews itself when they die, celestial
trees, plum-blossom Viennas; de Quincey said, shadowy
forests, endless savannahs, and pomp of solitary waters;
and a man whose brain is exquisitely moulded to perform
a delicate and complicated surgical operation has to throw
himself in the Danube because he is a Jew—I hope you
notice that I am not a Jew, my parents were Cumberland
farmers. Yet a general who has never done anything
except show men how to end each other's lives, a paunchy,
dimpled sack of flesh, and young male killers, are not
shunned as carrion. Extraordinary. Mrs. Pizetti, I
should like to live a long time; I want to see the psycho-
logical effect of the destruction of Europe. It's quite possible it will destroy too much, the survivors will be shocked
into sterility or a childish dementia. But suppose that
instead the survivors were shocked into truth, to knowing
inescapably that a man has only one thing of value, one,
one only, his own life, which is the same as saying his own
death. Every other thing he thinks he possesses, courage,

honour, power, isn't worth a damm, if you'll forgive me."

"You're really a doctor, aren't you?" Maddalena said calmly.

"What do you mean?"

"Well, you call yourself a herbalist."

The doctor passed his hand over his face. He must have powdered it before he came out; there were rifts of white sweaty powder in the wings of his nose and in the deep folds of flesh at each side. He had ludicrously small ears.

"I have a medical degree of Edinburgh University. Believe me, I never think of that now." He slapped his thighs. "I've led the life the animal in me intended to live." His voice rose. "None of these people could have handled the beast—I've wasted more energy, agony, sweat of fear on it than a dozen crucifixions—what's the good of it?—clouds without water, raging waves of the sea foaming out their own shame. I might just as well have given up at the start. Well, what are we here for?"

Maddalena poured out and pushed across to him a cup of black coffee. "You drink that," she said, in her flat voice, with its cockney intonations. "Do you good."

Her husband had hurried into the kitchen, now out again, and she beckoned him to come behind the counter. She looked at him with a searching steady glance.

"You're tired. Don't run about—*walk*."

Pizetti gave her an indulgent smile. "But if I walked I should burst," he said.

He went off.

"You're always kind to him," the doctor said. "You're a remarkable woman."

"There's nothing remarkable in being kind," Maddalena said dryly. "He runs about because he is impatient and obstinate, and wants people to enjoy themselves. We're going back to Italy before the winter, and a good thing we are."

Enid Jones looked round her as she pushed her way between the tables to the counter. You never knew;

there might be someone. As she crossed the yard to the café she had seen Mrs. Kerr standing at the bottom of the staircase leading to both their rooms. She had a man with her; "Good night," he said and went off, and Mrs. Kerr walked into the café.

There she was. She had seated herself on the only unoccupied stool at the counter, next to the doctor. Enid Jones pushed forward sullenly. If there's no room I'll sit on the floor, she thought, vexed. I can't bear m'feet a sec longer.

The doctor glanced round and saw her standing, with a fixed hostile look on her face. He got off his stool and waved to her to take it. He stood up, wedged against the counter, between her and the door of the kitchen.

"Much obliged," she said effusively.

She ordered coffee. Jean-Ann Kerr spoke to her and she answered insolently, as insolently as she dared. She was weakly afraid of the other woman's tongue. But Mrs. Kerr was in a good temper and only laughed— "Come off it."

"Afraid I don't get you," she said haughtily.

"How's the head?" the doctor asked.

She turned to him eagerly. "Not so bad now, but it's *been* awful. If you've never had a headache yourself you don't know what it is. There's time I wake up and I can't bear it. I keep saying Oh my head, my head. You know, I can watch it throb."

"I expect you're constipated," Maddalena Pizetti said quietly. "All the English are. It's their own fault, too."

"When I was a kid I used to have Gregory powder pushed into me," Jean-Ann Kerr said. "What's become of it? Never hear of it now." She leaned forward to smile knowingly at the doctor.

"Have you ever heard of Pope Leo X's Elephant?" he said.

"What's wrong with me is nervous," Enid Jones said. "I've always been nervous, since I was born. You feel how dry my skin is—I can't sweat. Not if it was ever so

I can't. And my headaches aren't like other people's. They're pure nerves."

"Why didn't you get married and make some man unhappy?" Jean-Ann Kerr said unkindly. "You're too soft to live. Softness doesn't pay in this world—unless you're married to a man softer than you are. If I was you I'd say less about my disabilities. They won't get you far."

"I didn't ask you for advice."

She put on a haughty expression, and drummed on the counter with her right hand, as if she were playing a piano. She wanted to impress on anyone watching her that she played. Not that she could play, but she wanted them to think so. The doctor especially. She ignored another remark from Mrs. Kerr. I don't like her, she thought; she's common. She was envious of the other woman; she was healthy, she had good clothes, she must be saving money. Let her—I don't care. She's nothing. I was running downstairs to the dining-room and a man said, Lovely legs that kid's got, look, and I told dada and he laughed and mother said, Oh he didn't mean you, he was speaking about some other child, but I knew all the time it was me, and dada winked at me he said, Look at that waiter he's got bandy legs, and we both laughed.

"Going out again, dear?" Mrs. Kerr said.

"I daresay," she answered, making her voice as ladylike as possible.

I don't know where she was brought up, but not in France I bet. Just say casually, I was educated in France. But he might begin speaking French, you never know, and I can't remember a word, not one word, gone like the dew on the somethingorother pass, gone with a flavour of hydrogen gas. Well, I remember that, I've got a memory like a clothes-horse.

She began to imagine herself talking French to the doctor. He was startled, fascinated. Of course now I look at you I can see you have foreign ways a foreign style. His eyes would get that fixed look. We'd go upstairs to

his room he'd lock the door and say in a deep voice deep
with emotion My darling has come to me Yes take me
take me you can't leave me now a faraway smile——

The doctor knocked against her elbow getting himself
out. He went off without apologizing.

After a minute she paid for her coffee and went. She
wanted to go to her room and lie down in bed with something to eat and then sleep. But she thought she would
give it another try, until midnight, and if she had no luck
then she would give it up and come in. She walked
briskly across the yard, holding her stomach in and moving
her body from side to side as she walked. I feel better
for that coffee, she thought. Well, here's hoping.

The last customer left, amiably escorted to the door by
Pizetti. He locked the door and drew the blind. Ten
minutes later he unlocked it for a moment, to drag out
two ashbins. The yard was dark and cool, but not quiet.
All the windows of the night club were open outside
closely-drawn curtains. The music had just stopped;
there were long intervals between the dances, to give
people time to order whiskey (in aspirin bottles) and
"fruit cup" made from a very poor champagne. The
laughter and talk went on in a noisy disjointed fashion.
To Pizetti the laughter of these English people was un-
natural. He believed they laughed out of a nervous
habit, and because when they were invited to enjoy
themselves they thought it their duty to make a noise.

Every window in the yard was dark except the room
belonging to the old German woman, the anarchist. In
this room there was a lighted candle standing on the
window-sill, a jonquil of light in the darkness.

It reminded Pizetti of an evening when he was a child,
and he was coming home alone, long after dark, and his
mother set a candle in the window of her room for him.
He saw it all the way up the narrow steep path to the
house. If it had not been for that he would have been

afraid. There were so many strange noises abroad in the immense night. But there was the candle, and a smell of thyme, and more stars than there were feathers on a cock.

He glanced up. There are no stars visible above London.

It came to him as an overwhelming need that he must go home. Not next year but this, he thought. His body was suddenly aching with love for—well, for what? Perhaps for his childhood and his youth.

Maddalena opened the window of their bedroom and called softly: "Gregorio."

"Coming," he answered, as he would have answered his mother. "Coming in a minute."

Towards midnight Pop sneaked downstairs from his attic over the Pizettis' bedroom. He had a quarter of a candle in his pocket. He lit it standing at the foot of the stairs, and began to search the ashbins Pizetti had put out. They were not anything like so good as the Screech Owl bins; Maddalena was too careful to throw anything away, but he found some dried mouldy beans in a paper bag, and stuffed them exultantly in his pocket. He blew the candle out, and began to sing a little under his breath.

> *"And thou I lov'd art gone*
> *For over the dark blue sea*
> *This heart is left alone*
> *That only throbb'd for thee. . . ."*

Holding his overcoat round him, he shuffled a few steps of a waltz, dragging his feet on the ground, his knees bent. He had been drinking from a bottle of port in his room and there was just enough warmth in his body to make him think of soft, rich summer nights, of a lamp behind the open windows of an old house, the scent of peonies in the darkness. Yet he had no wish to go back. Except in the early morning, when life runs low and sluggishly in the veins, he was quite content with New Moon Yard. He intended to live here for ever. For ever and ever, amen.

> *"We stood amid these bow'rs*
> *When last I wept adieu."*

He opened his arms to embrace the night, the burst of music from the Screech Owl, the sky, London. A yawn caught him, and made him stagger.

Time to sleep, he thought, and his mind—which was a rag-bag of other men's words—offered, *"the Quincunx of Heaven runs low, and 'tis time to close the five ports of know-ledge. . . . To keep our eyes open longer were but to act our Antipodes. The huntsmen are up in America, and they are already past their first sleep in Persia. . . ."*

The music stopped. There was a moment's silence, and then far away, outside New Moon Yard, a child began crying, against the night, against London, against the tor-rent of life. The old man listened to it with his head cocked on one side. It made him smile, and then it made him feel gently sad. I must write my sister a letter, he thought—forgetting for the moment that he no longer had a sister.

He stole back to his dark room at the top of the still darker stairs.

CHAPTER XII

ASHTON WATCHED Thomas bolt and lock the doors, not really noticing him, then went quickly into his room. Thomas followed him in. "I didn't know you were going to sleep here to-night, sir."

He drew the fitted cover off the divan, folded it, and turned the sheet back. Then he went to a drawer, took out pyjamas and laid them on the bed. "Will you have a cup of warm milk, sir? Or a drink?"

"I'll have a brandy," Ashton said.

He had drunk more than usual that night already, and he had reached a stage in which, while he had full control of his bodily movements, he had none over his impulses. He might decide to sit drinking for another hour, and keep Thomas hanging about waiting to see him safely in bed. It was five o'clock now.

While his servant was out of the room he sat on the side of the bed and began to undress. His brain was twitching with restlessness. The sudden feeling of dislike and contempt that had kept him from going off with Iris to her flat, as she certainly expected him to do, was turning to anger. She's every day as old as I am, he said to himself brutally; she's over forty and as hard and flat as a fish: let her find someone else to amuse her. He gripped his hands in a spasm of irritability. God send another war soon, he thought mechanically. His mind picked out an evening when he and that chap Fadds rode twenty miles into Amiens to have a woman. Neither of them had been in Amiens before; they got there at eleven and in the pitch dark streets Fadds kept flashing his torch in the faces of such women as were about. Most of them were impossible, awful, and he would say: "Pardon—cinq francs pour le dérangement"—and try another. But in the end they found a couple, and afterwards pushing along the roads to get back before daylight Fadds sang—what the hell was it he sang? He said he used to sing in St. Paul's choir before he went to British Honduras.

Though he did not know it, what soothed Ashton in thinking of another war was the idea of being accepted without question as a useful member of society. If there was only one kind of society which welcomed him, and that was a society in a state of war, then he was all for war. Really it was only by the way that war (any sort would do) satisfied his impulse to violence.

Thomas came in, poured out his brandy, and began to pick up the various garments he had dropped about.

"Plenty of people to-night, sir."

"Not the right sort," Ashton said irritably. "Bastards from Golders Green. Solicitors and I don't know what. Hardly a soul upstairs. Not a dozen." He meant the room on the top floor next the store-room, where he had roulette and *boule*.

Thomas grinned without opening his lips, and spoke with a self-assurance which surprised himself.

"Don't worry, sir. We'll manage."

He had been unemployed for six months when the Captain picked him up and brought him in on this job. He never sat on his butt waiting for the dole. He went on the road. It keeps you fit, and there are always chances— a job, a bit of poaching, an easy theft, anything but begging. His tight, smiling mouth and steady eyes were attractive to women; surprisingly often he landed jobs he could have kept if he were less restless. He had a half-formed plan in his mind. Suppose the Captain cleared out of this place, and took a pub on the river; he could work it up into a week-end and summer place. . . . If he gave me the run of my teeth, I'd carry on without pay for a bit, he thought, easily.

The moment to drop a hint of this plan had not offered itself yet.

"Manage be damned," Ashton said. He poured himself a second drink. "You can go," he said to Thomas. He saw Thomas hesitate. "Go on. Get out."

When he was alone he got up and walked up and down the room. He felt a twinge of pain in his left knee, and halted to rub it. He had never had a pain in his life, and never been ill. He had a splendid body, broad above the waist, with narrow firm buttocks. In the last few months he had noticed a thickening of the flesh over his stomach; it was no longer, as it had been, gently concave. Standing sideways in front of the glass fastened inside the door of the cupboard, he could see the change. Undoubtedly he was beginning to go flabby.

He felt an impotent anger. For the first time in his life he felt that he might not succeed in squeezing enough money by his efforts to get what he wanted. If I don't pull this off, he thought. He felt a flash of rage in his body. Someone, if he failed, ought to be made to suffer for it. He made a melodramatic gesture with his hands.

About six in the morning, Dr. Cleveland came home from wherever he had passed his night—and he passed more of them than he came up with—and stood in the yard, looking in his pockets for the key of his room. There was a steely brightness in the air; the sun had risen behind a sleeve of mist and was slowly unravelling it, so that the air was shot through with a reflected heavy light. It was already warm, warmer than yesterday.

He felt separated from his body. He saw it, brought into the yard from the street, in its grey clothes. The front of the house watched him from a gaping staircase; a torn newspaper had been thrown down. He had a consciousness, like a prick in the eyeball, of all the living asleep in these rooms and of the moment when each would begin to think like a child learning to walk and, alone, would assemble its idiot certainties to match its breathing.

There was scarcely a sparrow in sight, but a mob of them chittered under the gutters. Such a noise. It split his skull and reduced him to the state of infancy. He had no control over his mind; it went back, snuffling like a lost bitch, to a past of which the sole sensible content was a vague sadness.

Memory returned, insistent, through room after hired room, to reach this one. He had his hand on the key. He walked forward, feeling that the house followed him into his room; that when a blind in any window flew up, his hand was on the cord; his body turned on its back in every bed; his eyes stared at the ceilings. My God, do I have to endure this? he thought. And what a sell!

CHAPTER XIII

RANDALL GOT up at half-past six. He looked through the open window at the sky, and thought, Another hot cloudless day. Turning to dress, he caught sight of the letter which had been lying on the floor when he came in yesterday. It was from his mother. The address was typewritten and the envelope a thin one of the kind you buy in any shop as "foreign," but he would know who it was from at once if it had come in a heap of others. He had not opened it yet. He looked at the postmark, to see whether she was still in Pau, and left it. She would be asking him for news, teasing him gently because it was over a month since he had written.

She had once said: "You know, I have all your letters. You wrote more when you were a little boy than you do now."

He remembered the woman with the dogs who looked after him when he was too young to be at school. She and the dogs smelled exactly alike. They had the same eyes. Once a week she made him sit down and print a letter to his mother in London. He was obedient; he even took pains over the printing, but he was bored. There was snow outside, or it was summer, with bees droning under the window: whatever the time of year, he grew hot and the pencil became slippery between his fingers—IT WAS 5 INCHES ROUND WAS THERE ANY SNOW WHERE YOU ARE IF SO TELL ME. LOVE FROM BILL RANDALL.

As he moved about the little room he thought of Harriet with an emotion older than his years. It was as though they had been married for years, and he knew her so well that he could predict what she would say or do in any situation. She would argue and argue about leaving her absurd job, and in the end she would leave it, and probably she wouldn't tell him until it was done. And he was not

in a hurry.   He wanted to live with Harriet, in peace and
quiet, in his own house, not in this shoddy feed-outside
warren.   He liked the look of the house near the aerodrome.   (He imagined the ironic glance, turned instantly
to one of kindness, with which his mother would look at
it.   Let her, he thought.)   But if he could make this
flight he would put off marrying until afterwards.   Harriet
must wait.

His mind slipped past the trouble of persuading Rapp
that he ought to put up the money for the flight to the
flight itself.   He would have to find time, while carrying
on with his job, to make all the preparations, going down
to the works to watch the construction of the aeroplane,
apply for passports and permissions to fly over foreign
countries, arrange supplies, and work, with the maps—
how many times ?—over the route until it seemed that he
could fly blindfold to the Cape.

There would be the nerve-racking moments of the start,
and then the familiar, the still extraordinary sense of
escape, and of power.   But this would not last, because he
would grow tired; his mind, following the compass needle
and instruments, would harden against sleep and against
his body.   Towns, rivers, landmarks, would glide into the
circle of his airscrew, to be named and forgotten.   His
hands would move, smoothly and certainly, and his sleep-
tortured brain would carry the whole weight of the
machine as he held it between sky and the slowly-moving
and rolling earth.   If to save his life he were asked to
explain why he wanted to risk it for a record which would
not, in these days, bring even fame, he would have no
answer.   The answer was lost somewhere between his
finger-tips and his mind.   He knew that he wanted to
make the flight, that thinking of it poured an excitement
into his blood, yes, and a deep peace.   That was all.   It
was surely enough.

He knew a great many men with whom he could drink,
talk, play the fool, but he had only two friends, both of
them men years older than himself: one a test pilot, the

other an ex-war pilot who had become manager of an airpost. He would consult them about the flight, but he would not show any enthusiasm when he was talking to them about it. Nor even with Harriet.

Apart from this flight—which might never come off—and apart from Harriet, he had made no plans for his future.

His room was very untidy. Giulia, when she came in, would put the books into the shelf and fold away a jacket he had dropped on the floor. As he was crossing the yard to Pizetti's he saw Mrs. Caracas leaning from her window, her face red and creased, her hair in brown curling-pins. He smiled towards her.

"I say, I say," she called.

He stood still, reluctantly. "Yes?"

"I'm going to make a complaint," she said in an angry trembling voice. "I'm going to write to the landlord. That old man was hanging about the ashbins again last night with his candle. He'll set the house on fire. He's a fool, a lunatic. He ought to be shut up."

"Oh, I don't think he'll do any harm," Randall said.

"Carrying his candle. He'll have us burned down one of these nights."

A cat jumped on to the window-sill at her elbow, and she turned to speak to it. Randall went into the Café Bar.

Pizetti was busy washing the counter and the tables. He turned round when the young man came in, and smiled with touching warmth.

"Your coffee is almost ready. I never forget."

"Thanks," Randall said. He smiled at the Italian.

Maddalena came out of the kitchen with the pots of coffee and hot milk, and a cup. She watched him drop four lumps of sugar into the cup with no more than a sigh for his extravagance. Other customers found a cube of sugar in the saucer, and if they wanted more had to pay for it.

"We'll be in this evening, about seven, for a meal," Randall said.

"Well, I shall make you a *risotto*," said Maddalena. "And it won't be spoiled if you are late."

"Oh, we shan't be late. I'm going out afterwards." A sudden crazy excitement took him. "I'm going to fly to the Cape."

Mrs. Pizetti looked at him calmly. "What will your mother say?"

"I don't know," he said, still smiling. "What can she say?"

"Well, if you were my son I should tell you not to be an idiot." He doesn't know where he is going, she thought. To the Cape, indeed!

It was a quarter-past seven when he left the café. A little girl came out of Barley's workshop and walked, carrying a basin and some money, towards the café. She looked into his face as she passed. He gave her a friendly, embarrassed smile. He never knew what to say to children.

"You're out early," he said.

She hurried past him without answering. He wondered whether the mechanic at the garage had remembered to check the oil in his car, but when he reached the garage, behind New Moon Yard, he forgot to ask. He disliked driving in traffic. There was not much in the streets at this hour of the morning, but he felt distinctly happier as soon as he turned on to the bye-pass and then on a side road. The ragged streamers of early-morning mist had vanished. The hedges glittered with light as the sun fingered the young leaves. The fields ran over with light, and there were long shadows from the trees, lying like wings across the road.

He passed the same countryman at the same place and time every morning, walking to his work. Randall looked out for him. "Here he is." The man passed without so much as glancing at the car, and Randall thought, If he was big enough he'd brush us off the roads and out of

the sky like knocking away a wasp. Airmen joke about
the thickheadedness of farm labourers, but some other
feeling lies at the back of their contempt.

The air, rushing into the car, was warm and dust-dry.
He drove more quickly, and began to sing aloud, thinking
with familiar pleasure of his few minutes of aerobatics,
testing the Avro Tutor. It was his first job in the
morning. He was alone, and in the clear bubble of a day
like this, light running along the bracing wires, he would
feel a special happiness, a calm confidence in himself and
his skill, as though he were at the beginning of everything, body and mind cleansed by the air, by solitude.
He was perfectly happy.

CHAPTER XIV

WHEN ALFRED LINDER had to press for money owing
to him he felt, not uneasy, but unkind. He liked receiving money as much as most people, Jew or Christian—
he needed it, with so many little presents to make to so
many women who had told him the kinds of flowers and
stockings they liked, and with his wife's passion for gar-
dening. More, he was determined to have it. But he
wished that other people would pay their debts promptly,
and save him from having to write letters or pay calls
to ask for the money they owed him.

The proprietor of the Screech Owl owed him a large
sum of money. He bought bad cheap wine and never
paid for it. Linder pursed his full lips at the thought
of people pouring that rotten stuff down their throats—
and at such prices. But perhaps they deserved it. He
rarely entered a night club himself. He preferred quieter
amusements.

So now he must make another and more serious effort

to get Ashton to pay off part of his debt. He had written; he had remonstrated with that fellow Thomas when he came in with the order. His letters were not answered, and there was something very sympathetic to Linder about the ex-gunner porter, about his big solid body, twinkling eyes, and resolute expression. He is tough, a bit of a scoundrel, but he is very English, Linder said to himself. Like other Jews, he had a passionate love for the country he lived in. He would begin talking to the fellow and, before he knew it, he had accepted another order without insisting on his money. I am a damned fool, he thought, sighing.

This time he would run no risks. He would go across and insist on speaking to Ashton himself.

"And since I don't like the look of him——" he muttered.

Setting his hat a little too far back on his head, he walked across the yard. He stepped carefully—the yard was not clean, what with cats, overfilled ashbins, and dust from the street. He hated to soil his shoes.

It was just eleven o'clock. If he waited until later, Ashton might be out. Or that fellow Thomas would pretend he was out. But Linder had seen Thomas go out and come back with a copy of *The Times* and the *Daily Express*, and he was not buying these papers for himself. No, Ashton had spent the night at the Screech Owl and he was in now.

"Good morning," he said, affably, to the porter. "I should like to see Captain Ashton." He saw a certain glint come into the servant's eyes. "Now, don't tell me he is not at home," he added persuasively. "You see, I know he is. And it is only putting off the evil day. Go and tell him that I am going to wait until he is ready to see me."

Thomas drew his lips into a thin colourless line. He went off without saying a word. Alfred Linder sighed again. Dear me, he thought; it's going to be very unpleasant.

When he was admitted to Ashton's room he found him in pyjamas and dressing-gown. A breakfast-tray, on which was a glass and a half-filled cup of black coffee, was still on the table. The bed had not yet been made into a couch. The curtains were drawn over the window, and the electric light, a round glazed bowl let into the ceiling, filled the room with a hard light which had the effect of making it seem smaller. It was singularly more harsh and unflattering than the crude sunlight outside. Linder blinked.

"Well, sit down. What do you want?" Ashton said.

Another man would have been offended by this address. But Linder could feel the uncertainty in it, as well as the brutality and deliberate rudeness. He would have my teeth pulled if he could, he told himself. This insight into the other's harsh feelings did not make him angry. Perhaps, he thought strangely, I should feel the same if I were in his shoes. And by the way, they would be several sizes too large for me.

"You know that you owe me—you owe the Lunar Wine Company—a large sum now," he began in his pleasant voice.

"You agreed I should have credit," said Ashton.

"Three months' credit. It's close on eight already, Captain Ashton. I really don't want to trouble you." He had placed his hat on the table between the tray and his arm. He glanced into it, to avoid looking at Ashton, and stroked both his knees with a smooth, strong-looking hand.

Ashton detested him—because he looked well-off, confident, and secure. He would have paid to kick Linder's plump thighs, pressed over the edge of his chair. Why in hell's name did I buy from a Jew? He felt nearly insane with anger. He even blamed Linder for the fact that no one else would give him credit. They get hold of you like that, he thought. He looked down at the knuckles of his hands.

"I'll give you thirty pounds on account," he said with insolence.

Alfred Linder gazed at him with meditative, yet bright and calculating brown eyes. "Thirty," he repeated. He shrugged his shoulders.

Ashton trembled with anger. "Fifty." He felt his anger explode in the centre of his body—without sound, but there was a flash from it behind his eyes. "I can manage fifty. Not more."

"You know you owe us this money," Linder said softly. "I haven't asked you to make me a present of any of it."

He knew precisely what Ashton was thinking. And he knew that if he had not been a Jew the other man would at least have tried to make their conversation seem a meeting between men of the world. Yet the others would have pulled him up months ago, he thought. Why didn't I? But the answer was too far back in the past which had bequeathed to him his moon face, delicate hooked nose and womanly mouth. It was not entirely a distaste for dunning a client, or simple kindness.

"I'll write you a cheque now," Ashton said, getting up.

He sat down with his back to Linder, who took the opportunity to stare round the room. It made him shiver. I wouldn't live in this place for a fortune, he thought. One might as well sleep in a shop-window in Tottenham Court Road.

"Here you are." Ashton poked the cheque into his hand.

"Thank you—and good-bye," said Linder pleasantly.

He took up his hat, smiled with complete sincerity and kindness, and went out. Thomas, who had been hanging about the hall—probably listening—opened the front door for him, but made no response to his polite "Good morning."

Linder hurried across the yard. Watching from the window of the ladies' cloakroom, which looked on to the yard, Thomas saw him go into the shop; a minute later the boy who helped him came out and ran, in spite of the heat, to the street.

Going off to the bank with the cheque, Thomas thought. He stood still. Better not go in the room yet.

Two men came into the yard. One of them walked directly to the Café Bar. The other came towards the door of the Screech Owl. Both men were Jews, but of a different type from the manager of the wine shop. Thomas stared. We shall have to change the name to the Jerusalem Dove, he thought. He opened the door.

"Captain Ashton in ?   He's expecting me."

"Oh, is he ? " said Thomas. "How do I know that ? "

The fellow was small, and extremely nasty. Cuts your eyes out with a bottle, I shouldn't wonder. Thomas looked down at him with unflurried distaste.

"Ask him and see. I rang him up last night and said I'd be here to see him at eleven-thirty." The man yawned in Thomas's face.

"Name ! "

"Not your business."

Thomas gave him a gentle poke, which sent him staggering a few yards, and shut the door. He went to the window in the cloakroom. The man was disappearing into the Café Bar. After a minute Thomas heard the telephone ring in the Captain's room. He waited. One of his women, he thought.

"Thomas ! "

"Yes, sir."

Before he reached the door of the room, the Captain opened it and said sharply:

"What the devil do you mean chucking people off the step when I've arranged to see them ? "

Thomas stiffened his legs like a dog. "You mean the man was here a minute ago," he began quietly. The front door bell rang.

"Let him in now," snapped Ashton.

"I thought he wanted to serve a writ on us," Thomas said, without a change of expression. He went to the door, opened it sharply, and watched the man walk in. He took no notice of the fellow's jeering smile. "Come in," Ashton shouted. The door of his room shut.

Thomas moved quietly—he could walk as softly as a

cat—and stood close to the door. What did the Captain want with a man of his type? Although he admired and trusted Ashton he thought he was ignorant in many ways —it was the faint contempt an independent man of the lower classes has for his superiors.

He listened. The conversation inside the room came to him in snatches: he could not hear the other man at all —he spoke much too quietly—but the Captain's habit of repeating phrases he had not at once grasped was a help. Once Thomas had caught the drift of the argument he followed more of it than he heard.

To say that he was shocked when he gathered that the fellow was suggesting—as easily as though it were a usual business deal—setting fire to the place for the insurance, wouldn't be true. But he thought firing houses a singularly dirty crime because of the risk of burning some-one to death. He waited, without anxiety and with interest, for the Captain to kick him out.

The low rather flat voice said something he couldn't hear. Ashton's voice cut across it.

"What's that, what's that? Insurance companies settled for half? I don't understand you, Mr.—what's your name?—Franklyn. If they suspected anything why did they pay up at all, and if they didn't suspect—what d'you say?"

He didn't catch a word of the answer. In a lower voice the Captain said something about Ireland. Thomas felt queer—as though his stomach had dropped or turned in-side him. He was uneasy. He moved away from the door and went upstairs—out of sight if the door were opened suddenly. Changing his mind, he came down again and went outside and across to the Café Bar. He wanted to take a look at the second man, who had come with this Franklyn.

"Give me a coffee?" he said to Pizetti.

Leaning against the bar, he tried to see the fellow in the mirror at the back. He had to shift to the end of the bar to get him in. After a moment's scrutiny he

E

met the other man's eye in the mirror and realized that
he was being watched himself. The other's glance slid
away, with a quick movement of the eyelids.

Thomas turned to Pizetti. "Warm day," he said,
with his close smile.

Pizetti nodded and smiled gaily. He was feeling depressed, because his wife said she was tired, this London
heat tired her. He looked into Thomas's face with
friendly admiration. He never feels anything, he thought:
tough as a bear, no nerves, no feelings, no one he cares
for—ha, if I were only like that. He rushed off into
the kitchen to look again helplessly at Maddalena.

Thomas finished his coffee and went back to the club.
The door opened before he reached it, and the man came
out and made for the café. Thomas looked him in the
face. He had not the air of a man who has just brought
off a troublesome deal. Thomas swore under his breath.
Everything was all right. Only he'd been a fool not to
wait and see him thrown out. A bloody fool, he repeated
silently. He felt happy and went straight upstairs to the
store-room to finish the job he was doing. The door of
the Captain's room was closed. He would come out and
shout if he wanted anything.

Ben looked at Franklyn as he sat down. He guessed
that nothing had been settled. "Want anything to eat?"
he ventured. "It's twelve."

"Ask them if they've got any macaroni," Franklyn
said.

"It's an Italian place," Ben smiled.

Franklyn looked at him. "Well, ask them," he said.

Ben got up quickly and went over to the counter, and
rapped on it with his knuckles. Pizetti came out of the
kitchen, jerking his long thin legs, and said nervously:

"You want something, eh?"

"Well," Ben drawled. He was going to make a sar-
castic joke. He changed his mind and asked in his most

genial way if they could have a meal—"a dish of macaroni, and fix it with tomatoes——"

He waited, leaning against the counter. Pizetti had spoken to someone in the kitchen and came back immediately behind the bar. The door into the kitchen was pushed to. By just touching it with his foot Ben swung it open and saw Mrs. Pizetti stirring the macaroni (it must be that) in an iron pan on the stove.

"Nice place you got here," he said to Pizetti.

"You said that yesterday," Pizetti retorted.

Ben laughed good-temperedly. "So if I did. It is a nice place, isn't it? Better than keeping goats."

"Why should I keep goats?" Pizetti said frowning, and suspicious.

"Well, I never was in Italy yet, but I saw a picture of it once some place, the Plaza I think it was, yes, yes it was, I had the wife with me that time, and there was a shot of Italy—goats, dozens of goats, and a chap about your jig minding them. It kept coming back to it, and my wife jabs me on the knee, and says well, she says, I never knew there was nothing in Italy beyond goats. And she laughed."

He laughed himself. He had a pleasant laugh—"Ho, ho"—like a good-tempered and vigorous clown. Pizetti at first smiled reluctantly, then chuckled. Seeing the two men come into the yard again he had remembered his first suspicion, and half considered taking his boxful of notes to a bank. What had happened next reassured him. He had decided that they were a couple of debt collectors—crooks but, in this country, on the side of the law. He felt, not friendly but cautiously interested.

"If it wasn't in London, you are right, it wouldn't be a bad place," he agreed.

Ben sprawled bulkily across the counter. He was wearing a belt to-day, and it was too tight. He set it back a hole. "Ever been in Essex?" he asked.

"No, but I think we go back to Italy this year," Pizetti said. He had a sharp unexpected memory of Maddalena as a girl, standing against a tree in her mother's field, and the pattern of sun and leaf-shadow on her face, and her calm eyes looking at him. "Yes, this year," he repeated. His face took on an expression of fanatical energy. He rushed into the kitchen.

Before he could speak to her Maddalena put the tray with the dish and plates on it into his hands. "You don't want Giulia to take it, do you?" she said in a low voice.

"No, I'll take it."

He felt comforted for no reason. With a flourish of his free arm, he carried the tray across the café to Franklyn's table and set dish and plate in front of him. Ben followed him slowly, thumbs stuck in his belt, and sat at the other side of the table. He gave his friend a quick furtive glance, narrowing his eyes.

Now that he saw them again together Pizetti felt an unpleasant sensation in his chest. They were as tough customers as he had had in the place. He rallied and said cheerfully:

"There you are. Eat. Enjoy yourselves." He struck an attitude, smiling.

"Leave it," said Franklyn. He moved his hand very slightly on the table. Pizetti felt that he had been menaced. He went back behind the bar.

The younger man helped Franklyn from the dish between them, and then himself. "It's cooked fresh," he said.

Franklyn looked at him for a second without speaking. "Thinking of keeping a pub now?" he said.

"Well, now, Con, I just happen to like talking sometimes. We can't be all alike. I——"

"Shut your mouth, will you?"

Ben looked down at his plate and went on eating. Franklyn ate rapidly, with the very expression of a sheep tearing at grass. He became better-tempered as he ate. At last, rubbing a piece of bread over his plate, he said:

"Nothing doing there yet——" he played a stave with his thick fingers on the edge of the table.

'We shouldn't have come this far west," Ben said. "It's my fault. I just happened——"

"I can tell you what's wrong with that fellow," Franklyn interrupted, jerking his head very slightly towards the Screech Owl: "he thinks he's tough, but he's not tough enough. See? He's like all his sort. He'd steal, do murder, anything, it wouldn't mean any damned thing to him, but he couldn't bring it off on his own, without something at his back. See? He needs to be in his own class, and them all sticking with him. Then he's safe. They aren't sticking with him now. And for why? Because they haven't got a use for him, for any rough work, and he's no good except at rough work—see? So the Captain's out in the cold."

Ben nodded with a pretence of taking an interest in this account of Ashton. His own interest in him was simpler. Just as he had smaller ambitions than the older man, so he had a less or no need to prove himself by feeling contempt for anyone. He was cold-blooded, but he did not despise anyone. He and Franklyn had one deep-rooted feeling in common. They thought of their profession as more risky than a great many others, but not essentially different from them. They wanted the same things as other people wanted—a nice, paying little garage, a flat in Park Lane. In respect of their wants they were very ordinary members of society.

Ben noticed that a woman who had come in and seated herself at the nearest table was a tart. She was watching for him. As soon as she caught his attention she rolled her lips at him and winked. He looked her over without kindness. Going down fast, he thought. Perhaps sick. He looked away, turning his thumb down, with deliberate brutality.

All right, all right, Enid Jones thought angrily. She would have liked to shout something rude at him, but she was afraid. The insult made her miserable when she thought about it. She pretended to look through the window. Pizetti brought her her cup of tea and sandwich.

"Fine day," he said kindly and gaily. He was even sorry for her.

She turned round. "A fine day for Italians and monkeys," she said.

Feeling better now that she had been rude to someone, she sipped her tea. Its strong, coarse tang delighted her. She smacked her tongue over it, forgetting to be refined, and held a mouthful over the rotten tooth at the back. For a full minute she felt strong and well.

The Rev. James Daniel came in, looking round him with alarmed, yet unfocused eyes, rolling in their sockets like the eyes of a runaway horse, and seated himself at a table at one side of the two Jews. He looked at Enid Jones. When he looked steadily, seeking the centre of her body, the place under the breast-bone where the weak flame is kept alight and burning, he saw to his horror a worm. Even in spite of himself he had to speak to her.

He leaned forward. "You are in danger," he said to her, earnestly.

Enid Jones snorted with surprise. Then she assumed a dignified air and said haughtily: "Were you speaking to me?"

"I must save you with fear, and pull you out of the fire," Daniel said.

Now that he was looking at her with his ordinary glance he saw what she was, and he saw by her haggard face and the peevish drooping mouth that she was ill and weak. He felt as much compassion for her as if he had come on a draggled, dying animal. More. She had a spirit to be saved, and he did not believe that animals could be saved in the same way, though he believed, somewhere in him, that they had powerful spirits of their own.

Enid Jones had opened her mouth to retort, but Franklyn, who had been listening with a curious mockery in his look, turned his face full to the preacher and said: "You should mind what you're about."

"I know what I'm about," Daniel said.

Franklyn gave him the same lingering, cruel stare.

"Maybe you do and maybe you don't," he said. "But don't talk no more rubbish while I'm here. It gives me a headache."

He turned back to his food. The Rev. Daniel sat still. He rested his hands, black and thick like the roots of a plant, on his knees, and looked at the wall. Inwardly he was quivering with shame, because he had not answered the man according to his folly. But he felt weak—it was a long time since he had eaten, and he had been awake all night, on his knees in his room, rocking himself from side to side, praying. And this man, whom he could have broken with his hands, alarmed him. Never had he seen such a face of cold scorpion-like insolence and evil. Judas must have looked so, he thought: he tried to call up the image of the Shepherd, but it wavered, pale and weak, out of his reach. He kept himself still, letting the waves of blackness in his body submerge him. He drew strength from them; it was a strength on which he had tacitly agreed not to call, when he was ordained and re-baptized a servant of the Gentle Shepherd. Without fully under-standing why, Daniel knew that the bubbling fathomless black energy, like black water oozing up endlessly from a swamp, which he could reach when he wanted to, would very easily be the death of the Gentle One. He drew himself back, slowly, with an inward groan.

A woman put food in front of him and he ate.

He became calm. The defeat had been in his body, not in his soul. And it was to his soul that God had spoken, telling them to warn these dwarfs, insolent, threatened. Their end was very near. And although he knew he was to be saved, Daniel felt a shiver of anguish when he thought of the destruction of this room in which he was sitting. It was friendly—he felt more compunction for it than for the rest of London.

He paid his bill and rose to go out. Pausing at the table where Enid Jones sat staring vacantly in front of her, he said, in a quiet voice: "Remember. *And power was given unto him to scorch men with fire.*"

He went out. Enid had been frightened. She recovered herself and called after him:

"Go on, go it, golliwog!"

She looked round her for approval. No one had been listening. The two Jews got up, paid and went out; Pizetti watched them out of sight from the door. The heat reflected from the stones of the yard was visible as a faint discoloration of the air. At the very height of noon a film had come over the sun, so that what you got was a dense, dust-smitten weight of heat, pressing relentlessly down. It made the house itself, and the streets, appear dry and brittle, as though they might collapse quickly into a heap of grey ash. Pizetti thought longingly of his home. In the memory there are only clear skies. Above snow or above the green shoots of vines, always a clear sky.

Mrs. Caracas's big yellow tom was missing from his home. Since the day before. Enid Jones was trailing up the stairs to her room, past the old woman's door; it opened with a sudden click, as if she had been listening with it on the pop for someone to come past. She poked out, wiping her mouth on something, a dishcloth. "You haven't seen my lovely boy upstairs, have you? He's run off."

Enid said: "No." She stared through the open doorway into the room. It's comfortable, she thought. I like to see things with chintzy stuff round them, like that.

"I saw a room once done just like yours at Olympia."

"Well," Mrs. Caracas said.

"I had an engagement there. Queens of Story. I was an early one, called Jane Shore. I asked the boss one day, I said, Who was she, anyway? He said, Oh, her, she was a cow, she was kicked to death in a ditch in a white sheet, at Shoreditch. Hence the Town Hall. He was like that, assing round all day, joking. He had high spirits."

"One of the model rooms, was it?"

"Yes. It was sixpence to look at us. There was always

some onion saying things to try to make us laugh. You
were fined if you laughed."

She was standing right in the doorway now, looking
round. It was a change. Better than being alone. She
was going up to do her room, but it could wait. "Flowers
you got, too, I see."

"You can come in a minute and look at them," Mrs.
Caracas said. I shan't give her one, she thought; I can
see her number. She kept an eye on the young woman
when she made a show of smelling one after the other.
"Here, don't wear them out," she said with a sharp laugh.
And I hadn't asked you to sit down.

The room was hot, and the smell of cats and fish overpowered the other smells. She could ask me to have a cup
of tea, Enid thought.

"It's what I call a cosy room," she said in a pinched
genteel voice.

"Um," Mrs. Caracas said. "Yes, it's cosy, but I'm going
to leave." She stumbled against a chair, disturbing the cat
stretched asleep in it. "There, there. Mother's sorry.
Lie still. Mother's little sweetheart. Yes, I'm going to
live in the country. I shall take a cottage."

"Everyone to their taste, I always say."

Her fingers, exploring the padded sides of the chair,
touched something—a handkerchief? She pushed further,
feeling the dust and crumbs in her nails. A small flat
hard object. She worked the handkerchief over it. The
old woman was grunting, bent double, over another of her
blessed cats. Without moving her body she drew her hand
out. Don't look down. She pushed it swiftly up her
sleeve. Her heart was racing to kill her. After a minute
she stood up, holding the arm pressed to her side.

"Oh, are you going?" Mrs. Caracas said. She was
suddenly affable.

"If I see that cat of yours anywhere I'll fetch it."

"He's a wicked pussens. My other four are as good as
gold, but he's faithless. He's a corner. Out every night."
She smiled slyly.

"They're all alike—men." She kept on the same side of the old woman, who hurried her to the door, saying, "Mind *mind,*" when a cat jumped out in front of them. Half potty about them, she thought.

Going upstairs, she felt the thing hard against her flesh. If it was a pocket-book with a pound or two in that was good work. She locked the door of her room.

She could have cried with the disappointment. A dirty, torn handkerchief, and a small photograph. She picked it up. It was yellowish, fading. Two young women in big hats, dressed like in that picture *The Show Boat*. She turned it over. Bertha and self at Archie's.

"Bertha and self at Archie's."

In a spasm of weak rage she tore it across and dropped the pieces into the slop-pail. It was too bad. Everything's against me, she thought. Me trying to keep up and other people pushing me down. I hope her cat's dead.

As soon as she was alone Mrs. Caracas felt like a drop of something. To her shocked annoyance she found that the bottle she kept behind the drapery of the washstand was empty. "It must have evaporated," she murmured.

She put a coat on over what she called her rest-gown, and went down to the Lunar Wine Company's shop. Mr. Alfred Linder came out of the back room, smiling, wagging his head.

"You know it's out of hours," he said gaily. "I'll send you a bottle up later."

Mrs. Caracas's face fell. "That's no use," she said. "It's now I want it. I feel as if I'd pass out without a drop of something lively in me."

"I'll tell my boy to make you a cup of tea," Linder said.

"Tea? I don't want any tea."

She stood there, holding her coat over the welter of dirty lace, velvet, ribbons, that partly clothed her, one hand scratching her neck. The manager felt a sudden pang of pity take him. What has she, he asked himself, except food and drink to live for? She can have no other sensations, no other happiness. It seemed to him quite shameful that for heaven knows what reasons the State should deprive this harmless old ruin of her fun, and on an impulse of the purest compassion he exclaimed:

"Very well. If anyone sees us I shall go to prison."

"Who's going to see?" Mrs. Caracas said boastfully.

Her arm reached out and thrust the bottle deep out of sight in the mysterious jungle of her garments.

"There! Now where is it?"

"Dear me," Alfred Linder said, smiling roguishly. "I mustn't dare to think."

Mrs. Caracas was delighted. She went out of the shop chuckling, bubbling at the corners of her mouth, and pranced round to her room. Even her joints shared the joke.

In the middle of the afternoon the sun came out fully. It poured down on the glass dome of the Reading Room of the British Museum, and shafts of dusty light sparkled to the galleries. The air was tepid, heavy with the dry smell of the books. Pop, who read there every day, always sat in the same place, at the head of one of the spokes of double-sided desks. He was not following any line of research or study. He had long since given up pretending to be anything but an idle old man, and he took out books on any subject.

He turned the pages of one, slowly, and more slowly. His head was heavy with sleep, his ears singing. At last he gave up the effort; his head dropped forward until it was resting on his hands spread on the pages, and he slept.

He was walking ankle deep in a bog; the sun drew a warm scent out of the grass and reeds; buttercups and pale airy cuckoo-flowers glittered in the bright light. His father was standing patiently waiting for him at the farther side of the bog. "I'm coming," he called, "coming, coming." The road curved always farther from the railway station he could see below him, and if he missed this train there was not another until next day and he would be too late; heavy with anxiety he hurried on, and now he walked past the

arches of a bridge spanning the valley, enormous arches out
of sight over his head; the road climbed steeply between
walls and shops, and in a café at the corner higher up people
were drinking and eating quantities of chocolate and chocolate biscuits; the street was lighted, the large dress shops
glittering with light, tram-lines in the centre of the road
gleaming and curving, and then the darkened square and
the lane, and the indistinct room with his mother lying on
the couch, singing. He strained to hear the words; rather
than not hear them he sang them himself:

> "*Soft o'er the fountain*
> *Lingering falls the southern moon . . .*
> *Nita! Juanita!   Ask thy soul if we should part!*
> *Nita! Juanita!*
> *Lean thou on my heart.*"

"*Jua-ni-ta . . .*" He could not finish. The sadness
gushed over him in a warm flood. Hurrying in and out
of the narrow streets in the night, searching for something
he remembered, he forgot, knowing what was coming next,
and then it slipped, changing, and he walked on, seeing in
the distance the hills racing like dark beasts above the fields,
and all that beauty, all that tenderness, lost, betrayed, lost.

His gentle snoring had grown louder. Suddenly one
terrific snort burst out of him, echoing and re-echoing in
the dome. The woman at the next desk looked at him in
pained annoyance, and an attendant touched him gently on
the shoulder.

He started awake. Confused, he muttered a random
word or two and passed his hand over his creased moist face,
leaving a streak of dust. He began turning the leaves of his
book over and over, searching, pretending to search for
something in a great hurry. It was Bell's "Great Fire of
London," and still confused, and ashamed of having slept,
he muttered: "A day for a fire, a day for a fire."

In some part of his mind bog buttercups and "Juanita"
were still mingled like bright fragments of broken shells on
the floor of a pool.

Jean-Ann Kerr, wearing her going-out dress, a black figured silk with a short cape, was pouring the water into her tea-pot when the door-bell rang, a long imperative ring. She frowned. It was not the day for one of her regular clients who came in the afternoon. She felt vexed. I have enough to do, she thought, without being bothered at tea-time.

She opened the door, and saw Ashton. "Oh," she said. "Come in." He had visited her four times since the beginning of the year. She did not dislike him, but she resented his making use of her as a mere stop-gap. This resentment was quite illogical, and she knew it. She was not an unintelligent woman. And since she could not afford to turn away business, she injected a friendliness into her voice and manner which she was far from feeling.

She had clients with whom she was on terms of genuine friendship. Unlikely as this may seem, it was perfectly true. She gave an impression of reserve, and common sense, which was surprising enough in a woman of her profession to seem quite extraordinary. Any sensible woman would have given the man who consulted her on his affairs the same advice as she gave him. Because she was a prostitute he was overwhelmingly impressed by her shrewdness.

"Have you had tea?" she said to Ashton. "I was just making it. Or will you have a whiskey and soda?" She saw that he hesitated. "If you're in a hurry, I can undress at once."

"I'll have tea—without milk," Ashton said.

He sat down. He was not simple enough to accept her for a few minutes as a hostess, but he made the attempt. It pleased his vanity to think that he was equally himself in any situation.

"How's the club going?" Mrs. Kerr asked briskly.

"It's doing very well," he answered.

"Oh. I'm glad. Last time you were here you said you were worried."

"*Did* I?" he exclaimed. He was struck, not so much by her remembering, as by the fact that he had once given himself away. A sudden recklessness seized him. After all, to talk to a woman of her sort was like talking to no one at all. She was anonymous. He had had to struggle to recall her name when he was on his way here across the yard.

"To tell you the truth, I'm still worried. People come, but they don't drink enough, and there aren't enough of them. There's always a table for anyone who comes in after one o'clock. Yet the band's good, drinks are no dearer than they'd be anywhere else, and the food's better. Some people come regularly, of course."

As soon as he had come out with all this, he felt an extraordinary sensation of relief. Almost as though . . . He put his cup down, and took out his cigarette-case.

"Will you have more tea?" Mrs. Kerr asked.

"No thanks." He sent her a stealthy glance. Dresses neatly, he thought. You'd hardly know—yes, you would, though; there's something.

She had reflected. "You've never had turns, have you? A dancer?"

"No room."

"Who sees that you get into the weeklies? *Tatler* and that?"

"Well——" he hesitated. "No one specially," he admitted. "I sent invitations to all the apes and females who write the things, and some of 'em have been in the club." An expression of contempt, half put on, crossed his face. He knew he had not the right manner with the gossip and "personality" crew. He was either too off-hand or too expansive. "If this was a decent country," he exploded, "they'd all be put to work in camps."

Jean-Ann Kerr smiled slightly. She did not say: But then you'd have to find another way of making money. She despised him for his useless violence and because he was obviously going to make a failure of his night club; and yet she felt sympathetic. She could guess what he was feeling —the murderous rage, not against anyone, but against the vague menace of society. She could not say she had ever felt such rage herself—I'm too stolid, she thought, but if I'd been a man—why wasn't I a man? Wouldn't I have shown them! Ah, I'd have been somebody by now. Her contempt for Ashton returned hotly.

"You could arrange a special night," she said, slowly, frowning. "Get someone—get a woman over from Paris who dances naked, or as naked as makes no matter. Never mind about not being room. Jam the tables together. And splash it carefully—only ask the right people to come. You know—you've got to keep giving them something different. They won't go on coming to see the same faces in the same old room."

Ashton knew that she was perfectly right. He resented it. He had not asked her for her advice. Without knowing it he was savagely alarmed. If his want of success was so obvious that a woman of her sort knew it! An instinctive cruelty possessed him. He wanted acutely to punish her.

He put his cigarette out and stood up. He had not troubled to answer her.

"Well?" he said curtly.

Her expression did not change. "Let me clear these things away," she said. She crossed the room. After a second, and without turning round, she began to slip her dress off.

When he went back to the Screech Owl he shouted at Thomas to bring him something to drink while he changed his clothes for the evening. His head felt clearer, and he was light and easy in body. He had dismissed the woman from his thoughts as soon as he left her room. But the half-hour he had wasted on her had had an effect on his mind. In talking to her, he had crashed abruptly through the defences he had been putting up against his worst fears. Now that he saw it in this new raw light, his position was worse than he had admitted to himself.

The fifty pounds he had given Linder was the last straw. He could no longer reassure himself that he had money to pay the electric light bill when it came in. That was what the damned Jewish scoundrel had done to him. Tipped him over the edge.

He still had the lucidity to admit that it was not any trifle of fifty pounds that had finished him. But he loathed and hated Linder.

He began to think energetically about the offer that had been made him by his visitor in the morning. "Calls himself Franklyn," he murmured. Real name probably unpronounceable Polish-Russian.

Franklyn had said that the insurance companies involved in his fires had always compromised for half. But that was surely because all the fires he had so far arranged had been in the houses and factories of Jews, East London Jews. For *him* they would probably shell out the full amount, and when he had paid his bills, and Franklyn's percentage, he would still have a tidy sum in hand. Gives me time to turn round, he thought.

Abruptly he was seized with impatience and fury. Why am I in this mess? He looked round the room, longing to smash and destroy. If he could have fallen on Linder or Franklyn and beaten him mercilessly he would have done it, and felt assuaged. The circumstances of the only other time he had risked himself in a criminal scheme—he did not regard normal law-evading in a night club as criminal— came into his mind, adding flame to his fury. He felt himself a victim. It was not that he wished to behave criminally. He was being given no chance.

"God send another war, and send it soon," he ejaculated.

He knew the instant after he said it that he no longer had the nerve or the energy of body to enjoy another war.

He finished his whiskey and felt calmer. It depends on Rapp, he thought. Everything depends on Rapp. If he puts up a spot of money I'll carry on and I'll make a success of the damned place. If not . . . He began with an inflated eagerness to imagine the conversation with Rapp. He imagined it as though Rapp were a Chilean politician to whom he was selling aeroplanes. On this flattering assumption, it went with quite remarkable friendliness and suavity.

CHAPTER XV

RANDALL CAME for Harriet to her room about half-past six. She was not ready. He watched her moving about the room with awkward, surprisingly quick gestures of her hands and body. There was the anxiety of a child in her face to be prepared for him. He knew that he had only to remind her what he was doing that evening for the child to give way to a stubborn slow-thinking woman. It was too much in his mind. He had to speak.

"If Rapp will put up the money for the flight I shall go to Miles at Reading, to build me a special Falcon."

"Ah." She stood still. "It's to-night, isn't it?"

He looked at her with a smile.

"I wasn't pretending I'd forgotten," she said.

"But you hoped I had?"

"No. No, of course not. You wouldn't forget. It's your life, isn't it?" She hoped he would say, No, you are my life. Her throat was constricted and she felt breathless.

Randall looked at her with a blank expression. "It's more important than anything," he said mildly. A muscle twitched below his temples. It was sometimes the only inkling she had of the intensity of a feeling. He's afraid, she thought. He doesn't want to give himself away.

She seized the hair-brush and began to brush her hair before the glass. "Well, I hope he gives you the money," she said.

Randall laughed shortly. "He won't give me any money. I only want him to back the flight. He could do it without losing an eyelash."

Why should he give it to you? she thought. Suddenly she understood. He wanted so terribly to make the flight, that, as children do, he had persuaded himself that some-one was going to give it to him. Oh, my love, she thought. She could have broken into tears. He's safe, she thought, he won't be able to go. But rich men do put up money for flights.

"And there's so little time," Randall said. "A short time to live, and so much to do in it."

She put the brush down and went across to him. "I do hope he agrees," she mumbled.

She wanted to say there was nothing she would not give him. This flight, her own wishes, her future—anything— if it would save him from disappointment. This aching tenderness was new. She had never felt it until now.

"No. You don't," Randall said, grinning. "You'd rather I sat quietly at home."

She was hurt. She smiled brightly and said: "Now I'm ready. Shall we go? You have to change afterwards."

"No hurry."

He put his arm out. She moved away, still smiling. "Yes, let's go now. It's seven o'clock. I'm hungry."

She walked down the stairs in front of him, humming, and they crossed the yard to Pizetti's side by side, Randall slouching, she holding herself upright and very alert. Mrs. Pizetti had kept their table for them in the window. She looked at the girl and saw that she was only pretending to be happy. I was never so young as she is, she thought.

"I prepared the *risotto*," she said briskly.

"Good," Randall said.

While they were eating it, Harriet talked to him about the office. She had not meant to tell him yet about something that had happened to her to-day. She wanted to think about it first. But it tumbled out of her.

"This morning Mr. Shaw sent for me to go to his room. He asked me if I'd like six months in the New York Office. To learn something about American advertising."

Randall did not pretend that he was not startled. "What did you say to him?" he asked sharply.

"He gave me a week to think it over."

"Well, are you going?"

He is taking this quite seriously, she thought with relief. And at once she forgot that she had been vexed with him.

"Well, you see, Bill, the trouble is this," she said, anxiously, "I can't go to New York unless I'm going to go on working for them. I couldn't go and then leave to get married at once. It wouldn't be fair."

"Do you want to go?"

Her face changed when she smiled and was eager and confident. "I've never been to New York. I haven't been anywhere yet."

Randall looked down. "If it was only going there. But you know I shan't be able to stand you working afterwards."

"Bill, it's *not* fair!"

He glanced round, to see whether anyone heard her. "Do as you like," he said in a quiet voice. "I expect we'll end by living in a hotel together. Like my mother. Very convenient living in hotels. You don't bother about anything. Go down to dinner and come up again and go to bed. My mother used to sit writing in her room and tell me to go down into the garden. Have you ever tried to make yourself at home in a hotel garden, with a score of windows gaping at you from behind your back? It's grand."

"Bill!"

"All right," he said. "All right. Don't let's quarrel about it. You'll do as you like."

Looking round her for something to sustain her pride, Harriet caught Pizetti's eye. He came over to talk to them. Speaking in a whisper he told them that an Hungarian had been to see him about buying the lease of the café; he wanted it but he didn't want to pay for the goodwill. He reminded Pizetti that after the war Italy had robbed the Hungarians; he seemed to think this a reason why Pizetti should throw in the goodwill for nothing. "I said, It was not I, my friend, who robbed you," Pizetti chuckled. "Do I, I said, look like a man who has grown fat on my war gains? He is thinking it over. If he buys, then I am at home for the summer." His eyes sparkled. "Think of it! Summer in my home."

He darted away. Harriet and Randall smiled meaningly at each other. You couldn't watch him without affection, nor take him seriously. He was like a good, kind, well-meaning, sly little boy. Yet he had dignity. You respected him.

"There's that dreadful old man," Harriet said.

Pop looked round him with bright, cunning eyes. He saw one vacant seat at a table and he scuttled towards it making gestures with his arms, like a crab. The man in the other chair was the doctor, and the table was wedged so fast against the counter that he could only use one arm in eating. Pop drew his spoon and fork out of his pocket, but kept his hand on them.

"I remember this place when it was empty most of the day," he grumbled.

"If that's what you want, you can easily find it," the doctor said, yawning.

"I can remember London when it was emptier than it is now. You never saw such a town. There were window-boxes with flowers, and carriages in the Park, and a lady couldn't go out alone at night in the streets. There was a great deal more music. There were German bands, and Hungarian bands—and people walked more slowly—it's all very different now."

The doctor began to think, not of London in the 'eighties but of the small German city of Marburg where he had had part of his education. There the music was made by young men's voices. That was wild honey, he thought; the taste of a foreign city when one is young enough to make disgusting gestures handsomely.

"I suppose you never happened to be in Marburg?" he said. "I'm told the young men neither sing nor drink now—they're too busy marching. The plain fact is the Germans have never been civilized. They should be inter-married with civilized people, Frenchmen, Jews, the English."

"The first thing I saw when I came down from Cambridge to London as a young man," sighed Pop, "and mark you, it was just outside the station—was a big woman basting a little man for all she was worth. And when she was run clean out of breath, he up with her skirts and gave her a smack on a pair of black cotton drawers, and off the pair of them went into the nearest pub, as happy as laddie. I'll never leave this place, I said. I never have. Everything has altered, and here I am, warm in the very middle of London, and I'm going to live here for ever."

"What's your name?" asked the doctor.

The cunning in Pop's eyes took away from the innocence of a wide smile, exposing rotting teeth. "I can't remember," he said, chuckling. "It's a fact. I tried to remember the other evening."

The doctor looked at Giulia Pizetti, who had taken her father's place behind the counter. She was cutting sandwiches, pouring drinks and serving them with a joyous smile, she was pale and her eyes seemed larger than ever, and frank and direct, the eyes of a child more than of a young woman. The doctor caught himself pitying her because she still had to learn that life is bearable if you can get through it without wanting to love and be loved, and then he grinned at himself for an ass. He knew that he was trying by back doors to pity himself, and when he thought of himself, of his body, the notion of pitying that savage and stupid animal was ludicrous. Giulia looked up. She saw Bert coming in, with the Welsh chef of the Screech Owl. They came over to the counter and squeezed themselves in with difficulty between the doctor's table and the door to the kitchen. Simon asked Giulia for a cup of strong coffee. He took a quarten-bottle of rum out of his pocket and emptied the half of it into his coffee. The doctor caught his arm as he was pushing the bottle back.

"Hey. You came to see me a week ago," he said.

Simon looked down. "So I did," he said in an indifferent voice. "What of it?"

"Didn't I tell you that if you wanted to die at forty you should go on drinking black coffee and spirits and working over a stove?"

"Yes, you told me," Simon said, drawling, and rolling up his eyes so that he looked as though he had reached the ecstatic moment of a sermon. "But if I'm to die at forty I'm going to drink all the coffee and the rum, and good claret——" he passed his tongue across his thin lips—"my God, how I enjoy claret—that I can lay hands on." He smiled amiably.

"You're a fool," yawned the doctor.

"I'm going to work for another ten years," Simon grinned, "then make my wife keep me."

He had married a woman older than himself, a French-woman. She looked after him like a child, scolded him and petted him. She adored him. He was overpowered, physically and morally, by her; if he ever wanted to be free he would never have the energy to run for it. He took it out of her by ruining his health, and by the cynical humour with which he allowed her to gobble him alive. If they had had children she might have spared him a limb or two to himself, but she had no time, she said, for a child. So Simon filled the bill, pretending to be more improvident, more helpless to take care of himself, than he was. In a way he enjoyed it. And in another mood he knew, and it angered him, that he was being smothered.

Bert stood without speaking, fingering his glass, and watching Giulia as she turned to serve one customer and then another. He noticed the film of moisture on her temples and in the cleft of her chin. It made him dizzy. He wanted to throw his arms round her and to crush her body against him until a little of the pain left his, and yet he wanted to touch her gently, so gently that he would feel the moisture on her skin against his.

Giulia saw him looking at her, his rather clumsy lips pushed out, and his blue eyes staring. She smiled at him. Poor boy, she thought, liking him, half amused.

She had a minute to spare. Leaning towards him across the counter, she whispered: "This time, I think we are really going."

"Going? Where?" Bert said, staring.

"Why, home of course."

He never believed the Pizettis would go—simply because

he couldn't imagine that people lived in other countries from choice. But each time she spoke of it he felt the same pang of sheer terror and anguish. He felt as if he were going blind. In a second it was over. He felt the coldness of the glass in his hand, and saw Giulia's face close to his, so close that he could see the down on her upper lip and the flecks of brown on her full black eyes, and the shadow on her cheek of the long, intensely black eyelashes. He remembered that he had something to give her.

He took a folded paper out of his pocket and handed it to her. "It's over a pound," he said, in a low voice.

He saved every week from his wages, and from the tips he got when he helped with the waiting, and gave the money to Pizetti to keep for him. Pizetti kept it in an envelope in the box with his own money in the "office."

"How much is it now?" Giulia said, with a smile.

"Over twelve pounds. It's good, eh?"

"Wonderful," Giulia said, in a mocking tone.

"Yes, but it is good," he said, insisting.

She repented. "Of course it is," she said, warmly, smiling into his eyes. "Don't think I don't admire you for saving money—and for wanting to get on."

She had to run away to cut more sandwiches. Bert stood still. His heart was beating violently, and there was a foolish smile on his lips. The words she had just spoken worked upon him as though he were drunk. His head swam. Suddenly she came back, and said, laughing: "Look at those two—Mr. Randall—he flies aeroplanes, you know —and that girl; they're in love—don't they look terribly silly?"

CHAPTER XVI

SARAH HAD cut her knee badly, falling on a sharp stone in the cul-de-sac. She limped to the house, the blood soaking through her stocking and down her leg.

"Look what I've done," she said.

Usually Mrs. Barley made a fuss of a bad cut. But the hot endless day had been unbearable in the kitchen. She was sick to death of it. At half-past seven she had just dropped into a chair, and closed her eyes, when the girl burst in on her. The sight of the blood and the torn dirty stocking was too much.

"Oh, I'm sick of you all," she said, in bitter anger and weariness. "It's one thing after another, one thing after another."

Sarah was seized with dismay. She sat without a whimper while Mrs. Barley washed the place roughly and bandaged it. "What shall I do now?" she asked, plaintively. She was afraid, now, to do anything without an order.

"Go and fetch the other two, and stay in the workshop," said Mrs. Barley. "You're not fit to be out, with your clumsy ways."

So the three of them stood about in the workroom, not knowing what they could safely do. Sarah stood in the doorway and looked across at the Café Bar. She thought with an intensity that made her deaf and blind to everything round her, about the young man who had spoken to her that morning. He lived in the room above their bedroom: she began to imagine that in some miraculous way she appeared in his room; he was astonished by her beauty; sinking on his knees, he begged to be allowed to do something for her. What?—what then? He fetched things she wanted, he followed her everywhere. "My princess," he called her, in his deep voice.

She blushed. A flush of shame went over her body.

There was a dreadful thing—too dreadful, too shameful—never would she be able to forget it. When he passed her in the yard that morning one leg of her drawers was hanging down far below her knee—a button had come off at that side. She herself noticed it immediately afterwards, and he must certainly have seen it; she was disgraced for life in his and her own eyes.

She heard her mother come out of the kitchen and go upstairs to her bedroom.

"Let's do something now," Lucy said—in a loud incautious voice. She clapped her hand over her mouth, rolling her eyes like greenish boot-buttons in her round face. Hector went off into one of his hysterical fits of laughing. He became crimson in the face and staggered about the room, weeping with laughter.

Sarah took no notice of them. She wanted—she did not know what. An uneasy excitement had followed the feeling of shame. She would not think about the accident to her drawers again. She drove it away with all the force of her nature, and pulled the dream fast round her.

"Sarah, Sarah!" Lucy called, in a fright.

She turned round. Hector had set fire to a heap of shavings. Pale, yellow tongues of flame flew up. One shot out sideways and licked viciously at the floor. Hector stared at it with his eyes starting from his plump cheeks—as if it were a mad dog flying down the street.

Sarah hobbled quickly, snatched up a sack, and pressed down on the burning shavings with it. She was terrified of what their mother would do if she saw it. The fear of a thrashing drove out every other. Hector and Lucy were stamping on the separate flames of shavings scattered by the breath of the sack.

She lifted the sack fearfully. It was all out. They swept the charred remains out of sight with their hands, and pushed the blackened sack into a corner.

Sarah felt a throbbing pain in her arm. There was a raw-looking blister the size of a half-crown.

"Oh, our Sarah, you're burned," breathed Lucy.

"Hush! If she finds out——"

She felt obscurely that she was revenging herself on her mother by not showing her the burn. It serves her right, she said dryly to herself. If I died of it, it would serve her right. She triumphed. Yet she felt unhappy and bewildered—lost.

The watch on Harriet's wrist when she peered at it, straining her eyes in the dark room, said ten o'clock. Now she had been standing at the window for three-quarters of an hour, watching to see Josephine Rapp and her father arrive at the Screech Owl. I'm not afraid of her, not jealous, she thought, her head heavy with sleep and the effort of watching. The words rushed into her mind because she was tired. And at once her honesty—that Puritan self-tormenting legacy, given to her—forced her to think: You are not jealous, but you envy her the ease and lightness of her life, her self-assurance, the air with which she can walk into a shop and ask to be shown this and that garment—Would madam care to try it? and madam can strip her dress off without wondering whether the assistant will despise her when she sees—it's unimportant, nothing, Harriet thought passionately. None of these things matter. Think of poor women. She pressed her forehead against the window, and watched an elderly woman being helped out of her car by a man young enough to be her grandson. And is he?

Shall I recognise her? she wondered. She had seen Josephine Rapp once, when Bill, sitting with her in Pizetti's, said suddenly: "Look. See that girl going into the club. One of my pupils. She's as stupid"—he meant she couldn't fly—"as my boot, and terrifically rich."

I knew then, she thought, solemnly, that something would happen.

Shall I go to New York? She threw her head back. "To New York!" The words enchanted her. It was as though she stood outside a door in the darkness; opened it, trembling; wild horses leaped out, flinging their heads, and rushed away into the blackness of the great plain. She flew into the darkness with them. If I go there, she thought, my fortune is made. At this moment no life seemed so satisfying and splendid as one which led through the doors of fashionable hotels; the pages of *Vogue*; a first-class sleeping-berth in the continental trains flying towards the magical names of places; Vienna, Rome, Naples, Albi, Carcasonne.

And if I reject the offer, she thought, with a sudden cool certainty, they will take no further interest in me; I might as well leave the firm at once.

So she was being forced to choose. It was the moment. She thought of Randall. He drinks too much, she said abruptly. It was not really true. But the thought had been put into her mind by her mother and through her by each one of a long tale of careful watchful women. If you are not more careful, they said, it will be true. She pressed her hands over her chest, over the exhilaration and the pain. It is because he never feels safe. If he felt perfectly safe— she thought. It is his mother's fault.

If I became like her; if I were brilliant; if I had my life outside our life together—he would be as insecure with me as he must have felt, when he was a boy, with her, in that queer life of theirs. And even if it is nonsense about his drinking too much, he wouldn't feel safe with me. Simply because his mother, clever as she was, loving as she was, didn't do properly what she was ordered to do as his mother. She had failed, as completely as she would have failed if she had written bad books instead of good ones. Because a mother has to be there as long as she is wanted, to give everything, and then to go away, to draw back, her work finished. Mrs. Randall never finished—indeed, she scarcely began—her work.

But she wanted to write, Harriet thought. And it is unfair, it is horribly unfair, unjust, that women, that a mother—her thoughts flew off like rooks at a shot echoing among the branches—We shall have a child, she thought.

Where were the wild horses? Gone, scattered. Vanished in the darkness.

She was a child, standing in the little garden of their house, watching her mother, who was on her knees, plant the roots of red daisies and red and yellow polyanthus they had just carried home together from the market. Her mother's fingers worked, pressing the soil down round the plants. "Will they grow, will they grow?" the child cried. In her excitement, she pressed heavily on her mother's shoulder. "Don't hinder me," her mother said. She got up, quickly. "Of course they'll grow," she said: "come, Harry," and they went into the house together, the excited little girl and the small, easy, slow-thinking woman.

Harriet felt a sudden disintegrating pang. *That* girl was Josephine Rapp—now—stepping out of the car. She kept her back to the window, but Harriet was certain. She knew—without seeing the face she knew. The short, heavily-built man following her was her father. He turned round, and Harriet caught a glimpse of his face. He won't do anything for Bill, she thought at once, with relief, with an agonized pity. Oh, poor Bill!

For the moment, and rather than he should face this disappointment, she threw down New York, Vienna, Rome, recklessly, in ruins, into dust, and pressed roots of red polyanthus into the place. I won't go, she thought. She felt an overwhelming dismay.

I must go.

The main room, on the first floor of the Screech Owl, was painted a bluish white, like the inside of an egg-shell; the bar stretched across one end, with the little service lift, worked by hand, to the kitchen; at the other end a small and very competent Negro orchestra played, the leader smiling with an insolent or naïve good-temper as was expected of him; now and then he lifted up his voice and sang in French—he was French—a slightly indecent verse; there was a very narrow space for dancing, and the lights in the room, in contrast to the severe walls and the fake antique tables without cloths, were unashamedly rosy and sentimental. Women would appreciate that, Ashton thought. Actually, women have become so ruthless in spreading an artificial colour over their own that the lighting makes very little difference to them.

It was difficult to keep the room cool enough in summer. Open all the windows, and some air comes in, but it is air saturated with the breathing, the restless movements, and the smell of the bodies thickly lying asleep in rooms or still going about their business in the streets outside the Screech Owl. However, the tobacco smoke in the room itself overcame any less usual smells, and after they had breathed the air for half an hour people were accustomed to it, besides that many of them were a little drunk; no one complained of the air; there is no reason to believe that, let's say, an eighteenth century dinner-party in this room would have smelled fresher.

Randall had been sitting with Josephine and her father for almost an hour without any mention of his flight. He intended to bring it up himself if nothing was said. In the meantime he said very little. He was not good at small talk. He pretended to despise it, but he envied people whose tongues ran on in any company. As Josephine's did. She talked away; and he answered her when what she said called for an answer. Her father listened as though he were listening to a child: he smiled, and scarcely opened his mouth.

Randall felt that he must be making a bad impression. He looked once or twice at Eugene Rapp. Rapp was more impressive seated than standing. He was short, with a head a size too large for him. And he was completely bald, his head polished like dark ivory; he had thick eyebrows, and a long bland face. He looked like an intelligent priest. In a sense he was a priest.

"I don't approve of my daughter learning to fly," he said, suddenly, with a half yawn.

"But I'm going to be good at it," Josephine

smiled. She looked at Randall. "Don't you think so, Bill?"

"Quite good enough," he said, calmly.

"Nonsense! I'm very good." She went on smiling, but she was vexed. She thought he ought to have the sense to back her up. "Father is afraid I'll fall and hurt myself."

"It's silly and unnecessary," Rapp said.

"Well——" Josephine began. She broke off, as Ashton came and stood beside their table. He had greeted Rapp when he came in, then shrewdly ignored him for an hour, not to seem too eager. He had known Josephine by sight, but it was not until to-night, when she came in with her father, that he knew her name. Now he looked at her attentively. He saw that she was unusually charming and healthy. Except her lips, she was not made up; and if you touched her cheek you would touch really naked skin. It would be pleasant. Standing over her, he saw her breasts springing under a yellow linen evening frock.

"Is everything as you want it?" he asked Rapp. He tried to speak in a friendly casual voice, but he had a curious sensation at the knees. "The wine all right?"

Rapp had refused to drink champagne, and by good luck Ashton had a few bottles of hock Linder had sold him at the beginning. "Quite drinkable," Rapp said amiably.

"Good," Ashton laughed. He looked at Josephine. "Would you like to dance?"

She got up quickly. The moment before he came she had been bored and irritated. In a sudden revulsion of feeling she smiled into Ashton's face, delighted to have his arms round her. He danced well. He has a magnificent body, she thought. She felt a sensual helplessness and warmth in her own body. As they moved slowly, on the crowded floor, she began to imagine Ashton as her lover. She had been living without a lover at all for nearly half a year, and she was tired of this, and even a little depressed. Surely she was not any less attractive? She smiled to herself remembering a joke made by her friend Mary Coltz:

"She's been writing melancholy letters from Biarritz; I feel that no one has insulted the girl."

"What are you smiling for?" Ashton said.

"Nothing."

"All right."

"Nothing—a joke I heard." She wrinkled her eyes at him. "I like dancing with you."

"We're going on very well together."

"Why haven't you asked me before?"

"I wanted to," Ashton said.

"Sure?"

"Want me to do something to prove it?"

She felt an exquisite confidence, as though she were swimming in buoyant water. Her limbs moved in it without an effort. Her heart was beating violently and there was a sensation of breathlessness and a voluptuous pricking in her body. It was half fear, half excitement. She looked gravely at Ashton. From the corner of her eye she could see her father and Randall. The young man was sitting looking in front of him, with legs crossed, and a hand with its long fingers dangling, as if cut off, at the edge of the table. What does he think of? she wondered. He was like a faint pencil mark in her mind now. I shan't bother to take any more lessons, she thought. His youth—he was exactly her age—struck her as blurred and immature. She dropped him out of sight.

Ashton felt her body almost naked under the palm of his hand. It was agreeably round. She had small bones and they were covered. He had made love to women who were only a skinful of bones, looking older in bed than they did up.

"Ever been in Chile?" he asked.

"No."

He began telling her about a man he knew there, whom he had tricked into buying twenty thousand completely useless rifles, and how the man had shot at him afterwards in the street at night. He knew that the story would make her think him clever as well as reckless. A sharp memory of

Diaz pricked him, like a thorn under his nail, as insignificant and painful. He pulled it out.

"I'd love to go to South America."

"Better come with me," he smiled slightly.

"When?"

"When you like."

I could marry her, he thought sharply. Go about it properly and you can marry her and get on to something solid. She'll be as rich as God knows. I could do with that. He squeezed hard down on the excitement flickering in his brain. Go a little slow, he thought; you don't want to make mistakes.

Eugene Rapp watched his daughter with an ironical pleasure. He was wasting his evening, he was bored—but how charming she was. Not a young women in the room to hold a candle to her. He felt an almost painful pride and self-love. His dead wife, with her complaints, her ill-health, her over-bred voice, seemed to have had no share in producing this radiant creature. He recalled abruptly his first intimate sight of a room filled with men and women in evening dress, apparently enjoying themselves as if it were their duty. He was then a young clerk, and he had been sent by cab to the other end of London with an urgent message, and told to bring the answer to his employer wherever he was. There were delays and his employer was at dinner in his home. The young man had difficulty in persuading a butler to let him enter the room. He was wearing a shabby rain-coat, and he stood, holding his hat and a still shabbier umbrella, which he had not known he ought to leave in the hall, during the unending minute while his employer took the letter from his hand, glanced at the envelope and said dryly: "Why didn't you give this to a servant?" He had then to walk out of the room again. His intense mortification was swallowed up in rage that he could have been so foolish. But for this rage he might have contrived to forget the incident.

He felt only contempt for the men and women round him. To give himself confidence when he was younger, he used to calculate how much of any building in which he happened to be standing he could buy. Some part of his mind still played this game, but without speaking.

He had not troubled to talk to Randall: not because he meant to be rude or unkind, but for the simpler reason that he had nothing to say to his daughter's flying instructor. "Be nice to him," she had whispered, as the young man approached their table. She might have said the same thing about a pet animal she had brought into the room. Why talk to a man for the sake of talking—or of being nice to him? As individuals, men and women did not exist for Rapp.

The young man spoke. He looked directly at Rapp, as though he were concentrating an immense effort on these few ordinary words.

"Quite a decent place this, don't you think, sir?"

"Can't say I care for any of these clubs," Rapp answered.

"No?" Randall smiled slightly.

The smile reminded Rapp of his son who had been killed in the War. There was no other likeness between the two young men. Perhaps a great many young men smile with the same touching politeness when they talk to older people. It is a propitiatory gesture, an appeal, not for understanding —that is never what the young need—but to be allowed to live.

For less than a second Rapp saw his boy standing beside Randall. He saw him as clearly as we see in a dream the dead whom we have loved, and instantly forgot him. The dead who visit us in dreams elude us in life, always—it is always so. In the same instant he hated Randall murderously. He scarcely recognized the feeling. It showed itself and vanished too swiftly. He felt bored, and regretted that he had let Josephine persuade him to come with her.

"This place is coming down to make room for a cinema." It gave him pleasure to say this. Nothing had been settled yet, but he was confident. He would buy the site, and he would lease it to the people who wanted to put up a cinema.

F

Randall did not answer. He sat with his head sunk, wondering whether he should speak now, or wait for the girl to return. He did not know what she had said to her father about him. It never occurred to him that she had said nothing. His heart was pounding, and he felt a hard pressure behind his eyes and at the back of his head.

He cleared his throat. "Has Josephine told you very much about the record flight?"

Rapp lifted his eyebrows. "What flight are you talking about?"

Randall was sweating. He did not at once understand what Rapp said.

"I want to take a light single-seater to the Cape and back. It's worth doing just now. I can tell you why. It's only a question of the money."

He spoke in a low firm voice calmly, without looking at Rapp. He had lit a cigarette, and he pressed it out with a deliberate gesture, keeping his wrist on the table so that his hand remained steady.

"Waste of time," Rapp said.

Randall did not give himself away. He kept a quiet expressionless face; his lips came forward slightly, as they did when anything went wrong in the air; he looked once at Rapp, and then across the room. He did not let himself think.

"I don't agree," he said curtly.

"Weren't you in the Air Force?" asked Rapp.

"Yes."

"Why don't you rejoin? You can get back as an instructor." He felt a half-sensual, compulsive pleasure in destroying what he now saw to be a motive in Randall's mind. "A young man with your training ought to be in the Air Force. There's going to be war——"

His daughter's voice took him up. "Splendid! It'll be something to do at last."

He looked at her and felt vaguely uneasy. Her full, vivid lips were moist, and her body seemed to him to be standing up nakedly in its dress. He was shocked by these images, and felt cold.

"Don't hurry off," she said to Ashton.

"I'll find a chair," he said, casually.

"Have mine," Randall said quietly. He looked at her and knew exactly what was happening. He thought her unpleasant and boring.

"Half-past twelve. I have to be up again at five." This lie saved his face, he thought, as he turned away. Rapp had not taken the least notice of his smiling "Good night, sir."

He had not grasped the fullness of his defeat. He felt only confused and dissatisfied, but with such fury that he seemed on fire with it. Without knowing what he was doing he walked past the door to the bar. His mind was out of control, his mouth dry. The noise in the room split his eyeballs. A woman somewhere in the room was screaming with laughter like a mad parrot, stopping and beginning again. When he had wormed his way to the bar, between the tables, a man leaning there said: "Well, well. Randall, is it?" Randall recognized a man who had been at the Central Flying School with him; he had come into a little money and left the service: he was a curious fellow, unable to stop himself bragging. Most of his stories were true.

"Hullo," he said, amiable from caution, "I've forgotten your name."

"Call me Austin, as m'wife does. What will you have?"

Randall ordered lime juice and was given a weak whiskey and soda. He felt a hard tightness inside his head, as though a membrane was stretched to breaking point, and an impulse to hit and destroy things. He was not drunk yet. Austin began to speak to him in a low voice, exaggeratedly confidential. He listened, smiling. "I want you to meet the chap on my right. I brought him here—they all come to me, they do. He's booking pilots to fly in China. Yes, my boy. First-class passage out, and a thousand a month. Bring you back in the hold, ha, ha."

"Thousand what?"

"Pounds, my boy, pounds sterling—what did you think?"

"What do they fly?"

Austin sniggered. "Orange boxes, I think. Ask him."

The other man was a Dutchman, short, broad, freckled, with quick prominent eyes like frog spawn. He was sober. He said with contemptuous politeness for Austin that he didn't do business in night clubs—"but if you are interested come to my hotel, here is my card, don't ring me up, come any time between four and eight."

He slid one word into the next, with the nervous speed of a foreigner speaking good English. The tiny black speck in the centre of his pale eyes darted aside and a smile of derisive geniality came up to the wings of his nose and flattened out. Randall watched him with curiosity. The offer, if you called it that, might be fantastic, but in some way it restored his self-respect.

"A friend of mine agreed to ferry an aeroplane to Spain, Franco's half of the country," he said reflectively. "He got it there safely and they wouldn't pay his passage back. No end of trouble."

"You'd have a contract," said the Dutchman. "You get your contract in Paris and sign it there."

"Not here?"

"Don't go to Paris without consulting me first," Austin said, nudging him. "Give you some addresses—and, oh, boy, do I know Paris or do I know Paris."

Randall by now had drunk a second whiskey. His mind was alive with words; if he had not disliked both men he would have talked earnestly and fluently on the need to concentrate if you want to do anything. It was the truth and he had discovered it.

He left them and walked, smiling faintly, to the door and downstairs looking with surprised pleasure at the wooden panelling of the staircase; gave Thomas a two-shilling piece he found in his pocket, and stepped into the yard. The air in the yard was as cool as water after the room. He stretched his long thin body, and as he did so the conversation with Rapp slid into its place in his mind with a shock that sobered him almost completely. He realized it for the first time fully. Instantly defensive he thought: Josephine may still be able to do something with her father; she hadn't spoken to him, but I'll talk to her about it again.

A faint yellow light appeared at the foot of the staircase beside Pizetti's café. Pop slipped out, holding his candle, and began to search in the bins outside the café, his head wobbling from side to side on his thin neck, the flame of the candle almost touching his hair. In the darkness he hung quavering over the bins like a spectre. He started when Randall moved towards him.

"It's all right, it's only me," Randall mumbled.

"Who's me? Oh, it's the young man. You ought to be in bed," Pop said severely. "Go to bed, go to bed."

"Good night," Randall smiled. He glanced back from the entrance to his own staircase. I shall remember this, he thought, finding an inexplicable strangeness in the old man with his candle, in the night in the centre of London, seeing him without ridicule or a trace of pity, since the old man was freer than he was, safer and stronger, "and he will be alive when I have broken my back," Randall muttered, feeling his way up the narrow stairs to his door.

The first thing he noticed when he lit the gas was his mother's letter, still unopened, on the table. He opened it reluctantly and read swiftly the single typewritten page. It held nothing new. She told him that she was writing and described with quick, biting mockery the English colony in Pau—"all fascists to a dog"—and asked him with a teasing and half-awkward gentleness to write to her, "one of your long three-line letters, my little love, it's all I ask." She was afraid of vexing him and yet, at heart, she didn't care.

He dropped the letter on the table. He was suddenly tired and uncertain. In planning the flight he had been dragging at a stone fast in the earth and he would never lift it. He was confused between the certainty of his skill and shame in not being able to prove it in the way he had planned. An eager, baffled energy tormented him. He was afraid of failure, and his fear came from within himself, pouring through him like smoke. He thought with a

curious anguish of Harriet. "Give me, give me," he murmured, not knowing what he was saying. Leaving his
clothes lying on the floor he got into bed and lay shuddering
for a moment before he fell suddenly into a black, drowning
sleep.

Rapp had not even listened to the talk between his
daughter and this fellow Ashton. Captain Ashton, no less!
That placed the fellow for you—still using a title only
meant to see him through the War in a position of limited
authority. Abruptly he became aware that Ashton was
trying to draw him into the conversation. He gave him
half an ear.

"Miss Rapp was just saying," Ashton said pleasantly,
"that she has been in Germany this year, and that everything is well-run and everyone smiling and happy."

"Most expensive hotels are well-run," said Rapp dryly.
"In any country."

Josephine pouted. "Well but, daddy, we drove
hundreds of miles in the car, and even the children know
about Hitler and adore him. And the children are so
clean. Not like here."

"I don't say we want uniforms and all that over here,"
Ashton said, "but I do say we want someone to give a
lead. Stamp out all this socialist nonsense. If I had my
way, I'd——" He broke off. The cold brutality of his
voice delighted the young woman; her eyes gleamed with
admiration and interest.

Rapp said nothing. He despised enthusiasm and open
gestures of force and violence. He was of the opinion that
amateurs, savages, and Germans shout about their strength
for obvious reasons, and he would never subscribe to such
methods in this country. For one thing, they are unnecessary. A sudden sharp twinge in his back reminded him that
he had intended to see his doctor about the slight rheu-
matism from which he suffered, and in the same instant he
felt it impossible to sit here a minute longer.

"Time to go home," he said to Josephine affably. He beckoned the waiter. "I haven't paid. The fellow said he didn't know what the wine would cost."

"We keep this hock for a very few people," Ashton said, lowering his voice. "You're my guests this evening, please."

Rapp's eyes protruded slightly. He pursed his lips. "Nonsense," he said brusquely. "I'll pay for it."

"If you insist." He swallowed his mortification at Rapp's tone. Josephine had already gone downstairs to the cloakroom. She would be some minutes, and since Rapp seemed disposed to sit on at his table Ashton stayed with him. Now was the moment to suggest diplomatically that Rapp might care to interest himself financially in the club. It was now or never. Ashton stiffened the muscles of his stomach as he leaned confidentially across the table. Astonishing that he had ever thought Rapp as easy to deal with as a Chilean general. The two had nothing in common.

"I hope you've had a pleasant evening here," he murmured.

"As pleasant as I expected," said Rapp coolly.

"My idea is to run something rather different from the usual night club, where you're charged two or three guineas for a bottle of whiskey and ten shillings for a kipper with the fun of losing your money at a pin-table thrown in." He did not explain how the Screech Owl differed from any of these rivals except that the prices were not quite so high as the ones he quoted. "The place is doing very well," he went on, in a blithe tone. "People appreciate the fact that they're not skinned. But the fact is"—he tried to fix Rapp's eye, as if it had been the bright black acquisitive eye of a be-medalled South American—"the fact is I'm looking for a partner with a little money. I started with too small a capital to make the best of the place."

Rapp's thoughts during this speech were not so much scorn as amazement. He was astounded by the exquisite simplicity of the workings of Ashton's mind, as these had just been revealed to him. To think that Ashton could have dreamed of interesting him in this place—on no grounds except wanting the money. It was as mad as if, in his own poverty-ridden childhood, he had gone into a shop and asked for a toy because he wanted it and thought for that reason he ought to have it. The infant he had been knew better than that. And here was a grown man acting on the delusion. Rapp could not even sneer. He was confirmed in his belief that not more than a dozen men of any generation in any country understand the common reality of life.

For less than a second he considered Ashton as an agent for the Rapp Small Arms Company in Brazil. Ten years ago, he thought dryly, but not now—he's not up to it—not after this sort of thing.

He said with a certain tolerance:

"Scarcely a business proposition, these places."

Ashton was reckless enough not to take the hint. He lowered his voice again, and injected into it a sardonic assurance.

"I could soon prove to you that you're wrong about that!"

"Indeed!" said Rapp mildly. "I'm not in the least interested."

He rose, without troubling to say good night, leaving Ashton standing beside the table like a waiter, and went away.

Ashton was seized by a hatred so murderous in intent that he could scarcely see Rapp's retreating back. His brain throbbed and shook with it; he resented Rapp as much, no, more than he had resented the Jew, Linder. He would gladly have sent them both to the same unpleasant death and watched it carried out himself. If I ever get a chance, he thought, in confusion. Instantly he knew how powerless he was. There was nothing he could do to either of his enemies—no way in which he could punish them. He was impotent, trapped. In this country they have it all their own way, he thought dully.

Glancing down, he saw that Josephine had left a cigarette

case lying beside her glass on the table. He picked it up. It was small, marvellously flat, made of a black gold-flecked enamel, and lined with gold. He had noticed it in her hand because of the contrast with her nails, like pointed red petals. Heaven knows what she paid for it, he thought, with a sour rage. He turned his head and saw Josephine standing in the doorway. He held the case up, and hurried towards her.

"Bless you," she said, smiling. "I thought it was here."

"I was going to bring it to-morrow," he said, forcing himself to speak with off-hand gaiety. "I supposed you'd gone. Now you've spoiled my day."

"Which day?" laughed Josephine.

"To-morrow, of course. Actually to-day. I've lost my excuse for ringing up."

"Do you need one?" She gave him a frank, amused glance, with a hint in it of complicity in his plans. Ashton realized suddenly that she was more experienced than he had thought. Good, he thought quickly.

He saw her downstairs, but could not bring himself to go out to the car, where her father was seated waiting for her. She had agreed to lunch with him.

As he walked back across the hall he was thinking less about the young woman herself than about the life he could begin to live if he succeeded in marrying her. No more adventures. No trouble with women. No debts. He would pay everything up and begin afresh, with a good comfortable service flat, perhaps a house in the south of France, perhaps a country house in England, with horses, even a racing stable. He saw Josephine Rapp as part of a future securely and miraculously different from the disorderly present.

He felt a sharp, instinctive certainty that if the Screech Owl were to fail now she would lose her interest in him on the instant. Physically reckless she might be—and ready to throw herself to any reasonably attractive male—but she had more than a dash of her father's attitude to failure. She wouldn't think it pathetic—but simply that he had become dull and tiresome. She would drop him, perhaps with a twinge or two, but without pity. Yes, by God. The way to lose Josephine Rapp was to ask her to feel sorry for him. He took a violent resolution.

Thomas, who had been watching him with furtive steadiness while seeming to stare fixedly at a point on a level with his shoulder, thought: I believe the Captain's pulling us through; didn't I tell those two b.f.'s he could. He felt a quiet elation.

This one toss, Ashton was thinking, and then as careful as you like. A shiver of rage and excitement sprang through him. His hatred of Rapp turned suddenly to a bold alert gaiety. He felt an intense wakefulness.

During the evening a woman seated at a table near the door announced that she had lost her gold bracelet-watch. One moment it had been lying beside her plate on the table, the next it had gone, whisked away. She ordered François to bring Ashton to her at once. The waiter listened while Ashton questioned her in a polite, drawling voice. Her face was red under its powder, and she became very excited. "It was here—on this very place," she stammered, "I tell you it was here." She was more than a little drunk. She gesticulated with her lip-stick and a cigarette, so that ash fell into her glass of "lime-juice." Ashton snatched it up and gave it to François.

"Bring madam another drink," he said.

When François came back the woman accused him of taking the watch. "It was here when he changed the plates and it had gone when he turned round," she said, staring at him.

The waiter's pale face became paler. In a quiet firm voice he said: "I never saw the watch."

The man who was with the woman now joined in for the first time. He was more sober than she was, and he had listened with an ashamed smile to Ashton's attempts to soothe her. He swung round in his chair and said severely:

"But the lady's watch was here, my man. I saw it myself."

François looked at him with a calm stubborn expression. Inwardly, he was both angry and frightened, and angry because he was frightened.

"I never saw your watch," he repeated quietly. He was frowning. He did not look at Ashton. He understood perfectly that whatever the boss's opinion of the woman nothing mattered to him except to avert a disgraceful scene. Even in the clatter of so many people talking and screaming loudly with laughter her shrill rasping voice had caught the ears of the people at the next table. They were trying to hear what she said. The waiter made a desperate, drowning effort to recall anything that might help. He had served the table three, four times, perhaps five. During any of these minutes had he seen a watch on her mottled, fat, bare arm?

Ah, he thought sharply, I know! He took a step forward, opening his pale closely-pressed lips, and said softly:

"I think I know. The lady has left it in the cloak-room." He looked steadily into the woman's face. "You were not here when I brought you your—your lime-juice"—he wanted terribly to say, "your whiskey," and to tell her that she was ugly, stout, coarse and drunk. "I think you left the watch there."

"Pooh, rubbish," the woman said, raising herself in her chair like a fish in water.

"Please wait one moment," said Ashton. He smiled at her as though he found her charming, fascinating. "I will go and see."

He was gone about three minutes. The woman went on talking to her companion in a loud, gusty voice, and François caught the words "a damn clever trick," as he hurried past to another table. He felt the same loathing for her he felt for cockroaches, of which there were hundreds in the kitchen. He wished he could put his foot on her and crush her so that she cracked.

He kept half an eye on the door. He saw Ashton come

back and stoop over the table, giving the woman something—the watch. His manner had changed completely and the waiter could see the woman struggling to keep up her insolent expression. He drew near the table. Ashton sent him a warning glance and moved quickly away.

François waited, quite close to the table. The man saw him first, and looked away, confused. Then the woman saw him. She beckoned. He came over to her, bending his waiter's sleek head.

"Yes, madam."

"Fetch me some soda," she said in a tart voice. She had her hand over the watch lying on the table, and the waiter concentrated all his loathing on that hand, shapeless, fat, useless. Because of it he could not remain silent altogether. He felt bursting with indignation and contempt. He said in a voice without any feeling:

"Perhaps you better put your watch on—it's safer."

He walked off before she could reply, and sent Bert with the siphon. When he came back the boy whispered: "She isn't half creating, but the bloke with her says Shut up, you've done enough. But they won't come here again."

A little later François saw the woman seize Ashton's elbow as he walked past her and begin talking to him excitedly, but Ashton said nothing to him.

Towards four o'clock in the morning, when the last guest had left, the waiter went downstairs and spoke to the woman in the ladies' cloakroom about it. She was a stout friendly creature, with two voices. The one she used in answering François' question was her own, slow, deep and hoarse, straight from the Brixton street where she had lived since she was born.

"Lord, bless you, I'm not surprised, I'm never surprised at anything *they* do. I found it right off. I hadn't been in there since she was in, so I went in and there it was, she'd dropped it by the side of the seat—slipped off her arm, I sh'think. If she knew what she was doing when she was here, I'm a monkey from Peru."

"I could have lost my job," the waiter said.

"She wouldn't 've cared, not she," the woman laughed. "D'you know what, there's respectably-dressed women come in would steal the seats off the toilets if they could. See that French coin I've put in m' saucer? Yesterday there was two young women in here, one of them had a fur cape, and there was a sixpence in the saucer—I always keep something in, you know, to remind them—and what d'you think, one of them young women dropped twopence in and took out the sixpence. She did. As sure as I'm telling you! Oh, they'll do anything—anything. Some-one put that French coin in one night, an' I kept it, and I thought last night I thought, If they come again they shall have that to steal. Ah, the sinners. I often wonder what some folk live for. To see them in here in front of the glass you'd think they were all majesties, but if they've had children or if they're going to have children why do they come here drinking an' smoking an' showing off their bodies to any man that wants to look? Tell me that. I say, Tell me."

She went on talking as she tidied the room, her voice rumbling like a river running below the ground, like one of the rivers of which London is full, running out of sight below streets, under tons of stone, brick and concrete.

François listened to her, standing with bent head and pale, exhausted face, in the middle of the little hot room, while she moved, duster in hand and tongue wagging incessantly, round him. He did not want to move. He disliked the thought of going home, finding his wife in bed, sleeping as soundly as the dead; and he would have to undress by the candle and slip in beside her, and if by chance his arm touched her in the darkness she would draw back, even in her sleep shrinking from contact with him. He had spoken to her about it once, and all she answered was:

"But it's so hot at night now."

He saw her looking at him after she had spoken, trying to overhear his thoughts. Before all this happened he used to feel pleasure in the way she narrowed her eyes when she was thinking deeply; now it struck him as naturally deceitful. And then again he felt sorry for her. She might be as unhappy as he was. Probably she was afraid of him. I ought to ask her, he thought; I ought to say to her, If you want to leave me, go, go away, I shan't try to stop you, or punish you at all. He felt an anguish of loathing, like his loathing of the woman's hand on the table, but with it he was suffering unspeakably; he was in torment. He looked up and saw his own sallow and exhausted face in the glass, and thought, No wonder if she's grown tired of me.

"So you think a woman, a young, respectable woman, will do anything?" he said in a low voice.

The woman was putting on her jacket. She did not turn round.

"Eh?" she said. "What did you say?"

"A woman—I mean a decent woman—can do a nasty shameful thing," he repeated, looking down at his hands. He had no particular respect for her opinion, but she was of his own class and he wanted to hear what she would say. He waited anxiously.

"Is anything wrong with my jacket?" She turned herself slowly round in front of him. "Y'know my old fellow he said to me he said, Edith, if you wear that garment another week, I'll skin it off your back m'self. But, eeh, it's not so bad, now is it?" She laughed. "What with women and their watches and my old fellow I don't half have m'troubles." She looked at him inquisitively. "Why don't you go home? You look done up, you do. You go home and sleep, it's the best thing in the world. There's sometimes when I get into bed at night I could roar with it—m'legs and back all in one piece as if they'd never bend again. Sleep, sleep. I've never, no, had enough sleep, yet there's times I think what an ass I must be to spend more than half m' life sleeping when—you know what. Still—sleep. There's nothing like it, is there? Sleep, sleep, I say, sleep."

CHAPTER XVII

THE DAY came up clear, hot, blue. George Barley opened the door of his workroom at half-past six and stood for a minute looking up at the sky. One side of the yard was brilliant in sunlight. The scent of wood and wax rose in the dry air, in the early morning quiet. If he closed his eyes he could bring back the village road outside his father's workroom, and beyond that the green and the stagnant shrunken pool, white feathers fast in the mud. He felt suddenly happy as he stood there, seeming to stare vacantly across the yard. When he turned back into the workroom the feeling sharpened. For a moment he forgot that he was not beginning his life.

He went into the little kitchen and squatted raking the fire. Again he saw his father doing just the same thing at the blackened stone fireplace in his workroom. The memory gave him a deep sense of security and content. The kettle boiled on its gas-ring, and he washed his hands at the sink and wetted the tea. Then his eyes fell on the letter to the Insurance company, propped on the dresser.

He felt a start of guilt. It had waited all day yesterday to be posted. He knew why his wife had not reminded him. It was so that she could say: "I was waiting to see how long you'd let it lie there."

There was a roar of aeroplane engines. He went to the door again, hurrying himself, and saw a flight of six, lower than he had seen any. They had blunt powerful bodies and thick wings. The air seemed heavier, as though they were forcing a way through it, swimming against a current rather than flying. Their nearness, and the shattering noise they made, excited him. He always stared at aeroplanes when they came over the yard. If the children were playing they never even looked up.

"They don't know what's what," he grumbled. He was vexed by their indifference.

He took her tea up to his wife, set it down by her and hurried away. She hated tea which had stood.

During breakfast he showed her a letter from his sister. She was married and childless. She lived in their parents' old house and sold teas and refreshments. His wife looked down on her.

She had written to ask him whether Sally would like to bring the children and stay with her for a week in August. Mrs. Barley read through the letter with an impersonal attention, as though it could not concern her. She handed it back and said coldly:

"I can't go away in August."

"Why not?"

"You know why not," she said.

Sarah had been listening anxiously to the argument between her mother and father. She wanted to go to the country, to go anywhere—any change. Something in the tone of her mother's voice struck her. She means she is going to have a baby, the girl thought, vaguely. The thought had scarcely formed itself in her mind. She pushed it away, instinctively, not wanting it to happen. A baby would be a nuisance; she would have to pretend to like it and to want to help with it. A nuisance, *nuisance*, she thought with anxiety, angry with her mother, and obscurely, passionately, *for* her against the father.

She would not think about it. The future was a vast space round her, into which unpleasant thoughts could be dropped and forgotten.

Lucy cried out. Sent to fill up the teapot at the kettle, she had incautiously seized the handle of the kettle with her bare hand. It was very hot. A red weal appeared across her fingers.

Mrs. Barley rubbed soap on it, and told Lucy to get on with her breakfast. She had less patience with her second child than with the other two. Sarah was the first-born and Hector was a boy, but Lucy had no firm place of her own in her mother's heart.

The tears ran silently over Lucy's round cheeks. She

saw Sarah's lips mutely forming the word "Spunker," and made a terrific effort to stop them. One consolation—she could not help Sarah with the pots afterwards. Sarah washed up alone, but it made them late for school, and the little girls ran madly along the pavements, dragging Hector between them, his short fat legs flying out, gasping, face scarlet. They were often late. The cabmen on the rank at the corner used to give them an ironical cheer as they flew past.

Sarah had the letter to the Insurance company in the pocket of her dress. In the scramble she forgot all about posting it.

CHAPTER XVIII

HARRIET JUMPED out of bed when the aeroplanes passed over the house. She ran with quick awkward movements to the window and saw them cutting relentlessly across a narrow field of intensely blue sky. She had been startled. I hate them, hate them, she thought.

She looked at her watch. Before he went off to the aerodrome Randall was coming to tell her what Rapp had said. There would not be time to wash down in the basin, dress, and tidy the room. I must wash, she thought, and I must tidy the room. She was always afraid of offending him. He is used to such a different life, she thought anxiously.

To be ready sooner, she set the basin on the floor and stood in it, and sponged the cold water over her body. She brushed her hair, rubbed vanishing cream on the end of her nose and powdered it, thinking what a pity it is that the naked nose is not considered beautiful. She had put on a clean nightgown instead of the one in which she had slept, and then her dressing-gown, which was short and washed-out. She made the bed.

The room looked like the sitting-room of a boarding-house, prepared for guests who never sit in it.

When Randall knocked at her door she ran to open it. She hoped he would admire her in her nightgown. She was half innocent and half eager to rouse him so that she could feel surer of him.

He came in and said at once, as though he had rehearsed it: "No encouragement from Rapp. I shall have to have a word with Josephine."

"Oh," Harriet said. He had looked at her in an impersonal, smiling way that placed her hundreds of miles from him. She was afraid of saying the wrong thing. "Shall I make some breakfast?"

"No thanks. I've had coffee at Pizetti's."

"What did he say?" she asked in a low voice.

"Rapp? Oh, nothing much."

She waited, feeling helpless. In this mood she could do nothing with him. He leaned in the window, not looking at her. At least he doesn't pretend not to mind, she thought.

"Can you speak to him again?" she ventured.

"Oh, yes, I think so," he said, with an effort. She could not take away the sense of humiliation lying in him like a stone. He half resented her questions, yet answered her more easily than he would have answered his mother, who could have given him advice. Harriet could not advise him; she was too ignorant.

"What were those aeroplanes?" asked Harriet. She was ashamed that she had nothing to talk about.

Randall said carelessly, "Auxiliary Air Force bombers."

"Hateful things," she exclaimed. "How any man can bring himself to bomb houses, and streets with children in them, I don't know. It's not heroic. It's vile."

He was always startled by the sudden ferocious vehemence with which she came out with one of her few convictions. It made him realize that somewhere in her another Harriet, a stranger to him, was growing up slowly and painfully. This time he was irritated. He turned on her the contempt and indifference he had flinched from in Rapp.

"You don't know what you're talking about," he said icily. "A pilot has too much else to think about. He has to attend to his job and it takes all his senses, I can tell you. If people don't like being bombed they shouldn't start wars. It isn't the airmen who start them."

Harriet could not bear anger and disapproval in the flesh. If he wrote her an angry letter she could defend herself, but his voice made her ashamed. She drove back nervous tears. Standing there in her clean cold nightgown she felt very small and foolish.

"That doesn't change the fact," she said breathlessly. "The airmen who machine-gun children running across a field—as they've done in Spain—are cowards and beasts."

"War is idiotic," Randall said.

"Yes, yes," she agreed eagerly.

She thought he would now put his arms round her, but he did not move from the window, lounging there, looking half over his shoulder into the yard. She was bewildered. He is leaving me, she thought. But that would be easier than disapproval. With the complacency of youth she thought she could bear tragedy.

Randall jerked his head back. "Man I met last night over there asked me if I'd like to go to China. A thousand pounds a month they pay you."

"But—but what to do?" she said, astonished.

"Flying, of course." He smiled slightly. "You know neither side can fly, neither Chinks nor Japs. You'd be in more danger from your mechanics, if they were Chinese, than you would be from the other side. What I didn't like about it was—you sign the contract in Paris. No knowing."

Harriet stared at him in dismay. She was sick with fear. "You wouldn't go."

"Why not?" He felt a perverse happiness in tormenting her. His bewilderment and feeling of failure became less sharp. "Why not? Especially if you go to New York."

"How unfair you are," cried Harriet.

"I? What do you mean?"

"If I don't go to New York you won't go to China. You have no right——"

"I never said so," he retorted. "I don't make any promises."

"You won't promise not to go to China?"

"No. Of course not. Flying is the only thing I have. How can writing advertisements be your life? It's ridiculous even to think of it."

Until this moment he had not thought seriously of going to China. How many men survived to collect their second month's pay? And what could you do with a contract drawn in Paris if it were not watertight? Now suddenly he thought that it would be a way out of his perplexity and restlessness. No more harrying inapt pupils into the stage of nominal proficiency. No problems, except those that had to do with his job. He might survive and draw enough money to finance his record flight himself.

He imagined sending his mother a telegram from Paris. "Off to China. Love. Bill." What would she do? Read it and go on writing?

He saw fear and a perplexity like his own in Harriet's eyes. It did not make him sorry for her. She was too near him. He loved her with his heart and with all his senses, but she had no hold on his imagination. I won't make a bargain with her, he thought fiercely. If she gave him everything, *freely*, he would be—what?—happy? safe? You're a fool, he said mocking himself.

"We're always quarrelling," Harriet said quietly.

"Nonsense," he laughed. He roused himself to go away. "We're all right."

He put his arm round her. The stuff of her nightgown slid over her skin under his hand. He held her body against his, dragging her closer as he drowned in the heavy leaping waves of blood in his body and head, then let her go quickly, and went away.

CHAPTER XIX

PIZETTI WAS surprised to see the two Jews come into the café at half-past ten. He changed his opinion again. They must be opening a shop in the neighbourhood. They're trying to get Ashton's custom, he decided; that's why they asked about him the first time; but he owes money, they'll lose theirs.

They ordered coffee. When he brought it he said cheerfully: "Like this district, hey?"

"Yes, we like it," the younger man said shortly.

Pizetti felt that he had been rash. He went into the kitchen and told Maddalena that he would like to refuse to serve them. His sly peasant dignity was roused. She soothed him, and persuaded him that it wouldn't do to have trouble. "Not when we are going to sell the place," she said.

"You're always right," he answered, half vexed with her.

Franklyn glanced once round the empty café before he went on talking. He was in a good mood. The gratification he felt when a job had been arranged filled him. He never felt less out of joint with society than when he was busy cheating it.

"When he rang up—about half-past one this morning—he said, We'll fix it for next week. That'll do for now, I said; you don't want to discuss it on the phone."

"Next week?"

"What do you think?" Franklyn said dryly. "It'll be to-night. I don't give him time to change his mind or go and talk to someone."

"Yes," Ben said. He yawned widely. "Half-past one this morning I was taking Ruth to the hospital. She thought first she could wait, and then she said, No, we've got to go. That's where I was when you rang the first time. At the hospital."

Franklyn said briefly: "They've got to go through it."
He turned his hand over on the table, palm down, in a
gesture of closing. "Now listen, Ben. You've been round
at the back of the place. How many windows look out on
the place at the back?"

"Two, both on the ground," said Ben rapidly. "One'll
be a room in Ashton's own place. The other's the kitchen
of this café."

"Anything you noticed?"

Ben pulled at his mouth. "A lot of people sleeping in
the top rooms over here and over the other side," he said
slowly.

"You must have noticed them when you came here
alone, the first time," Franklyn said, looking at him without irony.

"Yes."

"Well, they can get out, can't they?"

Ben glanced through the window. "Plenty of staircases," he said slowly. He pushed his lips forward. "Yes,
I guess that's right, Con. I was just thinking."

"Get me some more coffee."

Ben walked towards the counter. Pizetti almost ran out
of the kitchen to meet him and placed himself in front of
the "office," his long thin body jerked sideways and backwards in an attitude of defiance. He laid his left hand
on his hip.

"You rheumatic?" Ben smiled. "D'you know what
you should do? Sod herbs in milk and drink it, see?
Any herbs you got by you."

Ashamed once more of his worst suspicions Pizetti
smiled at him lovingly. "All right, I will," he answered
in an eager voice.

Over his second cup of coffee Franklyn said with an
injured fury:

"Did you see Bergman's dead? Well, you didn't know
him when—at the time I remember him. Thirty years ago
when he was living next door with us. He was lucky. You
see he died worth two and a half million, after he's given

half a million to hospitals, and his daughter married a relation of royalty. If some of his friends he made knew what I knew about him. It depends if you're lucky."

He sat brooding with a sunken vicious humour. Ben kept quiet. He began to think of his wife waking him up in the stuffy darkness of their bedroom. Her voice sounded unlike her. It was a second before he realized that she was sitting with her back to him on the edge of the bed. He got up. "Is this it?" he asked. She said what she had been saying when he awoke. "I think we got to go, Ben." He wanted to turn on the light, but she said, "No, No," in an urgent hurried voice, and he thought, She's going queer in the head with it. The thought frightened him, because of the time of night, and being alone with her. When he was dressing, feeling for his clothes on the chair, she said weakly, "Perhaps we needn't go yet." He went round to her then and she said, "Why didn't you come before?" What does she mean? he thought. "You're all right, aren't you?" he said, heartening her, and he put his hand on her and felt her breathing, and the only thing it made him think was of a horse down in the road on a bad day. He felt fear, pity and disgust. So this is all of it, he said to himself, without understanding. He was sleepy and confused. With his hand on her the room seemed filled with the child going to be born, as if it were breathing the darkness. "If you shouldn't go yet get back into bed," he said quietly. She had changed her mind again. She began to dress, and they took up her bag she had ready and went down into the street, the eighth stair creaking as it did since he was a boy and lived in this house: he held her up because she was afraid of falling on the new linoleum in the passage. In the street she walked slowly, heavily, so that it was like walking with a stranger—nothing to do with him. He saw a cab in a side street, but she wouldn't have it. "Let's walk, Ben," she said. He walked eight miles to her one, with the effort of keeping step with her. It was not until he had left her at the hospital and was walking away that he began to feel about her again as if she were himself, and then he felt anxious. I could have said something, he thought sharply.

An age separated this café from their bedroom, the empty sagging streets, and the yellow-lit corridor of the hospital. He sat looking down at his cup, waiting for Franklyn to pull himself out of his mood.

Franklyn got up suddenly. "I'm going over to see Ashton," he said. "You wait."

He waited, half-dozing. Going on for twelve, he heard Pizetti talking on the telephone behind the bar. He got up and went over to the bar. Pizetti was speaking Italian and gesticulating to help out the words. He hung up with a flourish.

"Mind if I put a call through?" Ben said easily, stepping behind the bar.

Pizetti stood polishing glasses and listening without seeming to. "Queen Charlotte's? . . . I want to know if my wife, how my wife is, Mrs. Benjamin Abramovitch . . . Mrs. Abramovitch, yes." Standing with the receiver at his ear, mouth thrust out, stomach and gaudy plaid shirt thrust out, leaning against the wall, he was between Pizetti and the "office." At last Pizetti could stand it no longer. He wormed his way between the counter and the man's big body and began to dust off the tables.

The Jew came away from the telephone frowning. He stood looking through the door, his hands in his belt.

Pizetti went into the kitchen. "Look at him. Is he going to stay here all day?" he said whispering.

"It doesn't matter where they are," Maddalena said, in a low voice, calmly and soothingly, "they're living Ghetto lives, and you can't understand them. We're just as much strangers in this country, but we have got a country where we're not strange." She wiped her damp forehead, and spoke to Giulia in a sharp voice. "You're dreaming, girl."

Giulia turned her head, smiling. "I'm not dreaming. I was thinking about Italy." She plunged her hands again into the cold water and scraped away at carrots with such energy that her curls swung out like a merry-go-round.

At twelve o'clock Ben saw the two workmen leaving Barley's workshop. He had meant all along to try to make a separate deal with Barley. It was a small job, fifty pounds —but why not? He had a certain naïve vanity, kept under usually by his respect and admiration for Franklyn. He relished the idea of telling Franklyn that they could make a second rake-off by starting two fires.

It never entered his head that there was a risk in approaching Barley. Since he was doing badly, naturally he would jump at the offer.

He strolled across the yard to the workshop and stood a minute in the doorway, sniffing the dry hot smell of timber. It made him curiously happy. It sought and stirred a remote memory, so remote that he scarcely recognized it as a memory. It was perhaps not his but belonged to his Polish father. With it went a rippling light like water, soundless.

He saw Barley alone at the other side of the workshop. He was stooping over a bureau with a piece of glass-paper, sunk in what he was doing. He looked up with slow curiosity. "That's a nice bureau you got," Ben said loudly. He knew something about furniture. He did all the talking for some minutes, speaking very sensibly and energetically about the state of the trade. Barley nodded. "Business is bad," he said. His eyes looked past the other, and what he saw cannot have given him pleasure, since they filmed over —like dust covering the skin of water—to escape it.

"Why don't you have a fire?" Ben said, dropping his voice.

He saw the man's face change, to a look of listening caution. His vanity misread it.

Barley listened until he was sure he had understood the whole thing, and then told him to get out. He did it quietly, furtively, as if it embarrassed him. His air of embarrassment was almost ludicrous.

"What's that?" Ben said, malevolent. "What d'you say?"

"I said, Get out," Barley repeated.

Three children came noisily into the workshop from the yard and stamped across it into a room at the back.

"You should keep quiet, see?" Ben said. "You don't want anything should happen to you."

"Go on," Barley said, staring at him, "get out of my place." He put his fists ready, stiffly, like an old man.

The kitchen door opened sharply. Ben moved off, reaching the door as the woman said coldly: "Will you come to your dinner, then? It's on your plate." He saw Barley drop his arms and come to close the door into the yard.

Through the window, he saw Barley walk quickly, shambling, into the kitchen and shut that door as well. He stood in a stupor of contempt. Missed his chance, he repeated; missed his last chance, the old fool.

He went back into the Café Bar and sat down to wait for Franklyn. If he told Franklyn what had happened he would be for it. He struggled to forget it himself. His vanity was outraged.

He bought a packet of Gold Flake and asked Pizetti if his café was insured. Pizetti shook his head. "You asked me once already," he said as sharply as he dared. What next? he wondered.

"Well, you should be insured," Ben said. "If you were insured and you had a fire, see, that would be easy money. Or you don't need money, eh?"

"I don't need money!" Pizetti said. He made an expressive gesture. "I stay here in this café because they don't offer me enough yet to take over the Savoy." He said this partly from bravado and partly because this was one of the moments when his eight hundred pounds in paper notes in a wooden box seemed a small enough payment for so much hard work and enterprise. He had just read in the newspaper left behind by a customer that a rich woman had paid eight hundred pounds for a suitcase. A lifetime of savings for one suitcase, he thought, dumbfounded. It made him feel positively ill.

"I could arrange something for you," Ben said.

"I don't want an insurance," Pizetti said excitedly.

"I haven't no money for insurance." He went on with more calm: "You should sell your insurance to the next tenant. Next week or the week after or next month I clear out and go home."

"To Italy, hey?"

Pizetti said nothing. He was not in the mood for jokes about goats. Nor did he feel moved to tell this man that a wood fire even when it makes water pour out of your eyes is better than the smell of fog and dirt. And then, as a rich man, he would have a chimney.

Several people came in for lunch. Franklyn came back and said he would eat macaroni if it was ready.

"You like it with tomatoes," Pizetti said gaily. "I know. I remember."

"Well, get it," Franklyn said.

Pizetti flew round, serving the other tables. He tried to keep an eye on the two men without being noticed by them. He distrusted them more and more, but he was afraid to try to hear what they were talking about. They kept their heads down. It was the older man who talked, and the younger listened with his underlip thrust forward, a drop hanging from it. Pizetti was fascinated by this drop; he wanted to see it fall, but the man sucked it back and it formed again and again was sucked back and formed.

". . . that window you saw is the window of Ashton's room. It'll be open. The sort of passage outside is blind, only one way in, and there's nothing there. Some kids play there at night, he says, that's all, that's all. They'll clear off to bed. You come round to me for the doings about nine this evening. That makes sure, by the time you get it here, there won't be kids playing, nothing. Nothing. That'll be at ten. You'll go round *outside* with the box and put it in through the window. Leave it there. We'll meet at Martha's after midnight, say at half-past one, and have a meal, and be here at three. Yes, three. He's a fool. Four-thirty, he said. Or five. Four-thirty? I said, or five, you'll have daylight. You can't get away with it in broad daylight, I said. Well, there it is, he said, the place is cram full of people until after four. Tell them to kiss themselves good night and leave at two, I said. Well, it seems he can't, so what I did to save trouble and argument, I said, All right, have it your own way, make it five, I said. But don't you worry, I don't wait for anyone. We'll be here at three sharp and he can clear the apes out of it when the fire has started. And they can tell themselves goonight, goonight, goodnight, in the street. And goodnight. If their cars get in the road of the fire-engines so much the better, it gives it more time to burn. You can't work in daylight, I said to him; you don't see it, I said, but I see it, it's my job to see some things. So here's my meaning. . . ."

Barley waited until the children were out of the way, rushing out straight from the table to have time to play before school, and then he told his wife about the man.

"He said, I can bring the stuff to your place and they'll never find out the stuff I use, he said."

"Whatever next?" Mrs. Barley cried. She was thoroughly alarmed and upset. The dread of a fire was always in her mind.

"Why, he said, you can move that bureau out this afternoon; all you've got to do is count all the nails and screws in it and leave the right number lying about for the insurance jokers to count, he said, and claim for it, on top of the other things. He said, Isn't it worth all of two hundred, it's a beautiful piece? Yes, it is a beautiful piece, I said."

"Upon my word," exclaimed his wife sarcastically, "do you mean to tell me you discussed furniture with the man?"

Barley was taken aback. "No, that I didn't," he said quickly. "But he mentioned about the bureau and I agreed with him."

"You'll be agreeing to cut your own head off next," Mrs. Barley said. "And pray what else did you say to him?"

"I chased him off. He was going when you opened the door."

His wife looked at him, as though it were an effort to her to endure him at all. Her face was white and she was agitated. She could not quite control herself when she thought of the children and fire. She blamed him for it bitterly.

"You ought to have kept him, and fetched the police," she said in a sharp voice.

"I didn't think of it," Barley said. He hung his head, ashamed in front of her, because she was right, as usual, and his slow mind had let him down again. I am a proper fool, he thought.

"No. You think of nothing."

Mrs. Barley got up and began to clear the table, carrying the things to the sink. Her hands were shaking. She dropped a plate, and turned on her husband in fury when he began to pick up the pieces. "It's your fault," she cried, "you hinder me."

She felt that the heat in the room suffocated her. Turning away, she clung to the edge of the table and closed her eyes. What has happened? she thought, confused. Why am I in this place at all? She remembered running across a strip of grass to her mother, in burning sunlight. And now this room and her body heavy with her fourth child. And she did not want it. Suddenly she felt afraid that by not wanting it she would do it harm. She looked up.

"Where did the man go?" she asked.

Barley knitted his brows. "What? Oh—he went off, I suppose."

"I wish I'd overheard him," she said, still harping on it.

"I should've thought about going for the police," Barley said.

"It's too late now."

"Look, I'll wash the things for you," he said rapidly "And you can lie down a bit, see?"

"No, I'd sooner do them myself," she said at once. She was not a woman who could give in. "I'm all right."

"Are you?" he asked, wishing she would reassure him about many things.

"Yes, of course." She spoke in a gentler voice. "I'm perfectly all right, and we shall manage, we always do. But we can't stay here with this child—we shall be forced to move. You must think about it."

She watched him lumber out of the room slowly, into the workshop. Yes, and when he's thought about it for months I shall have to tell him what to do, she said wearily to herself. But she was not impatient now. His dependence on her moved her even when she had been exasperated by it. But what *can* we do? she cried; this time it's past me.

She said, "It's past me," but for all that she did not feel defeated yet. She thought she was too strong for life to finish with.

CHAPTER XX

THE SUN sent its burning arrows against every wall of the house. The afternoon heat was overpowering. It was like a flame licking the pavements. The stones of the yard scorched Charlotte Mannheim's feet through her thin shoes. She came in from the street, her head hanging like the head of an animal in the sun, and staggered into the dark entrance from which the stairs went to her own room. But she got no farther than the foot of the stairs. There she had to sit down, fighting for her breath. She laid a hand over her heart, to help it by the knowledge that she was listening. It was an old servant now. It had earned friendship. The days when she felt only impatience towards her body were in the past.

This time the attack did not pass as soon as she expected. In the end, afraid, she made her way blindly and slowly across the corner of the yard to the staircase leading to the doctor's room. He must help her.

She had to ring three times before he opened the door. He was an odd sight, if she had had eyes for it. His heavy face glistened with the face cream he had hastily wiped off it with the towel in his hand; there were strips of sticking-plaster across his deepest wrinkles, smoothing them out, and he had taken off and dropped one of those straps women wear at night to correct double chin. He had been using an exerciser for slimming and it was lying on the floor. As he opened the door he was fastening a dressing-gown round his body.

"Help me," Charlotte Mannheim said.

She was conscious of the doctor's thick hands. They dragged her out of the waves under which she was foundering, her clothes wrapping her like lead, but the shock of breathing the air again was too severe. The movement of her lungs sliced her body like knives. Let me drown, she groaned. Had she spoken at all?

At last she felt that she was all right. She sat up, and began to thank the doctor.

"Don't take any notice of my looks," he said abruptly.

She noticed it for the first time. She felt confused. "It's nothing, it's nothing," she muttered. She sat with her arms resting on her knees, trying to make up her mind to get up and go away.

"I'll give you a cup of tea," Dr. Cleveland said. "I can't do anything else for you, you know. Nobody can. It's too late now."

"Am I ill?"

"No, you're not ill," he said without embarrassment. "You're going to die, in a month or two, but don't be afraid. I'll look after you until then unless you have someone to do it. I don't suppose you have, or you wouldn't have come to me. I've seen you going in and out alone, too."

A feeling of emptiness that was almost ecstatic swept over her while he was speaking. It seemed that she held up her arms and wept with joy. Her life flowed from her, pouring over Europe into the twittering streets of foreign cities, into ill-lit rooms, into the sun-baked dust of roads, the naked glare of public halls, the café tables, prisons, platforms of railway stations. Throwing them from her, she threw off too the burden of all the men and women among whom she had parted her body.

"If I had my time over again——" she began quietly.

"You mean if you had your body given back to you."

"Yes if I could have it again I'd give it away minute by minute, to the same people."

"I don't know why you should," the doctor said, grimacing; he swilled hot water in the pot before he dropped the tea in. "Were any of them worth it?"

"All of them," Charlotte Mannheim said, firmly. "Men are born to be good, decent, friendly. They are forced out of their nature by the violence of governments. The men who killed my husband were ordered to do it. It would never have occurred to one of them to do it himself."

"Let me tell you," the doctor said eagerly, "that if I had been allowed to keep a certain person with me and to talk to him freely and honestly—or if he had been different —if I had brought him up to understand honesty—but there you are——"

"I never had a son," Charlotte Mannheim said.

The doctor was going to say, "Neither had I," but he changed his mind and said: "You're a German, aren't you? My mother was one, she gave me this nose I carry about with me; every single one of her ancestors had it in turn and when I think of them all poking their noses towards me through the earth, as supercilious as only the totally forgotten dead can afford to be, I'm delighted to think how they must detest me. I've disgraced their nose."

"Thank you for this tea," Charlotte Mannheim said.

"Don't hurry away."

"I'm taking up your time."

"Not at all. Besides, take it up, why shouldn't you? It's there lying about. I can't use the whole of it myself—nor want to." He looked at her with inquisitive interest. "Why didn't you see somebody about this"—he tapped his chest—"sooner?"

"I couldn't," she said, "I had Annie—I had a friend with me I had to take care of, and nurse. She was delicate. Last December she left me and went back to her family. I don't know why she did that, after all these years, but I daresay she wanted to hear her own language spoken round her; she wasn't at home anywhere, just as she was never really an anarchist, she only pretended to be, to please a man called Goltmann. Thomas Goltmann. You may have heard of him."

"No."

"He was my husband."

The doctor snapped his fingers. "Forgive me, I never heard of him."

After a long pause Charlotte Mannheim said:

"I realize that he was no more important than anyone else. I don't know why I didn't realize it sooner."

"Why think of it now?" Dr. Cleveland said with a vague gesture. "Can you believe it—that I still think about my looks? Can you beat that?" He began to laugh. "How old would you say I am?"

"I don't know," Charlotte Mannheim said wearily. "I'm seventy." She stood up, and set her cup down on the table. She noticed the neatness of the room, and yet it smelled—she wrinkled her arched nose—it smelled exactly like the guardroom in a barracks where she and Thomas had once passed a night under arrest, before being expelled across the frontier—a smell of cloth, sweat, and some metal. The odour of inhumanity, she had called it. Later she thought it was only the smell of men living without women, as they do during a war.

"Good-bye," she said, in a low voice.

"Have you a bell—I mean a hand-bell?" asked Dr. Cleveland.

G

"Yes—why ever?"

"Ring it out of your window when you want help. I may be at home."

"Thank you, but I shan't want help."

"It was what you asked me for when I opened the door," he said grinning.

I shan't ask again, she thought, stepping slowly down the stairs, through the furnace outside, and up the staircase to her room with scarcely an effort. She drew a deep breath. How marvellous to be able to breathe. She walked across her room, touching a chair, the table. For the first time in her life she thought, But this is my home. She opened the window at the bottom and propped it with the piece of wood she kept for the purpose. The yard came into the room. It had a dry, close smell, the smell of dust, oil, bread, of men and women living too closely together in scarred, narrow-chested houses.

"The smell of London," she said smiling.

She felt extraordinarily happy. Whether it is weeks or months, she thought, I'm content to spend them here. She drew a chair to the window, placing it so that she could see over the room and over the yard by turning her head very slightly to either side. Then she sat down, folding her hands, as though she had always been a patient woman.

CHAPTER XXI

ON HER way home at four o'clock Harriet felt tired and ill. In the office she felt dizzy, and was only saved from fainting by the other young woman's promptness. She tweaked Harriet's ears until they ought to have come off in her hand, and poured down her back under her frock a glassful of tepid water from the tap in the cloakroom. Then she suggested to Harriet that she could go home quietly, without asking anyone's permission. It was quite simple. "You go down the back stairs and if *he* sends for you I'll say you had to go to the printers'."

Harriet had no nervousness about cheating authority. And she really felt ill. It was not the fault of the fearful brutal heat. She had not been eating. The meal at Pizetti's, for which Randall had paid, was the only proper meal she had had this week. She was absolutely convinced that, unlike ordinary human beings, she did not need food. It was a sinful waste of the money she needed for other things—she had set her heart on buying a navy linen frock to wear when she went to the aerodrome on Sunday.

The walk through the streets was a physical torment, but neither she nor the people she passed had any reality for her. She was living through an unpleasant dream. She reached New Moon Yard, and saw the front of the house reel and slip sideways into blackness.

She was lying on the bed in her room. She knew that much, but she could not see clearly. A woman's voice said: "Oh, she's all right. I'll see to her." Indeed I'm not, I'm probably dying, she thought indignantly. "You are sure?" That melodious slow voice was Alfred Linder's. Surprise and displeasure drove away the grey cloud drifting in front of her eyes. She saw him standing in the doorway with that Mrs. Kerr. The door closed, and Mrs. Kerr came back to the bed.

"Feeling better?" she said.

Harriet tried to sit up, but the heaviness and weakness of her limbs frightened her very much and she let herself fall back. Mrs. Kerr laughed at the expression of alarm on her face.

"You're not dying."

The young woman blushed. "I've never fainted in my life," she mumbled.

"Time you began," Mrs. Kerr said. "D'you think you're immortal?"

Since this was precisely what Harriet did think, she felt oddly confused. She let the words fall through her mind,

like stones falling through water to lie on the floor of the
stream below the current.

"Thank you for bringing me up here," she said
earnestly.

"We got you up between us, me and your Jewish friend,"
Mrs. Kerr laughed.

"He's not my friend." She felt slightly ashamed of
herself, but she could not take the words back.

"I'll make you a pot of tea, then I must be off," Mrs.
Kerr said briskly. "If you take my advice you'll go to
bed and sleep. You'll be all right in the morning. Nothing
like sleep, is there?"

"I could sleep twelve hours a day," Harriet confessed.
She felt drowsy now. "But it seems silly to sleep so much
when you could be living."

"Depends what you call living. Some lives go as quick
as sleep; every day you think, I'll notice if I'm alive or
dead—but what of it? I remember looking hard at a tree
in the light, full of light, when I was a girl, and thinking
Now you've got that. But I'd nothing, nothing. It's no
use thinking you've *got* anything. The whole set of tricks
slips through your hands in a flash, a day gone, a year
years, gone. If you have money you can buy yourself
comfort, and that's something. What d'you hope for?"

Some impulse in Harriet sprang out, a beast leaping in
its cage. She echoed the woman's hard reckless zest. I
shall go to New York, she cried; I shall get money, more
than comfort—excitement. The words clashed in her
head, with the sound of trees in a storm. She ran beneath
them, tossing her arms, running away. A pang of grief
seized her. No—let me be quiet, she thought—*in re-
turning and rest shall ye be saved; in quietness and in confidence shall be your strength*. But what words, and where
did I hear them?

"Here's your tea," Mrs. Kerr said.

"Aren't you having any?" she asked awkwardly.

"No. I've had mine. I was just off out when you
came in the yard and fell." She went over to the glass and

began pulling her dress, wriggling in it like a snake in its skin.

If my mother could see her here! thought Harriet. She was overwhelmed suddenly by the audacity and strangeness of her life, which had brought her, already, a knowledge of things hidden—or so she imagined—from her innocent mother. She felt an arrogant pity for the woman gazing at herself in the glass. Nothing so dreadful will happen to me, she thought, with a hidden ecstasy. Other people do wrong foolish things with their lives, but I am not going to make any mistakes. An irrefutable assurance of joy sprang in her.

"I'll just rinse these pots for you," Mrs. Kerr said.

When she came from behind the screen, having washed the teapot and cup and left them to dry themselves, the girl had fallen asleep—suddenly—like an infant. She was half smiling, her head turned sideways on the pillow. Her young breasts were half naked. Mrs. Kerr had opened her blouse when they laid her on the bed. She had only a thin white cotton vest under it, very cheap. Mrs. Kerr was taken aback by the contempt it started in her now. That the young woman could wear such a garment, like a servant's, without being ashamed! Her head throbbed. She could not understand her sense of outrage. What's it matter to me if she covers herself with a dish-rag? she thought. She stared down at Harriet's shoes, dusty, and the heels scrubbed, dropped one on top of the other beside the bed.

Turning quickly to go, she saw the young woman's bag lying on the floor. She picked it up and looked in it, because it would have been silly not to. There was a notebook, pen, letters, a purse with a little silver in it, and in a small canvas bag a ten-shilling note and two pounds. Without hesitating a second, she took one of the pound notes and pushed it into her stocking. When she misses it she won't dare say anything to me, she thought, with cruel certainty.

She closed the door softly. Those shoes, she thought;

that cotton vest. All at once she saw herself tearing home from school with the other girls, and one of them began to tease her about her mother. The others all joined in eagerly. She was fit to cry with rage and shame. When she got home and her mother said, "Why, what's matter, Jeanie?" she ran at her and struck her, shouting, "I don't like you, you're shabby and ugly, and the house is ugly." Her mother had said nothing at all, not a word—only gone into the next room. And then she had cried and cried, and her mother came back and tried to soothe her, listening still in silence while she stammered, over and over, "I didn't mean it, I only love you, I love you, I didn't meant it."

Queer thing is, I did love her, she thought.

Come, cheer up, stir your stumps, she said. She pulled her fur over her shoulders. It was a good one, real fox, and the feel of it under her fingers comforted her. I'm going to be lucky to-day. She stepped into the sunlight with a quiver of pleasure. Ah, give me summer. A strong spring of gaiety and confidence leaped in her. She walked towards the street, with a slow deliberate smile for Alfred Linder idling in the door of his shop. Was he watching for me? You never know.

CHAPTER XXII

THE REV. JAMES DANIEL had walked across London to the docks. He had not eaten since noon yesterday. If he had kept still the sun would have fed him, but as he walked he began to be dizzy with hunger; his body played tricks on him; for moments he was insignificant, an animal padding through the undergrowth of a jungle; then he walked through streets he could have kicked aside with his foot and people scattered in front of him like ants. As soon a:

he saw ships' funnels he knew that, like Jonah, he had been tempted to go away from the presence of the Lord. He realized also that it was no use. He turned about and went back. About nine in the evening he was in Leicester Square, almost back where he had started that morning. He went and sat down in the garden in the centre.

He was in the pit of despair and weakness. It seemed to him that he had been abandoned; the force that had brought him here from New Orleans was being withdrawn; he had been deceived. To-day, for the first time, he had been awed only by the immensity of London. It was a wilderness of brick and steel, its roots in the depths of the earth, and a pulse beating in the steel. No one could destroy it, it was not Nineveh, not Babylon. He saw that the windows of the buildings were laughing, and involving him in their foolish joke.

So he sat in the centre of London, that is, in the centre of the world, and saw—what did he see? Vivid green grass, on which a pigeon strutted and tumbled like an urchin amusing a theatre queue; bright yellow tulips, pink tulips, more than half of them dead; water jetting from the mouths of dolphins like a secret word. Four great trees stood round the fountain, four black angels. Behind the railings of the garden cars and scarlet buses whirled in the inner circle of innumerable circles, one outside the other until the uttermost touched the circles spinning out from the sun and burst into flames. Ah—flames again! He saw now that they were very close to the garden; they flickered red and orange behind the trees; they whinnied like frightened horses; straining forward he could hear voices. News From All The World. Café de l'Europe. He felt his blood breaking down the paths and walls of its veins. Black light burst from his body. Of course, of course, he cried. I was right, I knew, I knew—I am right. This city, this country, Europe, the world itself, all were doomed; all would shrivel like paper in the breath of the furnace. He stood up and hastened into the Square. The sky at the end of Piccadilly quivered, a fiery striate cloud leaning above the houses.

It is coming, it is coming, he told himself, exulting. Lifting his arms above his head he cried out: "Woe, woe to this city."

A few people turned their heads to stare at him, but he did not shout anything more. In a moment he was forgotten. He walked blindly to New Moon Yard, hurried to his room, locked the door on himself, and began to pray.

Mrs. Barley had sent the children to bed at nine. They were playing one of their wild, savage games in the cul-de-sac at the back, and Hector ran home to fetch a stick they wanted. It was a fatal mistake. He came back with furious face, his underlip thrust out.

"*She* says we're to come in," he said, scowling.

They trailed home, disconsolate, and their mother hurried them into bed. None of them could sleep in the close airless little room. Even with the blind down it was not anything like dark. They kept quiet until they heard the door of the kitchen shut downstairs. Hector sat up, and mumbled:

"Go on with the story, our Sarah."

This was an endless story she had been more than a year telling. Its beginnings were already dim in the little boy's memory. He seemed to have been listening to it all his life. Sarah herself had forgotten when she began to invent it. There was a ball of silk in her mind from which she drew this bright glittering thread, without any effort. It was the story of three children, a boy and two girls, living in a dark wood without mother or father, who one day fell into the well at the end of the wood and found themselves alive in another world under ground. Here, chiefly by the cunning of the elder girl, they went through danger after danger without failing; they answered riddles, and escaped from traps set for them. There were aeroplanes and revolvers in the story, but there were also talking animals, staircases in trees, witches, kings' palaces; it was a peculiar hotch-potch of the old and the new, and the two younger children adored it. For Sarah it was so easy that she enjoyed it almost as much. When she was in a bad temper she refused to go on with it unless she were bribed by a "deed." The "deed" might be that Hector had to go upstairs to fetch her house slippers or Lucy to dry the tea-pots without help. They grumbled and did it. Whatever it was, it was worth it for the story.

To-night she began willingly. After a few minutes she broke off, with a look of consternation on her face.

"That letter," she gasped. "I forgot to post it."

"What letter?" asked Lucy.

"You know—that letter our dad gave me this morning. He said I was to put it in the box at the corner, because he said he wanted it to get there."

"Why, of course he wants it to get there," Lucy said. She began to laugh. "That's what you post letters for—to get there."

Sarah was too stricken to answer back. She got out of bed, stepping cautiously over the board that creaked, and felt in the pocket of her dress. There it was, the letter. Lifting a corner of the blind she read the address. Phœnix Assurance Company.

"You can post it in the morning, our Sarah."

"Go out and post it now," Lucy said, half under her breath. She looked to see how this crazy idea was taken.

"She daren't," said Hector.

"I'll go if I think," Sarah said.

"You daren't," echoed Lucy. Her eyes danced. "You daren't."

Without a word Sarah pulled on her dress over her short nightgown. She took her shoes in her hand. The other two watched her with a mixture of interest and malice. Lucy suddenly felt afraid of what their mother would do if she heard Sarah slipping out of the house now.

"Don't go," she said.

"She isn't going," Hector said.

"Yes I am then, and both of you be quiet," snapped his sister. It was unthinkable to give it up now. She would be disgraced.

She held her breath while she was opening the door. Slipping through as narrow an opening as possible, she closed it behind her and stood in the passage which separated their bedroom from their parents'. The stairs went down into the darkened workshop. She began slowly to go down. If she were heard now, or if her mother came suddenly out of the kitchen, she would catch the worst thrashing of her life.

When she was crossing the workshop in her bare feet her heart beat loudly. She thought fearfully that she might as well be knocking on the walls. It seemed impossible that no one but herself could hear it.

With immense relief she found the door from the workroom into the yard only closed, not locked or bolted. She drew it open inch by inch. Standing in the yard, she pulled her shoes on, and began to run, keeping near the house. It was still light outside. Her heart gave another jump as she passed the entrance to the next staircase of the house. She looked in and saw that big Negro going up; he turned his head, his eyes rolling in his dark face. Sarah flew past.

In the street she felt safe. She posted the letter and raced back. The worst moment of all was when she had to open the workshop door, not knowing what she would find. She waited a minute outside. Her stomach was in a knot of fear. Then she thought that someone, that Mrs. Caracas or someone, might be watching from a window. In an agony of fear now—she really dreaded her mother's angers—she put her hand on the door and pushed it an inch. All inside was darkness. She got in, closed the door, took her shoes off again, and crept up the stairs. As she reached the top she heard the door of the kitchen open down below.

She slipped into the bedroom and steadied herself to shut the door gently. Snatching off her dress she got into bed. The other two were lying down when she came in. Lucy started up and said: "Oh, our Sarah. I thought you weren't ever coming."

"Well, I've posted it," she said indifferently. She would not let them see what she had been through.

"Our Hector cried," Lucy said.

"No I never," said Hector. He spoke without turning round.

"You did. He did," persisted Lucy.

"Go to sleep," Sarah said. She lay down herself. In the relief from tension she was trembling, but she felt wonderfully happy, as though she had passed a difficult test. I'm not really a coward, she thought. Now surely everything would be different. She fell asleep.

George Barley looked at the clock as he left the kitchen. It was just on ten o'clock. Mrs. Barley had discovered that she had not enough tea in the house for the morning. She could not blame anyone else for her forgetfulness, but she was sadly vexed. Barley offered to go across and borrow from Mrs. Pizetti. "No, you'll only make a mess of it," she said, knitting her brows: "you'll let everyone in the place hear you asking for it."

"I shall not," he said, on his dignity.

"Oh very well, go then. If she isn't in the café ask Pizetti if you can speak to her. Say it's for your wife. And don't shout it out."

When he had reached the door of the room she said suddenly: "George."

He turned round.

"Don't mind what I say. It's all this heat—it fairly swithers me."

"I don't mind it," he said.

He crossed the workshop, in his slow heavy fashion. The room was very warm. He smelled the different smells of newly-planed and waxed wood. Outside in the yard the light was going, but it was scarcely cool yet. He walked towards the Café Bar.

When he was close to it he stopped and looked through the lighted window, looking for Mrs. Pizetti. He did not see her, but he saw the man who had come to him that morning and offered to set fire to the workshop. He was telephoning, leaning against the counter. His face was turned to the door but he was staring down, listening.

Barley drew back out of sight. After a moment's hesitation he went back without going into the café, and told his wife. She would know what to do.

She did.

"Are you sure it's the same man?" she exclaimed.

"Of course I'm sure!" Barley said. "I shouldn't forget his face in a hurry. Nor his shirt neither."

"Very well, you must go to the police," his wife said.

"I suppose I must." He hated putting himself forward.

"Eh, dear me, of course you must. And look sharp, too. We don't want a villain like that about the place. There's only one of them, isn't there? He didn't have anyone else with him?"

"No, there's only one."

"It's enough, I hope."

She was bustling round him all the time, making him take off his old jacket and put the other on. She hurried him away, and bolted the workshop door after him so that no one could break in and fire the place when he was gone. Then she sat down and waited in a perfect fever for him to come back. If it hadn't been for the children I'd have gone with him, she thought. She hardly believed that he could manage it properly himself.

Ben got on the underground at Old Street, carrying the box. He held it between his legs in the train and sat easily, a half smile on his lips. It amused him to sit there with the box. Next to him was an old man in the clothes of a tramp, with strips of canvas tied round his legs and over his boots. He had a delicate handsome nose, which he kept fast in a book. Ben looked inquisitively at the title. *The Secret Places of the Heart*—who'd have thought it?

He was concerned about Ruth, but in his present mood not worrying. She'll be all right, he thought. Think of something else. He thought, not for the first time, that it was a pity these boxes were made to be burned. Jointless, airless, water-tight—each one was a fine neat job.

He got out at Leicester Square and walked the rest of the way. He had to walk past the alley and come back, before he could slip in without being noticed. It was almost full night between the walls. In the wider passage at the back of the house there was rather more daylight left. He lifted the box through the open window of Ashton's room. The room, he saw, was empty and in darkness. He shut the window down gently.

Now he ought to clear off until it was time to meet Franklyn at Martha's. He hesitated at the entrance to the yard. Then he went in, and went into the Café Bar. He asked for a cup of coffee. "And I want to use the phone," he said to Giulia.

The café was crowded. He stood with his hand cupped over the mouthpiece and spoke into it under the noise round him. "... both going on well," he repeated, "that's fine." He had more to say, but the other end had no time for him and cut him off. He was left with his satisfaction on his hands.

Fine, he thought, fine—a girl, eh? He was sorry it was not a boy. Better luck next time, he said to himself.

He was excited. He stood himself another coffee, and then decided to eat something. He stood at the counter to eat, and smiled to himself. He looked good-tempered, yet Pizetti, who served him, felt a start of fear. Stick a knife in you as soon as look at you, he reflected nervously. He said so to Maddalena. She smiled, and patted his arm.

Ben was unwilling to move. He wanted to tell someone about his wife. But finally he left. It was dark outside and, after the heat in the café, cool. He walked quickly, humming below his breath, across the yard.

As he reached the archway four men stepped into it from the street; two were policemen, and another was as obviously a policeman in spite of his clothes and bowler hat. He recognized the fourth man a second later. It was Barley. "Yes, that's him," Barley said.

There was a door behind Ben. He pushed it open, stumbled in the darkness across an empty room and ran up the stairs. The police were coming behind him. He flung himself at a half-opened door. An old woman alone in the room started up and said rapidly:

"Was ist los? Oh, what is it? Is it the police?"

Charlotte Mannheim was half-undressed. She had an old grey dressing-gown round her shoulders, and she thrust her arms into it as she stumbled forward to shut the door he had left open. She was not in time to close it. The police pushed her out of the way as they came in. Anger and an old hatred sent the blood to her face. She shook with rage. She threw herself on one of the policemen, kicking him, and shouted:

"Get out. Get out of my room. Man-hunters!"

The policeman pushed her off and laid a large hand over her mouth. She bit it—with all her strength. She could feel her teeth in his flesh.

He swore, and shook his hand, shaking off drops of blood. Gripping her wrists he twisted her arms behind her back, and pushed and dragged her down the stairs behind the others.

She struggled. In the street she sank to her knees, so that they would have to drag her into the car. She noticed an old man standing in the circle of light round the street-lamp. He looked disgusted. "Can't you stop hurting her?" she heard him say.

The police shoved him roughly to one side. She would have spoken to him, but she was in the car. Exhausted, she fell forward and was jerked back. Tears of rage and pain ran over her face, and she tasted them on her lips.

Pop watched the police car drive off. He turned and walked, staggering as though he were drunk, across the

yard and began to go up the stairs to his room. He
changed his mind. He came down and went into the Café
Bar. He was not in the least drunk, but he wished he
could be—only he could not afford it, and besides there
was not time now. It was a quarter to eleven.

He saw the doctor at the counter and made his way over
to him. He's drunk as always, he thought; what a waste
of a human being! But then I, I'm not much to boast of.

"Well, how are you?" he said loudly.

"I don't ask you how you are, because I can see for
myself," Dr. Cleveland said, waving an arm. "You're old,
dirty; you have hardened arteries and the beginnings of
renal disease. One of these days I shall be exactly like you.
Well, what can I do for you?"

"You can hold your tongue," said Pop. He was
offended. Here he had been thinking about the man in
a human, civilized, friendly way, and he had insulted him.
What a beast! And what a shabby place this is, after all,
he said to himself. The disgust he had felt when he saw
the police twisting the arms of that old German woman
returned with doubled force. He took out his handkerchief
and coughed into it. Hateful, disgusting—I shall leave
this place to-morrow, he thought.

He forgot that it was the doctor he was annoyed with.
"I shall leave here," he said to him in a low voice.

"Oh, no, you won't," the doctor retorted. "You'll stay
as long as you have the will and the money to say where
you want to live. So shall I. Why the devil should you
go away? It's the same everywhere."

"You don't know what you're talking about," Pop said.
He looked into the other man's face and was startled for
less than a moment by its expression of fury and agony. He
forgot it at once. One can't remember everything. "If
I hadn't come here to live I might have had a respectable
position as a schoolmaster or a publisher or what not."

"Nonsense," Dr. Cleveland laughed.

"I mean it." He looked down at his hands. "My God,
how dirty my hands are. Why don't I wash them? The

fact is I've wasted my life, and now when I realize how vulgar, cruel, and beastly life has become nowadays I wish to heaven I'd been born a savage, a Malayan or something. There's a country for you! Anything will grow. No flies, or dust, no poor people, and the climate perfect. What more could you want?"

He rubbed his forehead. He was confused. Something had happened lately which had disgusted him, and he had already forgotten what it was. My head, my poor head, he thought; I really am old.

"Have you ever felt disgusted by yourself?" he asked the doctor.

The doctor stared at him without answering.

"Oh well, oh well, forget it," said Pop. "Forget everything."

"Why do you make a nuisance of yourself?" Dr. Cleveland said suddenly in a high screaming voice.

"I—I?" Pop stammered.

"Haven't I enough to put up with without your walking over me with your fly's legs? Don't I need peace as much as any other man? Don't I? Ah!" He bent forward and knocked his head on the counter. "Let me alone," he said, in the same voice. "I say, let me alone."

Pizetti came over to him and pulled at his shoulder. "Come, go to bed," he said firmly and gently. He looked round. "Help me," he said to a young man who was standing grinning behind Pop.

Between them they led the doctor to the foot of his staircase and left him to find his way up.

CHAPTER XXIII

ASHTON SWITCHED the light on in his room and saw the box lying immediately under the window. He pushed it behind the armchair, looking at his watch at the same time. A quarter to eleven. His mind jerked. At five ack emma. A moment later he thought, briefly: I've got the needle. It was precisely the feeling of apprehension and excitement mixed that he used to feel before an attack. He grinned.

Thomas came into the room carrying a registered letter. "This came for you this evening," he said. "I kept it, since you were out. I locked it up."

Ashton took it. "I'm late," he said energetically. "Had trouble with the car. Many people upstairs yet?"

"The place is about half full. Mr. Conolly and three friends of his came and went into the top room." He was getting Ashton's dress clothes out of the wardrobe as he talked. "I'd have had your things all ready for you, sir. But you'd taken the key of your room with you."

"It doesn't matter," Ashton said, without attending to him.

He had slit the envelope of his letter and was frowning at the single sheet of paper it had contained. Nice sort of registered letter, thought Thomas. He was disappointed for the Captain's sake; there ought to have been money. What fool would register an ordinary letter? He took Ashton's shirt out of the drawer and worked the studs into it. It came to him that the letter was a demand for money, sent in this way because all the previous demands had been ignored. He felt an intense contempt and affection, both together, for Ashton. His common sense revolted against Ashton's folly in starting the Screech Owl without enough money. He could have begun in a simpler way—he reflected again briefly on the possibilities of a small riverside place. But, no, he must risk everything on a chance that could only come off with incredible luck. He's like all of them, he thought; his eyes are too big for his stomach. It was Thomas's deep conviction, when he was still a soldier, that few of his officers had any *sense*, whatever other virtues they had. Why, only a fool, he thought, would have listened to that fellow offering to set fire to the place. He knew what had happened. The

Captain had been taken in by some windy talk and then —when the fellow really came to the point and explained his scheme—he had kicked him out quietly, because he knew he had been had.

Thomas knew nothing about Franklyn's second visit that morning. Ashton had sent him out of town on an errand.

Ashton dropped the registered letter in his desk and turned the key on it. He glanced at Thomas with an almost benevolent curiosity.

"Look here," he said abruptly, "what'll you do if we can't carry on here?"

Thomas looked at him with a stolid, unsmiling face. What'll *you* do, he wondered. "I shall be all right," he said. After a minute he asked quietly: "Is it as bad as that, sir?" Hasn't he anything left, then? he was thinking. But what a bleedin' fool!

"I don't know," Ashton said. He was speaking the exact truth. He had not thought of anything yet beyond getting his hands on the insurance money. When he had it he would decide what to do. The thought of Josephine crossed his mind again. "I don't know," he repeated, grinning.

"If you had any money at all," Thomas began slowly, "you could rent a place on the river or on one of the roads out of London—and work it up."

With an instinctive tact he refrained from saying at this moment that he was willing to work for nothing more than the run of his teeth until Ashton could afford to pay him.

"Yes, we might manage something like that," Ashton said lightly. Nothing was farther from his mind.

Thomas noted that he had said "We," and he felt a sardonic satisfaction. Well, he knows he can't do without me and he won't try, he reflected; seems he has that much sense. He said nothing more; it was not the moment. He finished putting away Ashton's clothes and went out to the hall. He had scarcely been there a minute when a man walked in and asked for Ashton by name. "Tell him my name's Rowse. He'll remember me." Thomas knocked on Ashton's door and, without going in, said: "There's a Mr. Rowse here, sir. He says you'll know him. Do you want to see him?" There was a pause, then Ashton's voice, clipped, slow.

"Send him in."

The man who came into the room was middle-aged, jaunty, well-dressed as to his suit. He was wearing as well a raincoat and a tweed cap. As Thomas shut the door behind him he heard Ashton say explosively:

"Why the hell are you wearing a cap?"

Ha, they were at school together, Thomas thought ironically.

This was not true. The sole relationship between Ashton and the man in front of him had to do with that one indubitably criminal episode in his post-war career. Ashton's irrelevant greeting surprised both of them. Why the devil did I say that? Ashton wondered.

"What the anything business is it of yours what I wear?" the other said, with mild truculence.

"What do you want?" asked Ashton.

He knew without asking. The fellow supposed he was doing well here for himself and intended to squeeze him. For a minute Ashton felt a horrible weakness. He was conscious of a weight in his stomach, and of a feeling almost of panic. He whipped up his anger. I've got to get rid of him, he thought desperately.

"Did you get my letter? Since I registered it, I imagine you did."

Ashton stepped forward and brought his hand down on the desk, flat open, with a crack. "Get out of here," he said, and with his other hand he took hold of the man's shoulder, feeling the arm thin and brittle under the cloth. Its thinness astonished him. Why, I could break it, he thought; I believe he's starving. He saw the other's air of truculence change to uncertainty and then to downright fear. He pressed cruelly on the bone and the thin layer of flesh round it. "Go on," he said, "get out, get out," and swung him round to the door. A wave of hate rose in

him; he felt the energy with which he could thrash and
kick the man out of his life. He let go of him. The man
leaned against the door for a second, opened it, and went

The pounding and jerking of his blood slackened. He
was warm, and an extraordinary breathless gaiety filled
him, a wild irresponsibility. Now he felt dead certain that
everything was coming right for him.

"Five ack emma," he said, choking with laughter.

He looked at himself in the glass—a fine figure of a man
Here's how, he thought. "Over you go, and the best of
luck."

He went upstairs to the main room. Looking from the
doorway he saw Josephine Rapp sitting at a table at the far
side; she was with the young airman. He watched her,
excitement pricking his skin. No reason why I shouldn't
have her, he thought; no reason why I shouldn't. He was
roused. Savagely now, he wanted her—herself as much,
no, more than the money. He began to go towards her,
pausing at one table to talk and then at another as he went.

CHAPTER XXIV

JOSEPHINE AND RANDALL had been sitting there
since half-past ten. She had asked him to bring her, and he
had agreed because innocently he imagined she was going to
speak to him about his flight. They had talked of a dozen
other things, jerkily, with lengthening pauses; she was not
making the faintest effort to be amusing this evening;
Randall was silent because he had nothing to say, except
on the one subject. Slowly, she became exasperated with
him. Even the fact that he was young vexed her. He is
stupid, a lout, she thought angrily. She looked at his long
thin body, in which every limb appeared to fit more loosely
than in other men's, and longed to punish him. Can't he
even sit upright? she thought.

Suddenly he said: "I didn't get far last night with your father." He forced himself to look directly at her.

"You wouldn't," she said indifferently. "He wants to buy this place—I mean New Moon Yard—and he can't get it. He's furious about it."

"Oh," Randall said.

Oh, she mocked him. And oh my God, how bored I am with him. He's thinking of his flight, she thought sarcastically. She could no longer pretend to be interested in it.

"I'm not going to fly any more," she said. "I'm tired of it."

He knew that he was dismissed and ridiculed. She might just as well have said plainly: You'll get no help from us, and you were a fool to think of it. He understood her. The whole of the frail bridge on which he had been walking for weeks collapsed, taking him with it, and he felt all the shock and horror in his body of the fall. He concentrated his strength on one thing—to seem unmoved. He would sooner kill her than show her what she had done. His bitterness was extreme.

"You might as well give it up as play at it," he said with calm irony. "You'd never have made a good pilot."

"You don't know," she cried, irritated.

"Of course I know," he said, smiling. "Haven't I been trying to teach you for weeks!"

She caught sight of Ashton at this moment. Instantly her anger against Randall turned to a piercing excitement. The change that came over her body when he spoke to her showed itself in her eyes and her gestures. And she felt the change in Ashton too. A tingling sense of triumph seized her; she looked at him with a gay ardent candour, and it was as though she were placing herself under his hands. She turned to Randall for a moment.

"You have to be up early, haven't you?" she said, smiling.

"Yes," he said, "but it doesn't matter." He felt choked with humiliation but he sat on, because he did not know how to get up and go away without awkwardness. He took no notice of the look that passed between Josephine and Ashton. Let them look at each other. At last, when he thought he would burst with suppressed fury if he sat any longer, he got up.

"Well, I must go," he said.

"Oh." She looked at him with a reckless brilliant smile. "Well, good night. It was so kind of you to bring me." She felt ashamed, relieved, vexed.

"Good night," Randall said. "Shall I tell them at the club that you're not coming again?"

"Yes, do." She laughed. "I don't owe them any money. I paid last week for another six hours. I've only used three."

"Afraid they won't give you your money back," he drawled.

"No, no, why should they?" Why doesn't he go? she thought, frenziedly impatient. Go, do go, her body said.

He went. He went straight out, across the dark, airless yard, to his room. The letter from his mother was lying on the top of the keys and the other things he had turned out of his clothes when he was changing. I don't want to answer it, he thought quickly, and he tore it up, tossing the pieces in the grate.

For no reason at all, he remembered a moment on a climbing party when he was at school. With another boy he had reached the top of a col before the rest. The other boy threw himself on the ground, while he remained standing, seized by a furious exhilaration which went through his body like a spasm of physical pain. He looked at the brilliant sky, at the shape of the hills on either side, at a cloud of astonishing burning whiteness and softness, and thought, I shall never forget this.

But why remember it now?

His sense of defeat overcame him. Half undressed, he sat down at the table and laid his hands on it, staring at them. What's the use of them? he thought. He remembered the quarrel with Harriet in the morning. I can't keep her from going to New York if she wants it, he thought dryly. I don't seem able to do anything.

Very well, then.

He decided to take Harriet on her own terms. They would marry and she would do as she liked, and he must make the best of it. He stood up.

Thomas watched without moving his eyes the Captain come downstairs with a young woman and take her into his room. The woman in the ladies' cloakroom peered out and saw it too. "A new one," she said under her breath, and looked at Thomas like a woman slyly calling attention to the gutter games of a child. Ashton opened his door again a minute later and shouted: "Bring me some sandwiches and a bottle of hock."

When he took it in to them the young woman was sitting on the arm of a chair, laughing, and turning her body about as she talked, like a woman pretending to dance. Her dress had no back, and in front only two strips parting in the hollow of her small breasts; she had long thin sun-browned arms. Thomas noticed all this without looking at her, and with a friendly cynicism.

When he had gone Ashton said:

"Will you eat now or—afterwards?"

"After what?" Josephine said, laughing.

She looked up at him as he stood almost over her; she felt flames like feathers parting this way and that in her body, touching her thighs, her small taut belly, her hard nipples. Her cheeks were burning, and her lips boasting with desire. Why play? she thought confusedly.

"Take this off," Ashton said. He laid his hand on her dress over her breasts.

She wriggled out of it, and took off the one garment she wore under it, kicking the sandals from her bare feet. Delight in him opened in her; she lifted herself against him and hung on him. She was not, he found when he was lifting her on to the bed, at all light; her body was slender but it was curiously solid. It was cold too, when he touched it.

She sat up with his dressing-gown round her and ate sandwiches with the frank greed of a schoolgirl. "Ah, these are good," she laughed. "How clever you were." She lifted her face. "Kiss me."

Ashton had dressed. He kissed her, running his fingers over her shoulders, acting a pleasure he did not feel any longer. Almost with anger he had realized that it was a mistake, he had never been in love with her: he loved so many million pounds, a comfortable flat, horses, that free secure life. He thought with a greedy passion about the safety, the full monotonous life he could live on Josephine's money. The image of Rowse, his shoddy jaunty good looks, crossed his mind; he felt contempt and disgust. Revulsion took his thoughts as far back as possible. He began to talk to her about his life when he was a boy, and then, afraid that he was boring her, he said abruptly:

"That man, you know, the porter, was my servant in France. I picked him up again quite by accident——"

"Oh, the War," she said, smiling. "It must have been exciting in its way." The smile lengthened to a yawn. "I was about six when it ended. I can't remember anything. Isn't it a shame?"

"You can't——" he began. He was stupefied. Of course —it was nineteen years ago. I'm in an awful state, he thought; what's happening to me? He felt strangely heavy.

Josephine questioned him about the club. She was intensely curious; she tried to probe into his life to find out if there were other women in it, but her comments on the Screech Owl were shrewd and searching. She might have been buying it. He lied. He told her that the turnover was regular and certain and the profits growing. He would not trust her with the truth about himself. He spoke casually about "my own income," as if it were apart from the club. As if he ran the place as a joke.

"Let me fill your glass," he said.

"Here's to to-morrow," she laughed. She leaned forward so that her mouth was close to his cheek. "We'll have a lovely time. We won't waste a day of our lives. You must come to Austria this summer when we go. You will, won't you? Promise."

She leaned against him, and he stared over her head, smiling, his face stiff, while he calculated how long his money would last. If he got as much as half the insurance money—and then there were bills. How long is it going to take me to marry her? he asked himself, with a dry excited triumph. He had no doubt that he would do it—it was a question of time. Time is the essence of the contract, he said to himself smiling.

François came into the kitchen and found Simon leaning against the table, smoking. Between midnight and one o'clock, people did not eat. About half-past one they began ordering breakfasts—kippers, eggs and bacon with fried bananas—on the hottest nights.

"Have you any coffee?" he said. "Give me a cup if you have."

"Headache?" Simon asked.

He poured two large cups of black coffee, one for himself. "No."

The waiter's colourless lips were drawn, his cheek twitching. He looked absently into Simon's face and said in his low voice:

"My wife has gone, d'you see, left me. When I got home last night she was gone. She had taken part of her clothes and left the others packed, for me to send on. There was a letter on the table in the kitchen. She put it there, you see, where I should get it at once. She——" He stopped. He was feeling as much agony as hurt pride. "Perhaps I should have known," he said.

Known what? Simon made a long face. "That's a bad show," he said with energy.

"Yes, I think so," François said quietly. "It is a rotten show. It's not right, not decent. Decent women don't run away—that's what I think." His pale eyes were stubborn, unmoving. "In her letter she said I should divorce her. I have to think about it. I don't know how, in this country—one of the regular customers, I know him, is a lawyer—I heard another customer say it. Perhaps I go to him and ask him to-morrow, I know his name." He paused. "What I think, you see, it's not a decent thing to do. Not what a decent woman should have done."

"I'm sorry about it," Simon mumbled. "You'll get over it, though."

"I think so too," the waiter said, after a moment.

He turned and went out, back to the room. On the stairs he stood still, trying to breathe quietly, to draw a long quiet breath past this knotted obstruction in his chest. He pressed his hand on it. Like his face, his hand was pale, firm, sensible-looking—and delicate and strong. It felt his heart beating and tried convulsively to press that down, too. His mind knew nothing about this: as he stood there he felt perfectly calm except for this agonized breath. I think so too, I think so too, he repeated. He almost felt relief that it was over, settled.

But, he thought, a woman like me would not have done it. It is because she had different ideas—she is not a woman like me. He meant that she was not of his class. She has disgraced herself because she knows nothing better, he thought, obstinately and quietly. If she came back now he would not keep her, he would send her off.

My God, I am sorry for her, he said to himself. His face twitched again. He felt a torturing regret and pity. Perhaps it is all my fault, he thought.

Simon got out the bottle of rum and two glasses, and was measuring it out. At this time Thomas generally came upstairs. "Ah, here you are," he called, hearing him on the stairs.

"Come up for my rum ration," Thomas said. His face wore its closed, scarcely perceptible smile.

"Well, good health."

"Good health."

"Franky was up here just now," Simon said. He gazed down his long tapering nose. "His wife's left, gone off with somebody."

Thomas grunted, "Ah." He was sitting down, knees apart, hand on his thigh, placid, sardonic, and reflective. "Glad I never married. No offence. Not my line. That's all."

The chef's smile was ambiguous. "Women," he said in his slovenly voice. "Women. They'll get at you if you let them, and in some other way if you let 'em know you won't!" He rolled his eyes. "Trust them," he said.

"You mean don't," Thomas said.

He felt the last drops of rum in his throat, and stood up. "That's good," he said. "Best thing in the world. Better than any of your women, good or bad." He stood with his head lowered. "I've often thought if we could run some place without women messing it up. The boss— me." He added: "And you and Franky, if you felt like it. Well—so long."

"So long," Simon said. And blast you, he thought. Blast the whole world. Blast everyone in it.

This brief commination service relieved and put him at ease with himself. You make your own life, he thought. Be damned if you do, he thought; and it comes to the same thing in the short run. Take it *and* leave it.

CHAPTER XXV

THE DARKNESS showed her only the folds of the sheet, like a retreating wave, and the window. She had the feeling that the four wings of the house, the warren of rooms as diverse as their tenants, held its breath with her— and breathed when she did. She sighed. She had not simply dreamed it, then. The knocks on the door were real.

Stumbling, she got out of bed and stood close to the door and said: "Is anyone there?"

"Harriet," Randall said quietly.

She unlocked the door quickly. "Oh, is it you?" she said foolishly.

"Yes, unless you wish it weren't."

He came in.

"Then what would you be?" murmured Harriet.

"Absent. Absent with leave."

She shivered, partly through being roused from deep sleep, and partly from one of those shapeless apprehensions that haunt the uncleared margins of words. "Never leave me." But, oh, why did I say that? she thought. She was ashamed as only the young can be ashamed of giving away the extent of their helplessness.

"I'm not going to leave you," Randall said. Since she was silent he persisted. "Why did you say that? Tell me—tell me at once. Why?"

"No, I can't tell you," she answered. "It meant nothing. I was asleep—you startled me, you know."

"Tell me, Harriet."

They were standing side by side in the dark room—it was absurd, Harriet thought—as though they had been strolling together talking and had only stopped to settle some point. She glanced at him stealthily. He was looking over her head towards the window. He is much too thin, she thought irrelevantly; his dressing-gown is too short, he must have worn it for years and years. Very gently, since she was afraid to touch his hand, she touched the stuff. It gave her confidence: more, it gave her a strange assurance of happiness to be here in the dark shabby room, sunk in the night, in London, as though this moment might persist forever, forever staring at the grey oblong of the window, as close to the young man as to be able to touch him if she wished, and yet free. We are free, she thought, with a fiery pride. I needn't be afraid. We are closer together now than we have been for a long time.

"It was because you didn't come to see me this evening,"

she said slowly. "I sat up, waiting for you, until ten o'clock. Then I was tired and I went to bed. I was very tired to-day."

"I was taking Josephine Rapp out to dinner and to the Screech Owl," Randall said abruptly.

"Oh." She was startled, then held herself rigid, waiting for the shock that must come next. Two evenings running—He is in love with her, she thought, not yet feeling the blow: she was borne up by the excitement of receiving it. So I'm too late.

She meant that she was too late with her decision—she had come to it just before she fell asleep—to give up New York. And now that, since she was alone, she could go to any corner of the earth if she wished it, she felt utterly uninterested. Everything was as flat as a worn penny.

"Let's sit down," she mumbled.

"I didn't come in to tell you because I hoped—I thought —it might mean that she had talked to her father about the flight," Randall went on. He was not listening to her, but he sat down. "I didn't want to come to you again with nothing more than plans. Not after this morning."

"This morning?" Harriet echoed. She was confused. She jumped up and stood trying to see his face clearly, to see whether it wore its normal expression of reserve and half-smiling indifference.

"We quarrelled," Randall said.

"Did we?" What does it matter—now? she thought, I shall tell him everything—everything. "Listen, please, Bill. Perhaps it isn't important—but I've decided not to go to New York."

"And Rapp won't put up any money for a flight. I ought to have known it. I was a fool."

I knew it, she thought. She did not know what to say. "What a shame," she said at last.

Randall smiled. He put his hand out sharply and made her sit down again, keeping his arm round her. "What did you say?" he exclaimed. "You want to go to New York, don't you? Why give it up?"

"Yes, I wanted to go." She was making an effort. "But not so much as I want to be with you. That is, if you still want it."

"Yes, I want it," Randall said.

He should have said more than this. He ought to tell her that he loved her more than anyone in the world. That he had come to tell her she could go, he would marry her on her terms. He struggled. The words would not come. He was only beginning to feel safe in her hands. He could not completely trust her—not at once—not yet.

"I have not asked you about China," Harriet said in a low voice.

"No. I'm not going," he said. "I wasn't going. It's too fantastic. Like my record flight," he said, in a different voice.

Harriet was caught by the pity of love. Oh, dear God, give him anything he wants, even risks, even danger, she cried.

She turned to him blindly. "Don't leave me yet."

"Not yet?" Randall said.

"Not for years. Not for many, many years. Let's be old with each other! Let's remember our lives when we're old!"

She was crying, but it was for some grief so buried in her mind that it was indistinguishable from some joy. We are not only animals.

"Shall I stay now?" Randall said.

Without waiting for any answer he made her lie down and he lay beside her. "Shall I stay?" he repeated.

"Is it my heart—or yours?" Harriet asked.

"What?"

"Yours, it's yours."

"Harriet, do you mind?"

"I mind nothing." I hear nothing. I see nothing. I am nothing, she thought.

Sitting on the side of her bed Mrs. Caracas worked a finger between each toe in turn. She watched with warm satisfaction fragments of black coming away as she rubbed, and brushed them off her foot on to the sheet. She did both feet, and sniffed at her fingers afterwards with a vague smile. She was pleasantly sleepy. Her old withered eyelids rose and fell like an infant's in strong light. It was not the light in the room—a candle burning on the commode by her bed—but the warmth. The window, opened for a short time at the full heat of the sun, had been closed now for hours, so that at midnight the room was filled with hot stagnant air.

Like Barcelona that time, she thought, with me and Bertha and two girls dressed-up French monkeys in that caffy as they said it was and we waltzed round between all the tables and a man and Bertha said Keep your paw off my —— and they all laughed not knowing a word what she said and the other man yelled out Kaygappo kaygappo right in my face I said to the French girl What's he mean kaygappo? she said God knows and I said Oh I thought it was French or some monkey talk or other and she tore my dress and the Spaniards shouting and laughing fit to split and Bertha doublemarched back to help me oh my God all gone all gone and the flowers on the whatedtheycallit the Ramblas hot it was sun flames a white wall with no windows burning slow thick black shadows in the church the fountain. Geese were they? Women. All gone all my triumph all my looks my legs you don't know when you're well off do you?

"If only Bertha was here," she said below her breath, "she'd help me."

If I'd helped her that time when I, she didn't mean it, not my fault at all not I could look up that boy of hers a man now children of his own I suppose wife house or if he's out of work I could but careful not let them think I have money that they can come begging wife not well children but help in small ways I might why not? not so lonely that way.

She saw herself in the garden of that cottage she would have soon, children standing decorously in a group beside her, eager clean rosy faces, smiling: she smiled.

Time now to go to sleep, she thought, sighing. She pinched the wick of the candle between wetted finger and thumb and lay down, pulling the sheet over the rough edge of the quilt under her chin. Her mind was placidly happy with odds and ends of feelings, dissolving into a fog of sleep. The smell of the dead wick came to her nostrils. She was lying in her mother's bed in the front bedroom. Half rousing she smelled the candle; then darkness; her mother's warm heavy body altering the shape of the bed, heavy arm laid over her. She wriggled her thin back until her bottom was pressed tight against her mother's stomach. That's right, the mother said, slurring the words, like a bee humming against the window: that's my good little Doshie, keep both of us warm to-night. Both. To-night. To-night. Till we meet again.

Sarah Barley woke, fighting and sobbing. She had dreamed again of the fire. In her sleep she pushed against Lucy, sending her against the wall, so that the little girl woke and said crossly: "Stop it, our Sarah." Then Sarah woke with a long-drawn sobbing breath—ah-h-h-h-h. It was frightening.

She was so hot, the sweat running over her body, that, still half asleep, she got out of bed. The bedroom door opened gently and her mother came in. She was in her nightgown, and she was holding the enamel candlestick from her bedroom. She shielded the flame with her free hand.

"What's all this?" she said in a low voice. "Lie down, Lucy. Sarah, what are you doing out of bed?"

She set the candle down on the chair by the door, and stooped to look into the little girl's face.

"It was—I thought there was a fire," Sarah said, abashed.

"Well, you see there isn't," her mother said. "Get back into bed."

Sarah got back obediently and lay down. She looked up at her mother, who seemed taller leaning over the bed.

The candle spreading a feeble yellow light behind her sent her shadow over the wall and ceiling. She was not angry. Tucking the sheet round the two children in silence, she turned taking up the candle to go.

"Now no more nonsense," she said in the same low voice. "Go to sleep."

She touched Sarah's cheek lightly and with a long glance at the boy, who had slept all through it, she went out, closing the door noiselessly.

Lucy was already dropping off to sleep again. She sighed and pushed the sheet away. Sarah did not move. She could still feel the roughened skin of her mother's fingers on her cheek. She was strangely roused. Something—perhaps the contrast between the mother leaning over her in all her strength and assurance and the indistinct old woman who was the mother in her dream—pierced her mind. It was like the contrast between the often harsh daytime woman and the soft-speaking reassuring figure of the mother at night. I have two mothers, she thought. Her heart contracted with love, but it was for the harsh, the ageing woman, more than for the other. It was as though without any understanding she had felt the poignancy of her mother's life, her middle-age, her thickening heavy body, her not yet defeated spirit.

For a short time she listened to the music in the night club across the yard. It stopped. She was sleeping.

CHAPTER XXVI

FRANKLYN STOOD outside Ashton's window in the cul-de-sac. Between the wall of the house and the other wall it was pitch dark. He touched the rough concrete facing of the house. It was three o'clock. He had waited for Ben, then come on without him. On the way he thought with a cold vicious anger about punishing him. After five years I didn't expect him to let me down, he thought. His garage, he said to himself with contempt. I'd give him garage.

Now that he was here alone, with the job to do, he put everything else out of his mind. Ben carried the tools for opening the box, and he had had to get others at an inconvenient hour.

He pushed open the window at the bottom and stepped into the dark room.

Opening the box and disposing of the powdered aluminium and paraffin-soaked wood-wool shavings was also Ben's job. Franklyn had decided when he was in the room in the morning where to plant them. He went quickly to work. His torch was of the kind which lights when set upright. He had placed it on the floor by the box.

He opened the window at the bottom as widely as it went, to be able to get out quickly. Then he moved the bed and piled the whole contents of the box against that wall, the inner wall. He prepared the fuse—what Ben called "the poke." As he was doing it the thought crossed his mind that it was a small room. He should perhaps use less. A shiver of hatred for Ben sprang through him.

Now, he thought.

He ran to the window. There was an explosion, not loud, between it and him, and a livid uprush of flame.

He sprang back. What did I do wrong? he thought. He stumbled to the door and across the hall to the door into the yard.

Thomas was running down the stairs. He saw the man bolting out of the room and went after him, but Franklyn was already out. Thomas turned back. Thick curling bolsters of smoke were stretching out of Ashton's room.

Franklyn ran across the yard towards the street. He was almost there when he saw policemen coming in under the archway. God! that's what Ben did, he thought. He ran back across the yard to the corner farthest from the Screech Owl and the street. A door opened when he flung himself at it, it had been pulled-to without fastening; he stumbled in the close darkness up the stairs.

The pain in his left arm brought him to a sudden halt. He had not noticed it until this instant. It was like teeth biting the flesh. I'm burned, he thought. He felt sick with it. He trembled for a second and went on. There was a narrow landing. He ran up the next flight of stairs, afraid now of his arm. He was thinking, I ought to get to a doctor.

On the top landing he stood still, taking a long tense breath. He could see nothing. Then he saw a skylight above his head.

"If I could reach that," he muttered.

A door opened suddenly on his left hand, and a man came out and ran down the stairs. Franklyn crouched. He could have touched the man by putting his hand out. The door through which he had come was half open. Franklyn walked into the room, where a woman, standing naked, had begun to dress herself.

"Get out," Mrs. Kerr shouted. She took a step towards him, as she was. She actually raised her fists. "I say get out whoever you are."

Franklyn stepped round her, took the backs of two chairs in his uninjured hand, and dragged them on to the landing. He placed one on top of the other, and climbed up to the skylight. It was open.

He got out on to the roof. His left arm was hurting him intolerably. He looked once down into the yard and saw that the fire was springing merrily in the angle of the building. It was spreading to the Café Bar. There was a boiling stew of people in the yard. The police had formed a line round the entrance to the club; women with necks and arms pallid in the glare were running out past it. Damn them, why aren't they burning? he thought with fresh hatred.

He was furious with all this scrambling about roofs and running. At my age, he said to himself.

Lying on his stomach, he slid the few inches until his

feet fetched up against the low parapet round the roof, and crawled along the gutter. He passed two windows. When he reached the end nearest the street the parapet came to an end. In any case he could not have got down anywhere here. There was another skylight. He dragged himself to it. Impelled by fear and rage he worked himself through it backwards until his legs were hanging through inside the house; the edge of the skylight cut into his stomach. He gripped the edge with his right hand. He was gasping. If the other side of the yard had gone up in flames at this second he would not have noticed it.

He let himself slide down, trying to fling his body sideways to save the injured arm. His weight wrenched his hand from the edge and he dropped. He dropped on to his feet. His left arm had scraped along the edge of the skylight and it was like a white-hot rake passing over it. He bit back a groan.

Doors stood open on both sides of the landing; the light was on in both the rooms. There were heavy footsteps below on the stairs. A man's voice, a policeman, shouted:

"Get outside. Everyone out of here."

A young woman ran out of the left-hand room and called: "There's only me, and I'm coming in a minute."

She had a suitcase open in her hand. She ran across the landing into the other room, leaving the door open, and began to shove things into it. She picked up a man's black overcoat and held it over her arm. Yes, I'll have that, Franklyn thought swiftly. His best, his only chance, was to cover up the blackened rags of his left sleeve and get out through the police as if he lived in the place. I'll take the suitcase too, he thought.

The girl started aside when he went at her. He knocked her down hard and snatched the suitcase.

Some person, a man, was running up the stairs. "Be quick, Harriet," he shouted. He saw the girl on the ground and Franklyn in the same instant. Franklyn pitched the case at him with the last of his strength, and ran back away from the stairs. In the light from the room he saw that a passage went along the back of the rooms on this floor. He ran along it stumbling and panting. I could have been along here ten minutes ago, he thought with rage.

He started down the other staircase. There were police on the landing below him. He had lost his nerve. He turned back. The chairs were still where he had placed them under this skylight. He rushed at them and climbed out on to the roof again, kicking them over with his foot at the last. His lungs were fit to choke him. All this at my age, he thought again, bitterly.

He lay huddled against the parapet. He raised his head and saw the head and shoulders of a man through the skylight. He got up, ran a few steps, and fell sideways. His knees were caught by the edge of the parapet. He threw his arms out and fell over into the yard.

Half out of the skylight, Randall saw it happen; he ducked involuntarily; but there was no scream. He let himself drop to the floor and ran back to Harriet.

The Pizettis were roused when the police came into the yard. Gregorio leaped out of bed at the moment a policeman started to hammer at the door of the café downstairs. He could smell smoke. He rushed at once to Giulia's room across the passage. She was sitting up in bed, and as he opened the door her face, pale in the darkness, turned slowly to him. She seemed terrified.

"Get up, get up," her father said urgently. "There's a fire. Can't you smell burning? The police are here."

"Shall we be burned?" she murmured.

Gregorio put his hand on her shoulder. Even at this moment he noticed that it was round and smooth like an egg under his hand. "No, no, of course not," he said. "But get up. We must go." He raised his voice. "Maddalena," he shouted, "the girl's frightened to death."

"I'm coming at once," Maddalena called.

Her mother's voice roused the girl from her nightmare of terror; she started up and took her clothes from the chair.

"Bring them with you," her father said.

He ran back to his own room. Maddalena was partly

dressed. She was pushing a few things into a pillowcase.
Smoke was coming into the room through the window.
Pizetti snatched the key of the "office" from the bed—he
slept with it under his pillow—and ran madly along the
passage to the back staircase, as narrow and awkward as a
ladder, that led to the kitchen. A cloud of smoke rushed
up to him. He plunged into it. Coughing and choking,
he stumbled half-way down. It was becoming hot. He
heard the rending noise of wood in a fire. Pressing his
hands over his mouth and nose he went a few more steps.

It was no use. He could not go on into a furnace. The
side of the café next to the night club was blazing; the
"office" and the farther side of the kitchen were in flames.
He felt his lungs bursting as he drew the smoke into them.
Maddalena, a cloth pressed over her mouth, dragged him
back just when he was going to collapse. "The box, the
box," he groaned. He coughed and coughed.

The common stairs leading to the upper floor and down
into the yard were at the other end of the passage. Smoke
came thickly from them. The flames in the café had
spread there already. Maddalena was completely calm.
"Come, we must go as far as we can—to the top floor,"
she said. She patted Gregorio on the back, and frowned
sternly and menacingly on her daughter.

The stairs to the top floor ended in a short passage between the two attics. One of them, Pop's room, was open
and dark. Maddalena knocked on the door of the other.
There was no answer. She knocked again, louder, and
called. Giulia was shivering, and her father put his arm
round her.

"Who's there? Whaderyou want?" Enid Jones said.

"This house is on fire," Maddalena said in a sharp voice.
"Get up. Open the door."

She had tried it and it was locked. She wanted to get
into the room, which was farthest from the fire, and shout
to the police to fetch a ladder. She had shouted once
already from Giulia's window, but the confusion in the
night club and their efforts to control it were occupying

the police so thoroughly that no one noticed her, and her voice was not heard above the noise.

Pizetti had run into the other attic. He came out with a chair and stood on it to reach the skylight. "We could get on to the roof," he said energetically, "and get along it to the next staircase."

"I can't squeeze through that," his wife said.

"Yes you can, mamma," Giulia implored her. "We'll drag you through. We shall be burned to death if we wait here."

Enid Jones had not answered. When Maddalena banged again on her door she screamed abusive words. They could hear her thudding about the room, and opening drawers.

Maddalena shrugged her shoulders. "You go on to the roof," she said to her husband. "You and Giulia go that way, and you can bring a ladder for me."

"Either we all go, or all of us stay," Gregorio said quietly.

Giulia only looked at her mother.

"Very well," Maddalena said calmly. "And if I stick in that place it will be your fault. Or mine for swelling like this. You go first," she said to Giulia.

The girl scrambled through easily. She lay down on the roof, her feet braced against the parapet, and helped her mother as well as she could while Gregorio pushed her from beneath. As soon as Maddalena was safely out, she sank down in the gutter behind the parapet in a fit of laughter. She was helpless with laughter. She infected Giulia, and when Pizetti climbed out he thought that both women were hysterical. He gazed at them in despair, and groaned.

"Every penny is burned," he groaned.

His wife sobered at once. "You go in front," she said to him in a sharp voice.

They crept along the gutter on hands and knees, round the angle of the house, to the next skylight, which was open. Pizetti got through it easily, and called out: "There are two chairs here on the floor. I'll hold them for you to get on to." He heard a stifled sound from the roof. "And for pity's sake don't start laughing," he shouted fiercely. He waited. His wife's legs, in grey stockings and grey cotton knickers, came through the skylight. He seized her feet and guided them to the chair, and she came slowly down. She was trembling now and leaned against him for a minute. In the meantime Giulia had got through without help. They went down the stairs.

Now that their lives were safe the full weight of his misfortune burst over Pizetti. He could have broken into tears. If he had had a knife in his hand he would have tried to cut his throat. Why go on living, without a penny, without hope, without courage? He had lost all three, and his future seemed blacker than this staircase. Maddalena knew what he was suffering. She said nothing. For the moment she was unable to comfort him and she needed comfort herself.

At the foot of the stairs old Mrs. Caracas was standing gaping towards a little group of people in the yard in front of the cabinet-maker's door. She turned eagerly to Mrs. Pizetti, clutching her wrist. "He fell," she said excitedly, "right off the roof. I saw it. I'd just that second got as far as here, and the policeman said, You can stand up now, can't you, ma? and then he fell. Coo, look at it, I said. You stop here, the policeman said, and off he went, leaving me to m'self. I might have dropped."

"What fell? Who is it?" Pizetti said dully.

"Stay with Giulia," his wife said. She stepped over to the group of four people. A man was lying on the ground. She knelt. "Is he dead?" she asked quietly.

"His back is broken, I think," a man answered.

At this moment Franklyn opened his eyes. He saw the woman kneeling beside him, and looked at her with hatred. He wanted to say, You pushed me over, but he was unable to articulate a single word. Then he saw Ashton.

"We've sent for the doctor," Ashton said. He was looking into Franklyn's face as he said it, and Franklyn stared back with a look of malevolence. A man, the police doctor, pushed himself between Franklyn and Ashton's face, but he saw it again when the doctor turned to speak to someone behind him. He saw that Ashton was murderously afraid of anything he could say. I'll ruin him, he thought. He tried to speak. The effort he was making was so terrible that he thought his voice would be heard outside in the street.

He had not made a sound. Maddalena closed her eyes for an instant, and made the sign of the cross. She got up.

"He's gone now," the police doctor said. "Pity."

It might have been Gregorio, or one of us, Maddalena thought, in fear. She glanced up at the roof and wondered how she had had the courage to crawl along it. Money, she thought recklessly, what is money compared with life? She would not feel like this always, she knew, but for these minutes she would cling to it.

She was hurrying back to her husband when her elbow was seized from behind. She turned round. It was the old man from the attic above their bedroom. Above what had been their bedroom. Flames were thrusting from the windows like jagged teeth.

"D'you see that?" cried Pop. "D'you see that? Why, I might have been up there, I might have been frying like a rasher, on both sides, if I hadn't happened to be out of bed when it started. I got up, well, never mind what I got up for, anyway I looked out of the window and saw a man running out of the Screech Owl and I thought he'd been chucked out. Then I saw a curl of smoke, just a finger coming round the door, and I thought My God, I thought, the place is on fire and I dressed and hopped down the stairs and people were running out of the club, and the police shouting Take your time, take your time, and my word it was lucky they were here. There'd have been a panic. I always knew it would burn sooner or later, but now where shall I go? Can you tell me? I don't know, upon my soul I don't know. And to think I might have been burned to death! I have nine lives."

He was scratching himself, and lifting his feet in excitement, like a hen.

"You didn't take the trouble to warn us when you ran out," Mrs. Pizetti said.

He was not abashed. "Oh, I knew you'd be all right," he said easily.

The fire had eaten deeply into the Screech Owl; it was blazing inside, and the heat from it had become unpleasant. Why isn't the fire-engine here? Mrs. Pizetti wondered. The police had shepherded all the guests out of the yard except a few men who were handling the cars into the street. Only a single car could get through the archway at a time, and the cars that had been got out first were still blocking the narrow street outside and the police were struggling to move them into a side street to let the fire-engines through.

In the yard Ashton was working hard—excited, happy, completely master of the situation. He was smiling, a slight excited smile. He and Thomas handled the cars together. He shouted his orders. "Here you are, man. Jump to it!"

Thomas jumped.

"Come," Maddalena Pizetti said to her husband. "We must go."

"Go? Where?" he said.

Then someone screamed.

"That woman!" Maddalena gasped.

Enid Jones was kneeling on the sill of her window, a narrow attic window, clutching the sides with both hands, and screaming, a thin breathless sound above the noise of the fire and the confusion.

The knocking on the door entered and had possessed her mind before she woke. She was a child lying in a bed with an iron rail at the foot; light poured through the window behind the rail, and there was nothing else, the light, the bar of iron, floating in the centre of space. She saw it one moment, with intense clarity; then she was struggling up in bed in her room. She heard Mrs. Pizetti's voice.

She began to sweat, her heart pounding. What's it mean? she thought in panic: what's come? She shouted.

"This house is on fire. Get up. Open the door."

She pushed back the bedclothes. It's what that nigger said. She felt giddy. I can't move, she thought.

Anger poured in over her fear. Open the door indeed. What a sauce! I shan't answer her, she thought. I'll not have them trooping in here to save themselves. What next! She stood up, swaying. Her soiled feet, yellow-white, the toes calloused, curled back from the floor. She heard voices again in the passage and felt pleased that she was ignoring them. Impudence, bawling at me like that. She walked unsteadily to the window. She had an awful dropping of the heart when she saw the smoke, and the moving heap of people outside the night club. Her legs felt weak.

She ran back to the bed. What'll I take? she thought. Jerking back the door of the wardrobe, she knocked the slop-pail and it splashed over the floor and her feet.

"I'm fed up with this bloody place," she shouted. "Fed up. Fed up. Well, you're going now, kid, aren't you? Going, going, gone. Where am I? Where'd I put m'bag?"

She felt over the table and touched it. All my money, she thought, sweating. She had pushed her feet into her pair of best shoes; the left foot felt queer, and she thought, I believe they're the wrong ones. She was too flustered now, her hands wet and trembling, to change. She took two dresses and a coat over her arm and stumbled to the door. The key had fallen down as usual. "Blast it," she said, "blast it, blast it." She went down on his hands and knees and felt for it on the carpet. The clothes she was holding bothered her, falling round her hands. She dropped them; and swept at them with her arm. "Get out of my way." Her hand struck the key and knocked it across the room. She heard it strike the wall near the bed.

I can smell the fire, she thought. She scrabbled on the floor again and found the key. She had dropped the bag.

She opened the door and ran along the passage; her legs were jerking. "Oh God, God, God, God, God."

She ran back from the smoke and heat of the staircase into her room. "Smoke—I can't see it but it's got in here now," she screamed. "Take it away, can't you. Take it away." She ran over to the window, screaming.

The ledge of the window cut into her bare flesh. After a minute it brought her to her senses. She made out Mrs. Pizetti and shouted: "Whadyou leave me for? Bastards. Saving your own dirty skins and leaving me to burn. Dirty aliens. Dirty foreigners. Aliens."

The smoke pouring from the Pizettis' bedroom over the café was streaked with flame. She screamed again. A man, a policeman, shouted something to her, but she was making too much noise herself to hear what he said. Then she saw Mrs. Kerr. She was dressed—even wearing her fox fur. She came forward, cupping her hands round her mouth, and called:

"You're all right. It's all right. They're bringing the ladders."

"All right, am I?" she shouted back. Resentment sobered her for a moment. To stand there like that, got up, and tell me I'm all right, when I. But it's always the same thing. Any lie—everyone lying to me and downing me because I'm not as bad as they are. She closed her eyes: and opened them again in fear.

"Keep hold, kid," Mrs. Kerr said in her strong sharp voice. "It's only for a minute now. You're all right."

I'm not, she thought; they're pretending. I'm going to fall. She tried to get back into the room but moving her leg made her feel giddy and she clung again desperately to the sides of the window. I'm alone up here. They let me stop here and went off themselves. It always happens to me like that, I never had a chance. Her sight went black. She thought, I'll jump down now and fool them.

"Don't shift about, kid. Only a minute now."

Terror seized her again, and she threw herself forward dumbly.

Stop, she thought, stop.

"Don't let Giulia see," Pizetti said.

"She's not here."

"Where is she, then?"

He began to walk anxiously across the yard. His wife pulled at his arm. "Leave her alone for a minute."

Giulia leaned against Bert when he put his arm round her, not because she wanted to but because he was steady on his feet and broad. It was as useful as leaning against a wall. He held her with one arm, the other hand stroking her hair. She was not crying, he saw, when she freed herself gently and stepped back.

"Poor Bert," she said, looking at him. "You've lost everything, too. Your money was all in with ours—in the box. That box!"

"Never mind," he said.

"You do mind. Of course you do."

"It doesn't matter."

He felt a pang as he said it—disappointment rather than another emotion. His plans, to begin training as a chef this winter, had shrivelled up with the money. He was out of a job now, too. His eyes glazed over, in the effort of thinking. Let be, he thought, shaking himself as he used to when he was a boy and his old man dusted him.

"What'll you do now?" he asked.

"I don't know," Giulia said. "They'll think of something." She smiled, and lifted her head back. "I shall try to get back into that shop. Or into some other shop— it won't make any difference, they're all exactly alike. I shall be a young lady again—*Miss Pi-zetty*. Can't you hear it? *What do you use on your skin, dear?* I tell them, Nothing, and they're offended. Of course, if you don't *want* to tell, they say. It's really dreadful. They're dreadful. They can't cook, they've never learned anything about it, they don't do anything."

She was laughing. Her eyes glittered with tears. She shook them away, and laughed, and patted Bert's cheek. "Forgive us for letting your money get burned," she said.

The fire was spreading. The house was full of wood, old wood, straw-dry. The Screech Owl was a bonfire, and Pizetti's place. The police began to clear the last few watchers out of the yard. Mrs. Caracas lifted a corner of the blanket she had folded over the cats when she pushed them into the dress basket. Her hands, trembling, passed over the warm fluent bodies. Two, three, four. Gone, she thought. No, no, not mother's best and brightest. She set the basket down and looked in it. Her face quivered. It was the yellow tom that was missing. He slipped out, she thought. It was when that woman fell, I was looking, not thinking about them then, and he must have flew like a shadow. Where, where?

She sent a frantic glance round the yard. Looking up, with anguish she saw him pushing his head and thick stout body between the flower-pots, on the windowsill of her room. She called, imploring him, in a plaintive voice.

"Come back. Lovely one. Sweet. Come, come, lovely."

He took not the slightest notice of her. She saw his tail, straight up. He's in one of his prides, she thought, with despair. Come to mother. He won't. Never in this world. I must. Before they lay hands on me.

Tucking the blanket firmly over the others, she hurried on shaking feeble legs into the house, clinging to the stairs with her hands to help her up. The glare from the Screech Owl lit her room. She stumbled across the room, calling.

"Pussens. Bad pussens. Mother's bad boy."

He turned his head back, and looked coldly, with fixed points of eyes, in her face. She tried to pick him up. He poured between her hands and rushed round the room, leaping in excitement from chair to bed and bed to wardrobe. Ha, he's mad, she thought. Panting after him, she caught her foot. I'm going to fall. It was a shock; she was a minute or two getting up. She let herself drop into a chair, closing her eyes, and breathed deeply.

The cat startled her, bounding on to her knees, warm sagging weight. How long have I? she thought, getting up. She coughed the smoke from her throat. Holding the creature tightly she stumbled on to the landing. Smoke rushed against her from the staircase, and a blast of flame. It's underneath in Barley's, she thought. All that wood. It's come, then. She ran back.

"God, Caracas, Bertha, save me," she said.

The cat slipped from her arms. She knelt in the window, her head leaning over the flower-pots of withered stalks.

Mrs. Barley had thrown bedding and clothes through the kitchen window into the alley, and some of the smaller pieces of furniture after them. She dragged them into the street and set the children to stand by them so that they shouldn't be stolen. After a short time Sarah could not bear to stand here out of sight of the fire. She left the two younger children alone and ran back into the yard, and stood just inside. If her mother caught sight of her she would be thrashed. But she could not help it. She *must* watch.

She saw her father drag out into the yard from the work-room a large desk partly wrapped in sacking. Mrs. Barley called him and they went back together and carried out the kitchen table and the large rocking-chair. Barley approached a policeman and pointed to the archway, which was guarded by two more policemen. Sarah cowered down in the corner. Her father was arguing with the man. Why won't they let him carry them outside? she wondered.

Her mother ran back into the house. Sarah was seized by an agony of fear that she would be caught there by the fire. But she came out again at once, carrying the tea-caddy and some other small things. She joined her husband and the two of them stood side by side, watching.

Sarah kept one eye on her mother for a time, but forgot her when the fire began to come nearer to the workshop. Now she wanted it to burn. A growing excitement filled her. It blew her out until she felt as light as a balloon. She thought that if she lifted upwards with her arms she could fly over the house as she did in dreams. Let it burn, she prayed. I want it to burn.

She watched with rapt intensity the flames reaching from the front of the house round towards the workshop, under Mrs. Caracas's room. Hurry, hurry, she thought, gripping her hands.

Randall came into the yard from the street. She barely noticed him. She heard him say: "We've cleared the street, the engine can get along." That's the fire-engine, she thought. It mustn't come yet, it mustn't. She thought that she would never get over it if she did not see the fire roaring to heaven through the workshop and their rooms. The excitement was unbearable. She folded her hands over her stomach to help to bear it.

One of the policemen caught sight of her. "Here, hop it," he said.

Rigid from the shock, she did not move. He put his hand on her and pushed her towards the street.

"Be off. Run."

She walked off stiffly. She was crimson with shame and disappointment.

Ashton caught sight of Mrs. Caracas's head in the window of her room. "Look at that," he shouted. He pushed Thomas out of his way and ran to the staircase leading to her room. It was too late. The heat and dense smoke beat him back. A fragment of blazing wood fell on his hand, burning him sharply. The floor of Mrs. Caracas's room crashed in, and a cat, flaming from tip to tail, leaped from that furnace and hurled itself crack on against the wall of the archway and broke its neck.

A policeman helped Ashton across the yard. A fire-engine had come up as far as the entrance. Other engines behind it were pouring water on the buildings, business offices, nearest the Screech Owl.

"Better go to bed, sir," the man said. "You've done all you can."

"Bed," Ashton said, choking and laughing. "How the devil can I sleep?"

His mind was jerking with energy. He saw everything, the fire, the street, faces, sharpened and distorted by his excitement. It was like an attack at night, the confusion, the fires, the pounding of his heart. The extreme sharpness of detail in things stunned him now that he had time to notice them. Where's Thomas? he thought. He turned and looked round him in the street, on both sides. Nowhere to be seen. Queer, he thought. He forgot him at once. By God, this is grand, he thought.

Once the fire reached into the workshop nothing could stop it, not even the water pouring into it. It poured into a furnace. Clouds of steam sprang out. George Barley stood inside the yard, almost where the little girl had been standing until a minute ago, and stared at it in a kind of daze. His heart was wrenched in a dull grief. He felt that his life was ending. He leaned against the wall as if he were too tired to move away. All that sound clean wood, he thought blankly. A fireman climbed up and stood on the bureau they had hindered him from carrying into the street, because they said it would be in the way. He gave a violent start.

His wife put her hand on his arm. "We must go," she said in a low voice.

She was sorry for him, but she had less than a notion of what he suffered seeing his work and his tools destroyed. She herself was glad it was going. If I hadn't made him pay that insurance, she thought, with a pang of fear and happiness. She felt roused towards her husband. It was as though they were alone together again, without the children. She wanted to think of something to comfort him. And she was impatient, too. Surely he can see it will be the saving of us, she said to herself.

"Come, we must go," she said again. "The children will be getting frightened."

The heat was too great now to stand and watch.

"Yes, all right," he said, as if in pain.

She put her arm in his and they made their way into the street.

On his knees in the empty room, the Rev. Daniel prayed in an ecstasy. No pleasure, no gratification he had ever

known in his life equalled the acute pleasure he suffered as
he watched the flames. He knew that there would be no
pain of burning for him. While all the other men and
women and children on earth ran up and down calling to
the mountains and the rocks, Fall on us; while trees
shrivelled and went out like dead wick; while pigeons fluttered into the fire and were destroyed; while the sun
became black as sackcloth of hair, and the sky departed as a
scroll, he, Daniel, would be going up by a whirlwind into
heaven with the horses of fire. "My father, my father!
The chariot of Israel, and the horsemen," he cried, in a
loud voice. "Thanks be to God, how lovely are the mes-
sengers. Comfort, O Lord, the soul of thy servant. The
same stone which the builders refused is become the head
stone in the corner, the head stone in the corner. The
day is at hand, let us put on the armour of light. Thou
that openest and no man shutteth, come and bring the
prisoner out of his prison-house, who sitteth in darkness
and in the shadow of death. Come, Lord Jesus! come,
Lord Jesus! Come! come! Suffer me not at my last hour
to fall from Thee. Amen. I go to meet the Lord in the
air. Comfort, comfort, comfort, He shall rise up at the
voice of the bird, and all the daughters of music shall be
brought low; He maketh peace in my borders and filleth
me with the flour of wheat, Hallelujah, Hallelujah,
Hallelujah, Hallelujah, Hallelujah, Amen, Hallelujah,
Amen, Hallelujah, Amen, Amen, Amen, Amen, Amen,
Amen, Amen."

Sweat ran down his face. His forehead was daubed with
dust from the floor. The heat became painful. Smoke, the
smoke of burning wood, came galloping into the room.

Mrs. Kerr walked beside the men who were carrying
Enid, on a rug with coats thrown over her, into the room
behind a tobacconist's shop. People were out in the street
from every house, and the police were keeping them back
behind ropes. Light was coming.

They had difficulty in getting her past the counter—it
was covered with newspapers and a sheet—into the room.

The couch was too short to put her there. They put her down on the table. The police doctor had looked at her in the yard; shrugging his shoulders, he said: "Take her out of here somewhere."

"Is she gone?" Jean-Ann Kerr asked.

He said: "All but. There's nothing to be done with her."

Well, I can't just leave her, she thought. She went with them, and they left her alone in the room. "The ambulance'll be along," they said, and pushed off, and there she was. Would they have left her? she thought.

She sat on the couch, smoking, and thinking. She lost her head; she could've got along the roof; or waited: the ladder came in the yard as she jumped—she never had any sense. She noticed suddenly that Enid was wearing odd shoes. Just like her, she thought. Couldn't even put her clothes on right.

The room, with its fly-blown electric light bulb immediately over her head, began to get on her nerves. I shan't stay here, she thought. She got up. No, I can't. Can't leave her alone. She sat down again, vexed with herself, with the other woman. Couldn't even kill herself properly.

Enid's eyelids flickered; they lifted, and stayed open. Holding her cigarette to one side, Mrs. Kerr leaned over her. "Feeling all right?" she said in a clear voice. I wish someone would come, she thought. I don't mind this, but I wish to God someone would come. It's not decent leaving her here. They wouldn't do it to anybody but a poor woman. If you're poor in this country you're only dirt. I'm not going to be done down by it; I'm going to do them all in the eye and come up with enough cash to spit on them. My God, I'll do it too. I'll make someone pay for what I've gone through since Kenneth—— She's trying to say something, she thought. Her heart jumped. "Feeling better?" she said again. "You gave us all a fright, you know. What'd you want to jump for? Never mind. Keep still now and you'll be all right in a day or two."

The other woman's lips moved. She leaned closer. "What did you say? Don't talk. You'll be all right."

"I never had anything," Enid Jones said, whispering. "They've all done me in."

She began to breathe quickly; then the change came over her face, and her breath roared in her throat.

Jean-Ann Kerr stepped back. What's the matter with you? she thought. I tell you she never was any good. Complaining to the last—as if it did you any good, ever. Who listens to it?

Randall was hurrying back to the house where he had left Harriet. She had cried from the shock when she was knocked down, and there was a lump on her head where it struck the ground. The fat Frenchwoman, a Jewess, with whom he left her, promised to bathe it.

He saw Mrs. Pizetti crossing the street towards him. "Did they get the doctor out?" she said, breathlessly.

"I don't know," Randall said. "I didn't see him anywhere."

"Then he's in his room . . . he was very drunk in the café. I must get him out."

She hurried past him, her strong delicate nose pointing forward as though she were following a trail. Randall caught her up.

"I'll go," he said. "The police won't let you in."

"Promise you'll go," she said, looking into his face with her sharp, calm eyes. "I ought to have thought of him sooner."

"Of course I'll go," he said impatiently. It was only a nuisance; he did not care whether the doctor, an unpleasant drunken fellow, was saved or not; but he could not behave as badly as his thoughts.

He ran back to New Moon Yard, and pushed his way through the line of police. They let him in because he had been helping. The firemen were still pouring water into Barley's workshop. Two of them were wearing masks. The flames were sinking, but thick acrid smoke rolled across the yard: the stairs to the doctor's room, the only staircase not destroyed, was filled with it. So was his room when they broke the door with an axe. Randall had to rush down to the clearer air in the yard. He came back in time to help the others drag the doctor across the room and carry him downstairs. The doctor's head hung over their arms, his face like a large clay-coloured fruit just splitting open. He was lying naked in bed and they wrapped the quilt round him. He weighed enormously, like a drowned man. Of course, he *is* drowned, Randall thought, drowned in smoke. They lugged him into the street, and the police doctor and his assistant began working on him. In the growing light, the scene reminded Randall of the effects of an air raid as he had seen them in a news film—the drifting smoke from the fire, the ropes keeping the crowd back, the men kneeling over a figure on the ground. It would be like this, he thought vaguely. Except that there would be more of us lying about, and less help. He felt suddenly, unreasonably, anxious about Harriet. Turning to go to her at last he saw her standing at the other side of the police cordon, looking at him. He hurried to her.

"Why did you come?" he asked sharply.

She was pale. "I was afraid. I didn't know what had happened to you," she said. She touched his hand. "Don't be angry."

"I'm not angry."

"Let's go, then," she said nervously.

He stood still. "Silly girl," he said. "What's the matter, my darling?"

He saw the look of relief in her face. Before he could say anything more, an old man, Pop, stepped in front of them. "I've been watching it," he said, eagerly, staring into their faces. "I've seen everything. Now I don't know where to go. I don't know what to do with myself. I could go somewhere and sleep, of course. I have money for that. But where shall I go?"

Harriet began to answer, frowning as though she were responsible for him. Randall interrupted her at once.

"You'd better find somewhere," he said curtly. "Come," he said to Harriet.

"Yes, I can do that," Pop said. He was offended. It doesn't matter. Nothing matters. . . . Really. Nothing matters.

CHAPTER XXVII

ASHTON HAD breakfast sent up to his bedroom in the hotel. He had expected to sleep late, but he slept for less than two hours, and at eight o'clock he telephoned for breakfast. He was excited still; he did not know how to spend the day in front of him after he had written to the insurance company. He could ring Josephine up and take her somewhere, but he had less than ten pounds in his pocket and very little in the bank. Would the company give him something at once, or did they make you wait weeks?

He strode up and down the room in the pyjamas and dressing-gown borrowed from the manager of the hotel, smiling, stopping at the table to swallow another mouthful of coffee and cram in toast and bits of grilled kidney. His left hand was bandaged and useless. He could not sit quietly. Between bites he read the newspaper. There was an account of the fire. West End Night Club in Flames. Four Deaths. Panic averted by police. . . . He frowned. For less than a minute it struck him as strange that the police had been in the yard as soon as the fire broke out. Almost as if they knew something was going to happen then. He grinned. Then they knew more than I did, he thought. I wasn't expecting anything until five o'clock. What a swine that fellow is. Was. Thank God he's dead. My luck, he thought, smiling. Time I had a bit.

He stood in front of the mirror and studied his face. I

look five years younger, he thought. Good. He felt younger; and tireless, confident.

"I've done it," he said. The excitement crackled in him again. He felt lightheaded with it.

The telephone bell rang. He answered it instantly, thinking of Josephine. But of course she wouldn't ring up now, she's asleep, he thought, hearing the man's quick impersonal voice.

"Someone here wishes to see you, sir. Mr. Cayley."

"Cayley?" he repeated. "Did you say Cayley?"

"Yes, sir. Mr. Thomas Cayley."

Oh, *Thomas*, he thought. I'd forgotten he had a name. "Send him up." How does he know I'm here? he wondered, idly.

Thomas stood just inside the room, as though he were waiting for orders. His big solid face and hard lips were guarded; there was an extra watchfulness about him this morning.

"Well, what is it?" Ashton said. "How did you know I was here, by the way?"

"I followed you this morning."

The devil you did! thought Ashton. "I didn't notice you," he said dryly. Anxious about his money, he supposed. "Well, that was a show," he said. "A proper night attack, eh? Well, what're we going to do? You leave me an address and I'll send your wages along as soon as the insurance blokes pay up. Like old times, eh? Waiting for pay to come up. It won't be long. If a quid is any use to you now——"

He turned to pick up his notebook lying on the dressing-table with his cuff-links and cigarette case.

"I can wait," Thomas said slowly.

"Very well." He put the note back. "What are you going to do?" he asked in a friendly voice. "No job at the moment, I'm afraid. But——" he hesitated. "I shall probably want a servant very soon." How soon? How long is it going to take me to marry her, to be safe? "If you don't get anything better," he said.

"I shan't want the job," Thomas said.

"Oh?" He was surprised and mildly irritated. "You've got something you can go to? Right."

"I haven't got a job, but I don't want one from you," Thomas said. "That's what I came to say."

He turned to go.

"Here!" said Ashton.

Thomas wheeled round again, facing him. He was stubborn, contemptuous, inarticulate.

"What the devil d'you mean?"

"I don't want to do any work for you again."

Sudden panic and anger started in Ashton. His mind jumped like a hare between them. "Damn you," he shouted. "What d'you mean? Get out of here."

"I'm going," Thomas said quietly. He turned with his hand on the door. "Don't get the wind up. I'm not going to talk. I only wanted to tell you I'm through. That's all. See?"

Ben had three hours' sleep between three and six. They began to question him again at eight o'clock. Sleep had restored him to himself. He kept a sullen jeering smile on his face until one of them said, casually, that Franklyn was dead. Now, if they had said that Franklyn had been talking he would have laughed. But—dead. He felt a helpless anger, the anger he had felt when they told him that his wife had split on him.

"You haven't seen her," he had shouted, jeering. "You don't know where she is. Try something newer."

"But we have seen her," the D.I. said. "We were talking to her half an hour since. I believe it's a fine girl. Congratulations."

Half an hour, he thought, stupefied. "What time is it?" he asked without thinking.

"The time now," said the D.I., "is two-fifteen a.m. Don't you want to sleep?"

"You bastards had her woke up in the middle of the night after she . . ."

A screen round the bed in the ward, and their whispers and faces round her everywhere, he thought; a shiver of rage and shame sprang in him.

"Bastards. Bastards," he repeated.

They were almost apologetic about it. "You've been in here since half-past ten," they said, "and you haven't talked. We had to do something. There was a nurse listening—matron or someone. We didn't worry her. She gave us some news. We know how many fires you and Franklyn raised this year and last. What she didn't tell us—maybe she was really telling the truth and didn't know—was what you're planning now. You tell us that, now, and we shan't worry her again. Well?"

Then, he had told them if they wanted to stop New Moon Yard going up they'd better hurry. His eyelids were jerking with anger. He had never felt less like sleep. And as soon as he was alone he dropped off, suddenly, like something falling, a stone. . . .

"You did it," he said, looking at them.

"Did what?"

"You did Franklyn in."

"Not a bit of it. He dropped off the roof. Spine. We weren't even after him then."

He chewed this over for a minute, hating them. He hated their hard cocksure bodies. He hated them for being on the right side of the fence when he was on the wrong, and for being able to punish him for doing no worse, he deeply knew, than they did themselves in other, respectable ways. He felt bursting with anger. The thought of his wife lying there in her weakness, flinching from them, their breath on her, jerked at his stomach. He wanted to vomit the breakfast he had eaten.

"Bastards," he said again mechanically. "Harassing a woman after she . . . It's not decent."

"Raising fires isn't a decent job," the D.I. said, suddenly and sharply. "There were people sleeping in the yard.

Four of them lost their lives. Even for you and Franklyn it was a dirty piece of work." Why, the place looked like an air raid, he thought.

How many years will I get? he wondered. Years, years. Doing time. His mind spun in circles. Time. His body revolted against its punishment. To be deprived of days, weeks, months of active life; of his wife's life. Of his child's. I shan't forgive it, he thought.

"What d'you want to know?" he asked sulkily.

"Who employed you to start the fire last night . . . this morning?"

"Bloke in the night club. Ashton."

"Who made the arrangements with him? You? Franklyn?"

"Con did."

"Any proof?"

"Oh, he signed on the dotted line," he said. "You'll find the letter in Con's office."

"Don't play the fool, Abramovitch," said the D.I.

"I'll telling you," he bawled, losing his temper. "You'll find it. It says if he, if Franklyn brings off the deal arranged—selling a house is what it says—he takes twenty per cent. Signed, Ashton. Con likes to have something signed, no matter what." He looked round their faces with the same helpless anger. "Signed, Ashton," he said. "You ought to let me off easier if I help you out now. What else d'you want to know?"

"I don't want any breakfast," Harriet said. "I'm not hungry."

"We'll go to Legrain's in Gerrard Street and drink coffee."

"Will it be open? Half-past eight?"

"I don't know. Come and see. It has the best coffee."

"We'll go straight to the Corner House," Harriet said abruptly, with decision. "Open all night. I don't want to be turned away anywhere."

The place was full of an exhausted tepid light. They chose a table near the wall, and Randall ordered fruit and rolls with the coffee. "Go on, eat," he said. "Do as I tell you."

"I don't mind these places," she said, looking round. "In fact I like them. I like the faces, with their lives cut into them. If I could write I'd write down what happens here during one hour—the people who come in and sit down, with dozens of their selves standing beside each of them waiting to be taken in again and walked off with. That girl over there—she might be me. She might be thinking of her childhood, of her mother, of a pink daisy root with soil on the flowers, of a hole in her shoes, of something she's ashamed of."

"Or of a man," said Randall.

"Very likely," she said.

"You can write when we're living together. I'm going to see that man about his house to-day."

He watched her without seeming to. Is she going to go back on it? he wondered. You can't trust anyone. His eyes were careful.

"I can't write," Harriet said. "There are too many writers anyway. Too many unnecessary books, words. Nowadays things are more important than words. Do you suppose I could learn something? It won't take me all day to clean the house, and get dinner. I'll do that. But if I had something as well——"

"Do you want to learn to fly?"

"No," she said, after a minute.

He was relieved.

"I'm not quick enough," she said in a low voice. "I should be afraid."

"Nonsense."

"No, it's true. I can bear some things—but I should be afraid of being killed."

Randall looked at her schoolgirl's long awkward hands and loved her and them. "I'll take you up," he said. "I won't kill you."

"All right. But what can I do myself? What can I learn?"

"Are you thinking you're going to be bored?"

"No," she lied.

He felt bewildered suddenly. Nothing is simple, he thought. He saw his mother, writing, writing; pushing the hair off her face with a jerking hand; her eyes distant, coming back slowly to him. What did you say, darling? You don't listen. I was writing. All right. No, tell me what you said.

"Shan't we have any children?" he said.

Harriet's knees shook. "Do you want them?" she said.

"I don't know. Not particularly. If you do."

She thought in the same instant, What a bore, and, Of course I want children—yours; your seed in me. "Yes, we must," she muttered. "But not just yet, Bill. Wait and see what happens next year."

"What could happen?"

"I mean a war, of course." She remembered the face of a Chinese woman seen on the pictures: the street behind her had been burned, it was still smoking; she was looking at something in her arms; her face reproached not death but her life. Blotted out, hundreds of children. Obliterated by explosive. Not mine, not my child, thought Harriet.

"We'll wait a year," she said. "If things are no worse then."

"You're shaking," Randall said. "Why? It's going to be all right. We're going to have a fine life."

"Do you think so?" She smiled at him with sudden triumph, half closing her eyes. Mine, she thought. A pulse throbbed inside her again; her cheeks flushed. Mine. I shall be married next month; I can write to them at home: I can be proud. He looks what he is. There must, she thought secretly, be something about her since he wanted to show her to people as his wife. She felt a sharp, serious confidence in herself.

"Of course. Don't you think so, too?"

"You're sure you want to marry me?" she laughed. "I'm obstinate—and very clumsy, and I don't know what to say to people."

He smiled reassuringly. Gaiety, kindness, were between them in the air. They were already different, because surer of each other. In the end nothing matters, he thought, but to feel safe with one person; one is enough. If you can be sure of nothing else now, and you have this, you can be happy. Happy? Content, at least.

"I'll try not to let you down," he said.

"And I," she said quickly.

"We must be married at once. As soon as it can be managed. You never know nowadays how much time you have. We'd better not waste any."

"Ah, time," Harriet said, sighing. "I should like to live"—she hesitated—"to live—that's all—simply to live," she said, with a little laugh.

"We'll manage that, my girl," Randall said.

Their hands, clasped across the table, fell apart. They became aware again of the lifeless overheated air; of the noises of the café, of the street; of the listless black-clothed figure of the waiter; of excitement in the day.

"Time to go," Randall said.

Eugene Rapp read *The Times* with his breakfast of strong Indian tea and toast. It continually vexed him, because he thought it namby-pamby in its attitude to the lower classes, but other papers were worse. Turning the pages irritably after he had read part of an account of the bombing of a little town in Spain, his eye caught a paragraph about the fire in New Moon Yard. More than three-quarters of the building was gutted; the Screech Owl Club, a Café Bar, a cabinet-maker's workshop, and the rooms above them. He folded the paper and told his servant to ring up Mr. Godbell at his private number.

"Is that you, Godbell?" he said, when the solicitor answered. "I thought I should catch you. Look here.

Did you see in your paper that that house in Soho, New Moon House, has been burned out? A piece of luck, eh? I want you to see his Grace's secretary at once, this morning, and buy the site before anyone else moves. What's that? No, no, of course they can't preserve a house that isn't there, but there's the other fools, the slum clearers. Yes, of course. Well, you'll see to it at once." His voice became jovial. "Time, my dear fellow, is the essence of the contract. Yes, I daresay you've heard it before. How's your boy? Good. I thought he'd see sense. Good-bye."

He ordered fresh tea, and drank it, blowing his cheeks out. He liked to put pieces of crust in his mouth, then fill it with the hot tea, so that he got the taste of soaked bread. He was delighted by the prospect of defeating the slum clearance monkeys. It was a little thing, a very small transaction, this purchase of a cinema site: it had become important only because he had been hindered. Now that it had dropped into his hands he would sell it again and forget it.

Feeling pleasantly full, he stood up. I'll look in at Asprey's, he thought, and choose a little something for Josephine, a surprise. Windfalls all round this morning, he thought, smiling with pleasure.

Pop implored the man to let him squeeze through the barrier of planks and ropes into the yard. "What d'you want to go in for?" the man asked. "All right. But don't be too long in there or you'll get me in trouble, see?"

He slipped a plank out of the ropes and let Pop step into the yard. The old man stared round him, his eyes blinking in the strong sunlight. He took a few steps forward, swaying as he went. It had never occured to him that the bins Pizetti had put out the night before would be burned, but there was no trace of them outside the blackened walls of the café; they were either destroyed or they had been dragged out already.

He walked disconsolate as near the house as he dared,

looking into the holes of the windows.   There was still
smoke rising from a corner of the Screech Owl.   As he
watched it, it seemed to twist and swell inside his head; his
eyes dimmed with it.   He remembered the old woman
taken off by the police in her grey dressing-gown the day
before.   No, no, don't think of it, he said; it was nasty.
Think of something else.   But what?

Where shall I go now? he thought, turning round and
round, like a stick twirling inside his thin clothes.   In the
whole world, why need my room have been burned over
me?   Is there any justice in that?

And what a day, what sunlight!   He loved heat on his
dry bones.   They say we're done for, he thought more
cheerfully: it's the end of the world; England's finished, no
more of it, no more of us.   His eye caught a gleam on the
ground.   He pounced.   A two-shilling piece.   Delighted,
he thrust it out of sight quickly.   You waited for me, he
said, holding it affectionately inside his pocket.   Now he
felt that the country would at least last his time.   And
after that, what did it matter?   He hurried away.